The Flawless Skin of Ugly People

The Flawless Skin of Ugly People

A Novel by
Doug Crandell

Distributed by Holtzbrinck Publishers

FIRST EDITION

Designed by Jason Snyder

Library of Congress Cataloging-in-Publication Data

Crandell, Doug.
  The flawless skin of ugly people : a novel / by Doug Crandell.
    p. cm.
  ISBN-13: 978-0-7535-1299-9
  ISBN-10: 0-7535-1299-8
  1. Overweight persons--Fiction. 2. Georgia--Fiction. I. Title.
  PS3603.R377F57 2007
  813'.6--dc22   2007025177

10 9 8 7 6 5 4 3 2 1

For Nancy

Acknowledgments

How do you thank a person who saves your life? I was near defeat, and writing was all that worked to quell a deep longing to "belong." Robert Guinsler, my agent, threw me a lifeline. I took a deep breath and returned to the world, tired but hopeful. Thank you, Robert. May you always have your kindness reciprocated tenfold.

I am grateful to Ken Siman, a fine reader, talented writer, and enthusiastic publisher, and a guy who still sees the world like William Carlos Williams did. Ken believes life is better lived when done so with the aid of great writing.

To Ann Espuelas, thanks for making me a better writer, and for caring about the book as much as I do.

I'd like to thank Kennedy Crandell, Nancy Brooks-Lane, and Walker Lane for tending the farm, and for their love, support, and laughter.

This novel began at the Virginia Center for the Creative Arts. The time I spent there on the Goldfarb Fellowship was invaluable, and without it this book would have stayed only a nagging idea in my head.

Finally, for all of us who feel misplaced in this world, here's to real beauty, the kind that can make you whole again. Cheers!

The bottom line is that (a) people are never perfect, but love can be, (b) that is the one and only way that the mediocre and vile can be transformed, and (c) doing that makes it that. We waste time looking for the perfect lover, instead of creating the perfect love.

—Tom Robbins, *Still Life With Woodpecker*

PART I

....

one The letters arrive with her new weight printed in each corner. Week after week they appear, as if Kari really believes this is the way normal people live. The lined paper, the same kind we wrote love notes on, seems imbued with our adolescent past. It's as if I can smell her lip gloss smeared right down into the pulp, the Dr. Pepper kind she wore the night of our eighth-grade dance. When our lips touched during REO Speedwagon's "Keep on Loving You," I wanted some salty Fritos to go with that sweet cola kiss. Maybe even a Ding-Dong. We ended up at her dad's place after that dance in 1982, scarfing down junk, high on each other and giggly, food in our braces as we kissed and groped.

Kari is not shy about telling me how we both are at fault for how our lives have turned out. In her last letter, the one that broke the 200-pound barrier, she simply wrote: "We've known each other too long, Hobbie. We know too much about the people we could have been."

I click the leash on our dog and step outside. Terry's paw gets caught in the strap and as I bend to release it, he tilts his head like a captive. "There you go, baby," I say, helping him step free of the tangle. It's rained all night and the front entrance is treacherous, an inch of freezing water on the steps, sealing leaves below the ice like decoupage.

Our pooch has lost weight like Kari. I promised her I'd keep him slimmed down, since for years we fed Terry the same bad food we ate. Terry's been on a strict one-meal-a-day diet for nearly a year now, except for the treats I slip him. His dry food smells like eggs. It's pure protein. That's what Kari is all about: "Protein makes muscle, soft carbs double and re-double, make your health vanish," at least that's what I think she meant. In one of the letters she wrote that very thing, but slipped and instead of writing "vanish" wrote "make your health famish."

A few drier leaves somersault across the paved driveway. Terry pulls hard against the leash, which makes him wheeze slightly. As per our routine, I stop and let his mongrel-Dachshund body take a breather. The little guy sits down, looks up at me under his elephantine ears, and sighs loudly, then stands back up, attentive. The icy drizzle has started to make its way into flurry form, giving the air around us a lint-filled look. Blackbirds chatter from above, roosting on the scrawny limbs of a craggy tree. There are paw prints in a muddy spot near the drive, big ones, and they've appeared only in the last couple of weeks. I try and call Terry to me before he spots them, but it's too late. He sniffs the spoor and I swear I can see movement out of the corner o f my eye.

This is a rental house, just across the state line between Georgia and North Carolina. Kari had strict orders; I couldn't be in the same state with her. So I've settled into an outpost in the North Georgia Mountains, exiled from the woman I love. Terry yaps for me to pick him up after he's gotten good and scared. I stoop and lift him to my chest, pull the extra-large raincoat over his body. He snuggles into me like all the other times we've made this trip to the mailbox, his warm belly comforting against the cold. Often I show him the letters or read to him that Kari has asked me to rub his ears for her. I don't ever read to him when she writes in block letters: "DON'T FEED

HIM SNACKS!!" Kari's handwriting looks the same as it did in junior high, feminine and optimistic, an outlook that has now become almost obsessive. I fear that her new view of the world, lean and disciplined, won't include me. But since I can't write her back, she knows nothing of my worries. There are lots of things she doesn't know after six months without me getting to talk to her, or write her, or try and slip an e-mail her way. Early on, when she'd been gone only a few weeks, I tried to use our AOL account, but no luck. The e-mails I sent her had been deleted, and in the next postal letter she told me she was never going to read them, I shouldn't waste my time.

Terry wriggles deeper into the coat, his breathing becoming softer, eyelids heavy. Before, when Kari was around, I didn't really connect with him. He was her dog in every way; he'd wag his tail when he caught a glimpse of Kari in her pink robe, pant whenever she spoke his name, and while his heart is pure and he'd do some of the same things when I was around, I could tell that it was out of pity for me, a gentlemanly courtesy. But since Kari's been away, Terry and I have bonded. When I look down from the bed in the morning, and I see his long nose and dark eyes, whites showing where the skin sags, as he sits obediently on his small haunches, my heart is filled with compassion. I love him. He's the one who saved me from despair.

The flurries have turned to larger flakes, floating down from the gray sky in a slant. It's 12:15 and the red flag on the mailbox is still erect; the mail truck hasn't come yet. Just as I brush back my coat sleeve to look at the time again, I hear the truck gaining speed to make the steep hill of my road. I sort of know the driver, see him at the grocery store in town, near the ballpark on Sunday afternoons, and spot him sometimes at the movie-plex when I sneak Terry in to watch a matinee. He's young, a slacker, and has the look of a person who has just gotten out of bed. I often wonder if he's in limbo like I am. Is his loved one in another state, shrinking down to half her size?

Terry pricks his ears when the brakes on the truck chirp and the mailman lurches up to the box. The mailman doesn't really look at me standing there; it's more like a quick glance, fast but inquisitive, like all the other looks I get, or more exactly put, that my face gets. But he means no harm, I can tell. Snow covers Terry's head, a sprinkling of white powder. I can hear his chops smacking as he tries to eat the cold flakes from my hand; his tongue is warm and slippery on my knuckles, soothing. The mailman leans out of the doorless side of the Jeep and removes the bills I'd left there, tucks a bundle of mail inside, and flips down the flag with some effort. Everything creaks in the newly fallen snow. I wave and the mailman shoots me another speedy gander and a guilty salute. The truck puffs past us, up the road toward the only other house on this gravel bylane. Terry squirms in my arms and bristles, producing a concise yet mean yap in the direction of the vanished truck. He's a ferocious dog once danger has passed. It makes me laugh, like when I chase him around the house playing hide-and-seek.

I hesitate at the mailbox, take in the stillness of the outdoors. It's all new to me, this rural seclusion, but that's not what Kari thinks. In one of the first-month letters, she made it clear. "We've been hiding out from the world since we met, Hobbie. We've grown up being scared together. It's got to change." It's those kind of sentences, the ones she writes with love and pain and a little force, that make my stomach churn.

Once, a few months ago when it was still very warm, Terry and I didn't go get the mail for three days, trying to ignore the letters.

Finally, when we resumed our routine, the letters were even more difficult to take when read all at once, so Terry and I made a pact; we shook on it actually, his small paw barely lifting an inch. We told ourselves it wouldn't happen again. The letters would be retrieved daily, even if it felt like it was killing us.

My face hurts in the colder wind now blowing in from the north. The new sores and cracking scabs tingle and sting, a sensation that after all these years I am still privately embarrassed by. When Kari and I would go swimming in college, the chlorine felt like acid on my face. It was supposed to help, though, dry things up, etc., but I felt only more cracked and etched upon than ever, and tender, especially around my lips.

The mail catch today reveals a new log cabin catalog, an electric bill, and Kari's daily letter. Her cursive writing on the front sinks my heart. The space where her return address should be is blank as always, even though we both know exactly where she's writing from. Terry wants down. I stoop and place him softly on the ground. He picks up his paws when he senses the snow and patters toward a hoary bush to "tinkle," Kari's word for pee. Terry trails his nose over some more tracks in the snow. We have a black bear that has tipped over the garbage and sent poor Terry into a tizzy. It's terrifying. I've always thought of bears as land sharks, and although our bear is not a grizzly, he's no less scary. I worry he'll hurt Terry; the bear is skinny and desperate, and leaves his gamey scent in the air like a warning.

I tear open the envelope at the end and extract the letter as if it were a knife from a sheath. Under the cement-colored sky, I unfold the page and instinctively look to the top right-hand corner where once again it will be dog-eared. The weight is there: 171. In her curlicue writing, down near the center of the page, it reads: "I will be released sometime soon, but I am not certain about coming home. I'll just have to see."

Something cold and dark passes though me, over me, under me; it comes from everywhere, fills and empties me all at once. Terry is now sniffing the yellow oval he's made in the snow. As if he's heard his name, he perks his ears and trots toward me, his awkward tail wagging faster than his legs move. I bend and pick up my pal, my throat tight with emotion, the cold making it seem even more stuck, my Adam's apple frozen in place. It's silly, but I don't want Terry to know Kari's written such a harsh letter, so I stuff it and the envelope into my hip pocket as if he can read.

Before we can turn to head back toward the house, a FedEx van pulls into the lane. The driver nearly hits us as he swerves to miss an icy pothole. He yanks back the emergency brake and steps out. "Are you Mr. Hobbie?"

I nod.

He thrusts an overnight letter in my direction and flips a handheld gadget for me to sign. I take the stylus and try and sign while I hold the letter and Terry at the same time. I can feel the driver's gaze on my face. Is he one of those guys from high school who would call me "Pizza Face"? When I finish signing and look up to offer a smile, he jerks his eyes away to avoid being caught staring. This is why I've not been able to disobey Kari and simply drive to see her during visiting hours. It would mean having strangers search my face with disgust and wonder, sometimes point, or even have them yell, "Hey, Clearasil" when I'd walk down the sidewalk to the entrance of the building where she's staying. Other than work, I rarely go out, avoiding people as much as possible. I shop the 24-hour Wal-Mart, rent movies from the Internet, and basically stay hidden as much as

I can. Having to endure people's stares is what has made my job so tortuous. Sometimes I dream about pulling on this magical mask that makes my face flawless, giving me a mug that can float easily from one social situation to another, free from people's judgment.

The FedEx man reverses out of the drive. The overnight letter has the bank's HR department's return address printed on the label. It's gotten so gloomy outside that the nightlight on the utility pole clicks on. It's supposed to snow enough to accumulate two inches. In the failing light, Terry lovingly licks my cheek, a sign I take to mean he wishes to heal my wounds. The wind picks up some more and Terry and I both smell the bear. It's our joint fear that makes me run toward the house.

two All night the winter storm rattles the windowpanes. At nearly 3 a.m. I wake to find Terry shivering at the foot of the bed. He isn't really cold, just putting on some good theater. I don't like to let him sleep with me because he will snort and roll over a hundred times an hour, and because I'm afraid I'll want him to sleep with me all the time. But in light of Kari's news, I relent and let him climb aboard. I bounce in and out of fitful drowsing. Insomnia isn't new to me.

Graduates of the inpatient weight-loss program in Durham where Kari is include: James Earl Jones, Buddy Hackett, and Harry Wayne Casey, better known as K.C. of K.C. and the Sunshine Band. When I joked with Kari and began singing, "S-A-T-U-R-D-A-Y, night," she replied with a grin, "That's the Bay City Rollers, dork." At the edges of sleep, I see them all boogying, gesturing Travolta-style toward the ceiling. Instead of acoustic tile, James Earl, Buddy, and K.C. all watch as the skin-like surface of the ceiling in my dream erupts with pus.

I awaken, finally, after a heavy pimple on the ceiling splats down to the dance floor. Next to me, Terry is snoring like a piece of stalled woodworking equipment. I nudge him, exactly the way I interrupt Kari's midnight sawing. At every apartment we've rented on bank tellers' salaries, the places where over the years we've grown to become common-law spouses, Kari would nearly stop breathing several times a night, waking up in the morning with much less rest than she needed, sleep apnea robbing her to exhaustion. We've lived in lots of America's suburbia: Detroit, Colorado Springs, Indianapolis, Pittsburgh (our hometown, the place that nearly killed us), Minneapolis, and the list goes on. The suburbs are where we've lost ourselves, hidden out with Kari's weight and my face. She's right in that regard. "If we live in the suburbs we'll just be another couple that hates their lives. No one will bother us," she used to say. This rented house, in the North Georgia Mountains, is the first time I've not lived within a block of a strip mall. Here it's like out West, full of militant groups and backwoods societal dropouts. It's beautiful, but scary.

Terry turns onto his back, dinger and soft belly for all to see, and begins snoring even louder, his thin eyelids shuddering like hulls in a breeze. I pull him toward me, careful not to wake him, and he stops snoring, but another noise takes over. It's a rustling sound combined with thumps and muffled grunts from somewhere near the back of the house. I toss the covers aside and put my feet to the cold wood floor. The sound comes again two times before I can slip on my robe.

I creep down the hall, leaving Terry's snore behind and getting closer and closer to the other noise: thump, bang, thump. The fluorescent light over the kitchen sink flickers as I head toward it. The banging sound suddenly becomes more distinct. I reach the sink and peer out the window toward the deck. The black bear is pawing the turned-over trash can, his beady eyes gleaming red from the porch light. Bears should be in hibernation, at least that's what the game warden said, but he also pointed out that the warmer winters of late have confused the animals, thrown off their internal clocks. For once, I am glad Terry is dead to the world in my bed; he'd be in a yapping psychosis if he knew the bear was outside gorging himself on a Jimmy Dean sausage patty box.

I switch on the other security light on the deck and the bear rears up. It's big, but obviously malnourished; the ribs are showing and its fur is ragged and tattered. My hand shakes as I flip the switch on and off like the game warden told me. All I want to do is dial 911 and get some real protection. The flashing light makes the bear slowly return to all fours, but not before exposing its long teeth. More snow has fallen, and the ground and deck are covered in a fluffy blanket. I watch as the animal lumbers toward the slope behind the deck and disappears into brambles and saplings.

I am afraid sleep will again elude me. There's a slice of key lime pie in the refrigerator and some cold milk. On the kitchen table sits a stack of nearly all the Kari letters. I pluck one near the bottom, from months ago, slip the letter out, and place it next to me while I eat. I find my reading glasses on the table and polish them. The corner of the letter reads 275. There are more words in her early letters, but like her weight, they've become fewer and fewer, just bite-size now.

"Dear Hobbie, I don't know if I can do this or not. I'm scared and this place is full of depressing people. I'm depressed. Today we had three sessions of therapy. The food is horrible and I am tired. I miss you. I can't imagine six months here. I sometimes want to escape, break out, which is stupid I know, since I can leave anytime I want. But I can't really. If I leave here and don't stick with it, all we'll ever be is underdeveloped. Lots of people here have kids, and they seem more grounded because of it, not like us, stuck in adolescence. I think of you always."

I put down the fork and take a swig of milk from the jug. The house is quiet again; only the hum of the refrigerator can be heard. My legs have goose bumps. I fold the letter back along its crease and return it to the envelope, plucking another more recent one from the pile. The weight reads 183 and there's no introduction; my name is not even written, just this: "Maybe we've used our skin as an excuse to compromise."

I am surprised each time I read and re-read the letters to find that they bring up a whole host of emotions. This letter made me mad at the time, unable to plead my case, counter her philosophical points like we always have when we've argued. The anger all comes back sitting at the table alone, the piece of pie gone. I reach for another letter and get the one that simply says: "177, but I still weigh almost fifteen pounds more than you."

I put all the letters back and clean up my mess, place the plate in the sink. The thought of Kari not coming home turns my stomach. We'd planned on seeing one another immediately once she hit her target weight, which on Kari's 5' 7" frame is 140 pounds. The idea of a weekend in North Carolina together to plan our next move is the one thing I've looked forward to; it's kept me going. Kari would talk on and on about it, as we ate salads for a whole week before she was due at "fat camp," her words, not mine. But as soon as she lost 40 pounds the letters changed, and since then she's mostly offered up pithy philosophical statements. But in some of the letters she gets more concrete with her assessments. She told me that her therapist said she was a control freak because of her demand that I not be able to contact her. I kind of liked the therapist saying that, and love Kari for telling me.

Kari's always been honest, so much so that I could take her word for it when she said my face was what made me Hobbie. In fact, she said that going by my first name, Leonard, didn't feel right and that Leo didn't fit me either. From then on, I've gone by my last name. Kari didn't lie and say my face was handsome in its own way, or rugged like my Aunt Rosie used to try and convince me in high school. Nope, Kari would stroke my topographical cheeks and ask me if it hurt.

I tried Accutane, but the bank we worked at didn't cover tellers that were considered part-time, and they kept both of us at 32 hours week, just so they didn't have to pay for our insurance. In fact, we didn't really stay at any of our bank jobs long enough to get insurance. But that's a cop-out, too; the truth is I didn't like how the medicine made me feel, and it turned all my skin into a scaly mess. Later, I tried almost every concoction out there. Kari would go through the whole list of the most recent regimen some quack had recommended: Did I put on the medicine, swallow the vitamin D pill, visualize a clear and perfect face? If I answered no to any or all of these, she just kept stroking my face, not at all judgmental or grossed out at the red lumps and white cysts. She never seemed to care the way each morning my face emerged as the profile of a different person, the swelling highlighting new features, a broader nose, a cheekbone higher because of infection, or an eye temporarily forced further into hiding. Kari has known me so long, from eighth grade right up until now in our mid-thirties, that she's used to it.

I can recall the specific swelling and contours of my face one morning when we were 15½, driving permits tucked into our jean pockets, Kari in a short skirt, her strong legs tanned darkly. That was when we told each other the secret. I felt cleansed and dirty all at once, but also giddy that we'd shared. I wanted to hold her hand. It actually wasn't as large of a coincidence as it seemed then, and now after all these years it's embarrassing to think how we were amazed at our luck, the chance to share something horrible together, not real-izing it was commonplace at Washburn's Tabernacle Church. The deacon had molested us both, and lots of others, but we were kids and believed it was our own private tragedy, one we thought made us closer. In fact, the night before she left for Durham, Kari said with nonchalance, "We were so stupid to think we're the only ones he got to, Hobbie. Do you think that's why we've stayed together so long?" She asks those kinds of questions all the time. Hard ones. They can't be answered, or romanticized. She knows neither of us can explain how we ended up here. Or at least I can't. If Kari can now, after the therapy and weight loss, she's apparently not coming home anytime soon to enlighten me.

Finally, after avoiding it all day, I open the FedEx package and see the termination forms for what they are, just a formality. I won't sign and return them. And Kari would back me up on this. The bank in town, First Union Southern, is firing me. The papers state: in-subordination. Which is true, basically. I didn't want to work the front cubbyholes; I specifically stated I preferred the drive-thru when I took the job six months ago, after Kari left for Durham. The trouble started with a new manager, a guy with perfect skin, flawless teeth, and naturally wavy hair he wore in a loosely styled cut. He didn't know the first thing about our kind of lives. Kari always says, "They're a dime a dozen. Tellering is just like fast food, but instead of tacos or burgers, we handle tens and twenties, same thing, and they're easy jobs to get. Instead of yelling, 'The fries are down,' we say, 'The deposits are up!'" Kari laughed and playfully slugged me in the arm. She'd said, "If we get experience tellering, we can move anywhere. We can see all the major cities, and do our own thing. It pays crappy, but the world will always need tellers, Hobbie." I didn't tell her how awful it would be for me to have customer after customer approach my cubby and stare at my face while I counted out their 50 bucks in fives. But just like always, Kari mentioned it before I could. "People don't even look at tellers anymore, they're too busy filling in their checkbooks or talking on cell phones." For a while, when we worked at a Citizens Trust Credit Union in Toledo, she would apply her foundation to my face each morning, trying to conceal my worst spots, but before long I quit getting up early enough to let her give me a makeover. If I could do things over, go back in time and try to be a better man, I'd make certain to be up at the crack of dawn every morning so her soft hands could make me less grotesque.

Through the window, I can see more snow falling, swirling inside a cone of brightness from the security light. Before long, just as I am about to go back to re-read a letter from when Kari weighed 210, the bear returns. I wish the house were made of metal. I'm reminded of a haunted house, how your whole body seems to spasm with fear. I get up and creep to the kitchen sink, making my body compact, hoping I'll be negligible. I flip the light on and off, but this time the bear ignores me and decides to carry the bag of trash into the bushes. He's hungry and willing to eat what there is.

three Morning has finally come. The snow is pristine across the yard, crystallized and as bright as copy paper, and for some reason, I think nothing bad could happen on a day like this. With a hot cup of coffee in my hand, steam rising toward my face, I open the front door. The trees and fence posts in every direction sport two inches of stiffened fluff; sometime in the early morning hours, a freezing rain fell, not a lot, but enough to glue the snow in place, keeping it from whirling freely in the strong wind. I sniff the air and detect nothing but wind-scoured cold, and yet I realize something is unsettled in me. For several moments I just stand and stare, hoping whatever is out there will see my lingering as courage.

I close the door against the wintry mix in just enough time to keep Terry from shooting onto the lawn. Together we trek through the house to the sliding doors that open onto the back deck. We step out cautiously. The bear has managed to leave a nice mess on the ground, but for the most part, our waste—the cardboard boxes of Terry's Moist-n-Meaty dog food and my microwavable dinner containers—has disappeared, rotting now in the belly of the bear. I hope this was his last forage for grub, but I'm not certain; in a day or so, it will be back in the 50s and he'll still be skinny and voracious.

Terry barks at the sight of the strewn garbage, then whines until I pick him up. Back inside, I warm his food in the microwave and add a cup of chicken broth to his bowl, and then go to the bathroom for a shower. In the mirror, I examine my face. Not much is new: A few overnight whiteheads have formed a tribe, and several crusty scabs are in the final stage of healing, but that's par for my bumpy course.

Terry sleeps as I dress and watch the news. Atlanta is in a tizzy about the inch of snow there. Schools are closed, and salt and sand trucks are on the interstates. I switch to the weather channel to find out how Durham fared in the storm. To my surprise, three and a half inches have fallen and I instantly picture Kari tasting it with her tongue.

I feel stuck. There have been a hundred times when I've packed a small bag and started for the car, only to put the keys back on their hook and slip to the bathroom mirror. My anxiety shows on the festers of my cheeks, along the harshly squeezed bridge of my nose.

I turn off the television and watch Terry's chest rising and falling with his noisy breathing. His sleeping position reminds me of a baby, even though by human years Terry's already well into retirement. He's almost 10 years old and it shows in the chivalrous gray beard he sports and the peppering of white hairs that line his swayed back. With nothing to do but contemplate Kari's most recent letter, and anticipate the one that should come in the mail today, I decide to call her father.

Roth Francis is a man who perpetually confuses me. Ever since junior high he's alternated between acting like I'm interesting to regarding me as if I were a statue. One birthday I'll get a card from him that has a long and touching paragraph, written in his hard-pressed cursive, and the next he'll forget it altogether. He's the same way with Kari. He either pours it out or clams up. But he worked as the accountant at the Washburn Tabernacle, and he, more than anyone, knows what we've had to do, how we've had to live, even though he won't talk about it.

Roth doesn't speak much of Kari's mother in front of me. After we moved to Atlanta from Colorado Springs to be nearer to him and his faulty heart, he said at Thanksgiving that year, a little too much whiskey sour in his belly, "Kari, your mother wasn't a perfect woman, but she wanted you to have a life without her fouling it up." Then he left and went to his bedroom to nap while we cleared the table. Kari ate scraps from the plates as we worked, her face blank, her large body bumping carelessly into the counters, the fridge door, the open dish-washer. The next day, while we kissed in the shower at our apartment, I tried to caress her ample hips where small bruises had appeared from where she'd knocked around in the kitchen. When I tried to touch them like she'd done the burnt-out stars on my galactic face, she swat-ted me away, saying, "Don't, they're ugly. My legs are huge."

The phone rings once. Roth answers with a boom. "Hello," he says with genuine enthusiasm. "How can I help you?" It's as if he's still in the church annex answering calls with faith and determination.

"Hi, Roth. It's Hobbie. How are you?"

"Can't complain, son. How 'bout yourself?" Roth has toned down the vigor in his voice, and I can't tell if it's because he's relaxed about talking to me or disappointed.

"Fine," I say as I watch Terry slowly move into the foyer, his fur mussed and his small eyes sleepy. He approaches me and sits down by my feet, weakly wagging his tail. I'm distracted and don't know how long I've been silent when Roth speaks up.

"I said, what do you need, son?" I often wonder whether he thinks that what happened to me, the only boy on the deacon's list, was due to some masculine defect on my part. Terry whines to be let out. It's cold, so I decide he'll simply pee outside near the door.

"Hold on," I tell Roth. I crack the door, and Terry meekly steps onto the icy porch and makes his way down the steps. Roth is still talking.

"If you're calling about Kari I've not talked with her. You two ought to have worked out a better system before she started up there." He sounds annoyed, and really, he should be. I've not pro-tested much at our arrangement, yet I've called him weekly, some-times more, to see if he's had a phone call from his daughter. He's mentioned our poor communication setup before. Years ago, after the church decided to let the deacon get away with what he'd done, Roth sent Kari away for almost a year to her grandmother's in Colorado. Back then, at 15, we thought our lives were over, not being able to talk on the phone for hours, but now it's fine with her.

I apologize to Roth for the inconvenience and watch out the slim pane of glass by the door as Terry hikes his tiny leg to urinate in an unspoiled ridge of pure white snow. His brown body looks like a mole on some giant's flawless, milky facial skin. Roth breathes into the phone, as I continue, though not intentionally, to ignore him, preoccupied by Terry outside.

"What's her weight now?" he asks, which he doesn't do often, but I've confided in him about the letters, how they arrive with the tally in the corner. I start, "She's about…" but stop. I notice Terry hunkering down in the snow, almost burrowing into it. I can barely see him through the glass now, when out of nowhere a hobbling mass of black cuts across the white lawn, lumbering toward Terry in no particular hurry.

I drop the phone, already knowing what I am seeing but not able to get my brain to register it completely. I can hear Roth nearly shout, "Son, are you there? What in the hell's going on?" I yank a flimsy umbrella from a blue and white waist-high vase and charge out the door. The black bear looks weak and wild. I flay my arms and shake the umbrella in his direction, but his large paw has already been lifted, now falling toward terrified Terry. My breath is coming fast and shallow. Terry's muffled whining is all I can take. I run straight for the bear, umbrella hoisted like a spear. The bear picks Terry up in its mouth and tosses him like a dishrag across the slick snow. Blood surrounds the bear like drips of paint.

Before I know what I've done, the tip of the umbrella jams into the taunt neck of the mangy thing. At first the bear jumps back and shakes its head. Then it rears up on its hind legs and growls and takes a step in my direction. I whisk the umbrella in a circle over my head like a ninja and let the bear have a hard smack upside the shoulder.

I turn slightly toward Terry and without thinking, take my eyes off the bear. A quick blast of relief gives my whole body an adrenalin surge when I spot the mailman pulling up. But just then, as I am waving frantically to get his attention, the bear pushes me to the ground. I can see Terry turning circles in the red snow and the mail truck bounding toward us just as a sharp, ringing pain registers first along my arm and again across the terrain of my face. I think to myself, "Go ahead. How much worse can you make it, just leave Terry alone." Then everything turns quiet and dark, and there's finally some heat in all the cold.

four I wake up in an igloo, one eye open. My mind tells me that's what it is, at least. The bed and walls and even the television set appear to be fashioned out of nicely packed snow. The blanket over my legs is also made of snow, but it's just a dusting, light and airy. I open the other eye and try and focus. In the doorway the mailman is reading a comic book and slugging back a soda. Suddenly, I have a vision of Terry as a white stuffed animal, his insides poking out of a torn seam along his belly. How is he? I sit up too quickly and feel sick to my stomach. The hurling sound I am holding back gets the mailman's attention and he stands up straighter off the doorjamb.

"Hold on, I'll get a nurse." He's still clutching the rolled-up comic when it occurs to him to grab the waste can. I upchuck nothing, dry heave and spit. I retreat back into the pillows as if truly dying. My mailman says again, louder, "Nurse?" In a flash, he's out the door and stomping down the hall.

My forearm feels tight. I find that a broad swatch of gauze covers all the skin from my wrist up past my elbow. I try and say something to myself, call Terry's name, but nothing comes out. My lips are numb, as if I've had a root canal. My neck is as stiff as a metal bar. The television begins to melt, turn back into the black plastic Sony that it is. The silent weatherman is all movement in front of the map, areas of pink indicating snow.

A nurse wearing pastel blue scrubs strides into the room, a face full of gleaming teeth. She's got flurries and frost in her hair, white light dancing from it. My mailman has had to jog to keep up with her. She approaches the bed and lifts my arm without asking, takes my pulse, all the while smiling, lips lifted from those ice-block teeth. She places my arm near the bedrail and says, "Better shut this off. Your heart rate is slow, sir." She twists the knob on an IV and motions for the mailman to sit down. He does as he's told, all wide-eyed and attentive.

"Sir, the postman brought you in his truck. Do you remember what happened?" She's got a southern drawl, a nice one, and brown hair in a ponytail.

"Yes," I finally manage, the words thawing, breaking out. I can remember a snippet of the ride, lying in the front seat, bleeding onto a stack of mail.

The mailman stands and says, "Bud, you, like, almost got eaten by that bear, dude." Since I've been in town, I've only seen the mailman, never heard him talk, but I figured he'd sound this way.

"How's Terry?"

They both look at each other briefly.

"Oh," the nurse sighs, "your dog."

The mailman steps closer and says, "Dude, I'm not sure. I dropped him off at the vet's after I got you here. They didn't tell me anything, so I came back to the hospital."

The urge to touch my face is both irritating and embarrassing, as if I can't even forget about my acne in the care of a nurse. I reach up and run my hand across one cheek; it feels strange. There's a new ridge with brambly sprouts poking out in several directions, puckered and tight. The nurse smiles down at me with real empathy and takes my hand. "Sir, that dern ole' bear ripped a pretty good cut on your face. Eleven stitches, and a slight concussion, but you'll be as fine as wine, sugar," she says with a wink, placing my hand on my chest as if I were on display in a casket. I wonder whether she was in the room when the doctor sewed me up, if she was privy to the wisecracks I assume the attending ER doc made when he started. "Geez, might as well leave this guy's face wide open, what's he got to lose, you know what I'm saying!" Even a bear clawing my face can't make me forget the acne.

The mailman smells of marijuana as he comes closer to the bed. "Dude, when I floored it at the bear he took off real fast, like, you know, he was scared, too."

"Thank you," I say in a tone that sounds too dramatic, but truly, who knows what would've happened if he hadn't come along. "I've got to see how Terry is. Do you have a number for the vet?"

"No, dude, but I can stop by there if you want. I gotta get the rest of the mail, like, delivered." It's too hot in the hospital room; a warm blast of air eddies over my head, and it feels as if I could drown in it.

"Yes, please," I say as he stares at my face. Is it the sutured, raw skin or the bumpy zits and puffed-up boils he's taken the opportunity to scope out?

"Dude, I'll check on the man, Terry, see what's up with him." He keeps right on staring at my face, and I want to crawl under the blanket and hide. Finally, he says, "Man, that cut looks wicked. Take care." He meanders toward a bag on the empty bed next to me. "Oh, I almost forgot. You got mail." He hands over two letters addressed in Kari's handwriting. I frown at the sight of blood on them. "Yeah, you kinda, like, bled all over them, dude." He hangs his head. "I don't know what I'm gonna do with the other stuff with blood on them. Have to call my soop." He wheels around and hightails it out of the room.

The nurse prepares a yellow mixture in a plastic container. She approaches my face, whipping the stuff like cake batter. "This is to prevent infection. He didn't get you too good on the arm, just a nice scratch." She spreads the salve along the stitched flesh. It feels cold, like menthol, and stings. I secretly hope she'll use her expert knowledge to caulk my entire face with the yellow, smelly stuff.

"Do you have any family we should call, hon?" the nurse asks, squinting at me, the wooden tongue depressor buttering the salve gently over every centimeter of the cut. She is average size for an American woman, which Kari has emblazoned into my mind, a size eight. Her face is perfectly round, and she has bothered to wear lipstick.

I don't know how to answer her question. Do I have a wife? No. Do I have a significant other, someone whom I've been in a relationship with for over 20 years? Yes. Will she come and get me? No, she's not let me talk with her for six months. None of these answers seem to make sense. And once again, I feel that familiar internal pull, the one that tells me to ignore Kari's wishes and do what I think is right, but it also tells me not to risk it, just like I've always done. Finally I say, "No, not really," which feels like a betrayal.

Finishing up, the nurse tells me, "Well, you shouldn't have to be here long. Just want to make sure that bear doesn't have rabies. The game warden is probably already out there by now. If it's one of those citified bears, they'll kill him in no time."

I am taken aback at her callous tone, but then again, she operates within the confines of life and death every day, so I assume she's only being practical. I picture my poor Terry with rabies, his mouth foaming madly with white froth, a tiny, tiny version of Old Yeller locked in the corn crib, barking, unaware that his owner must put him down through snotty proclamations of love and devotion. The pain medicine is starting to fade.

"Do you know the name of the vet in town?" I ask, realizing that in the six months I've lived here, I haven't taken him there yet. He doesn't like going, and like an indulgent parent, I avoid making him do things he dislikes. The nurse is focused again, wiping the excess salve onto the lip of the open container, scraping each side over and over until it's entirely cleaned off. She removes her latex gloves.

"I'll call the one I think it is and see if we can find out about Mr. Terry. You rest now," she commands.

She's out the door and off to tend to another patient before I can say thank you. Alone, I am curious about the cut on my face, wondering whether it'll make any difference, perhaps shock the skin there so much that it wouldn't think of producing any more acne. I touch the whiskery sutures again, the loose ends like the coarse legs of a fly. If a bear can't dig out what's there, how can I? Processed-food smells creep in from the hall, as an attendant slowly rolls a stainless steel cart door-to-door. Suddenly, I am famished; my stomach churns and growls, empty and sick feeling.

A young man with a fu manchu pushing the cart pops his head in and asks, "You wanna meal?" I nod heartily. He wheels his cart into the room and I'm expecting him to say something like: "My cousin had real bad zits. You tried tar paper?" It's the kind of thing I get all the time. But instead he says with sympathy, "That looks awful, man." Still, I'm not certain what part of my face he's talking about. I wish they'd bandaged my whole head like a mummy's. He arranges the tray on my swivel table, careful not to hit my bandaged arm. If he were to give advice on my acne, that would make him only the millionth person in my life to offer up some supposed secret cure that will leave my face as fair as a Teen Beat boy's, my soul absolved of any wrongdoing.

"Nope, never tried that," I say, even though he's not actually said what I had him saying in my head.

"What?" he says, as he prepares my tray. He places my carton of grade school milk next to my plastic spork and lifts the cardboard lids from the apple pie and cube of steaming lasagna.

"Sorry," I say, "I thought you said something else." He nods, probably assuming I'm still out of it from the drugs. The truth is, I'm tired and worried to death about Terry. I think only for a minute of calling my own parents, but my father ended up leaving Pittsburgh to find work, and we didn't see much of him after that. A phone call here and there, some money, but by the time I entered high school, he was gone for good, worn out from my mother's unchecked mental illness. Calling her right now would be an exercise in the absurd; she'd be drunk, unable to even understand it was her son calling.

I've already taken a cautious bite of the lasagna and picked up the garlic bread when a voice booms through the air.

"Watch it, sonny, or you'll be in Durham with Kari before you know it," he says, cracking a joke about my picky eating habits. Roth acts as if he doesn't even see the attendant trying to get through the doorway, shoving right by him without a word. I stop chewing, the stitches not giving to the motion of my jaw, like they might just pop out and lay the wound open all over again.

Roth pulls up a chair and plops down. He's still in decent physical shape for his age, except for the heart condition that runs in his family. He's not a big man, but his arms are muscular and he likes to work out.

"Damn, Hobbie, you scared the living crap out of me, son. I tried and tried to call you back, but there was no answer. Figured I'd better call the police to check on you. The dispatcher told me what had happened." Roth shakes his large head and sees that I am not eating at the moment, just staring at him. "Eat, you'll need your strength."

five Sometime during the night they've pulled my plug. I awake in the early hours of the morning and find that the IV stand is gone and that the soft skin where the needle had been is covered with a bandage and a cotton ball, a deep purple bruise peeking out. The hospital room is enchanting, and while that's hard to believe, it's awash in an iridescent glow, a perfect setting in which to hide from the world.

The curtains are open and the sun is coming up in a blaze of bright orange. Some of the snow has melted, but from the bed I can see that a few limbs still have white tufts on them, delicate, dripping water. I look around the room and spot the chair Roth sat in, now folded up.

I feel lonely and abandoned, half-thinking Roth would've kept up an all-night vigil. It's silly, but I'd hoped this would bring us closer.

The cut on my face is pulsing but not unbearably painful. The idea is funny to me. *The bear cut is not unbearable.* I wish Kari were here so I could share the joke with her, also so that she could baby me some over the cut. My mouth is dry and I want some cola. I look around to find a button to push for the nurse, but only black switches and portholes for respirators, suction devices, and EKGs come into view.

I can't remember falling asleep or Roth leaving, but I can recall our conversation. As I sit in the quiet hospital bed, the rush of heat coming from the vents the only discernable noise, I ponder his challenge. "You don't go get her now, Hobbie, who knows where she'll go. You two grew up together; now's not the time to be growing apart." Why was he so sappy? Over the years I've always taken his inconsistent emotions toward us as disapproval, so why's he so willing to have us together again?

I prop myself up in the bed. Kari's bloody letters that the mailman left are on the swivel table untouched. With Roth around, and my head chock full of medicine, I didn't get to read them, and now I want to consume them more than an ice-cold Pepsi. My hands are weak as I tear open the end of the first letter and notice right away that it's missing the printed weight in the corner. I turn the paper over and search for it, like a monkey that has been conditioned. The lined paper is blank all the way to the bottom where Kari has written: "I love you, Hobbie, I've got to face that."

The next letter is covered in more dark blood, the envelope heavier. I don't bother to gently tear the end off but simply rip it at the edges. I unfold the paper in a rush only to find the corner blank again. At the top Kari has started as if she's going to write a long letter. "Dear Hobbie," but after that it's just a few sentences. I notice she's not used ink but opted for a dull pencil. The writing is difficult to read. It reads: "It's over. Weight doesn't matter anymore. There's so much more that's weighing me down. Your Face, my Weight, the DEACON, my dad, our fear, our love, all of it's so heavy I can't conceive of losing an ounce of it. How can I still feel all this bulk after losing so much?" I turn the page over and find a lipstick kiss, smudged but still intact, a dark crimson color I recognize; it makes Kari look sultry and fine. My throat hurts, the emotion stuck right in the center. I need to see her, let her know I'm okay, see that she is, too, hold her in my arms, and talk all night.

I put the letter back in the envelope carefully like it's a relic. It's almost 8 a.m. and I have to get out of here. There's a whistle outside my door. I look in that direction and see no one. I figure it's an attendant using a secret code to call his co-worker for a joint on the freight elevator. A slight knock gets my attention again. A hand and forearm reaches to knock again and disappears.

"Come in," I say, becoming annoyed, thinking it's perhaps a hospital volunteer doing his best at bedside hilarity.

"Special delivery, sir," a voice says, an obvious attempt to sound disguised. The mailman steps into the room and says in a baby-talk voice, "It's me, Daddy. I came to see you." He's holding a squirming bundle of bandages in a blanket, a wagging tail. Terry whines, nearly leaps to the bed. I can't help but smile at his eagerness. The mailman smiles, too, a gap-toothed grin as he ambles toward me, boots unlaced. "Dude, I just picked him up. The vet says he's luckier than shit, man. Says if that bear hadn't gotten interested in you this little dude would have been history with a capital H."

Terry looks tired and scared as he climbs into the bed, nestles up to my side and lies down with a moan. His back is covered in gauze. I stroke his ears and inspect his legs. I was wrong; they weren't broken. That's a relief, but it breaks my heart to see him in this condition. The mailman keeps smiling, looking down at Terry and me in the bed, as if he'd healed us himself.

"Thank you so much for bringing him," I say. "But how'd you get them to give him to you? How'd you get him in the hospital?"

The mailman steps back and shifts his weight. His hair today is not slicked back; it's unmoussed and hanging around his face like a Dutch boy's. "Dude, everybody trusts mailmen." He puffs up his chest, mocking his profession, and says, "Besides, they wanted me to give you the bill." He hands me a sheaf of dot matrix paper and a letter from Kari. "No blood this time, dude."

He sidles to the door and says over his shoulder, "Got to get on the road, make up for the stuff that didn't get delivered yesterday." The room is quiet once again. Terry licks my hand as I whisper to him. The poor guy looks so much smaller all swaddled in gauze. Normally, I'd worry about hospital rules, but I'm too tired to care, so I think of how assertive Kari would be in this situation and it gives me a streak of defiance. I stroke Terry's bony head slowly, just the way he likes it. Before long, he is snoring, a sound that activates my basic optimism. I lie in the bed and listen, close my eyes, too, and drift off.

Less than a half-hour later I pop my eyes open at the noise of a floor buffer revving up. It's a sound I associate with the Washburn Tabernacle, more specifically, a horrible memory there. And now the memory is back, full force.

I've been asked to stay after youth group to help with mopping and polishing the floors of the basement. I love to do it. Riding the buffer as it swirls across the gray linoleum makes me feel like I'm on the ocean. Roth is in his office, punching an adding machine, tallying up the sabbath's tithed dough. I can hear his fingers hitting the keys as if he were mad at the devil for making people give so little. On his desk he has a picture of his daughter, Kari, in seventh grade, same as me, but I've not met her yet; however, I've seen her beautiful picture when I've dusted for him. Now his door is closed and I'm alone in the large room where a worn area rug lies on the floor. The deacon is somewhere upstairs helping two girls practice their readings for the upcoming revival; the tent is already set up on the lawn next to the John Deere dealership. Pittsburgh is cold and it's been raining all day, the silver droplets clinging to the church windows. My dad dropped me off on his way to a second job that would finally get the best of him; he'd been working extra to pay off my mother's credit card debt, and he was starting to give up.

I move the dusty rug and marvel at the concentric oval rings of sand underneath; they're like a maze made by ants. I sweep the dirt into a dustpan so I can rev up the buffer. First I mop, then dry the floor and put down a polish that feels good to sniff. Later, a couple of kids will be busted huffing it and get expelled from the youth group. Much later, one of them will end up being killed selling crack downtown, but by then Kari and I and even Roth will have been gone a while; we'll hear the sad news from one of Roth's old church friends. I remember the time that same kid and I split a funnel cake and he let me in on what girls liked about French kissing. He's another lost child of the tabernacle now, grown up and gone.

I plug in the buffer; a spark pops and a tiny fizzle buzzes like a bee from the socket. I approach the buffer as if it's a mechanical bull.

I place my feet on the outline of two solid shoes and turn the switch on. I'm going slowly in a circle, feeling the slight brush of air over my face, where my skin has recently started to work itself into what it is today, but I've not yet heard it called *acne vulgaris*.

I'm getting dizzy and my stomach feels jittery. I've not eaten much, only a couple bites of hot dog during the youth group gathering. All at once, the buffer stops dead and tosses me off gently. I press the button and when that doesn't work, I glance over at the wall where I'd plugged it in. The deacon stands there, holding the plug in his hand like a dead mouse.

I can still hear Roth tapping away at his figures inside the office. The basement of the church feels as if it's gotten colder and my stomach is for certain upset; it gurgles and I feel sick.

"I think the floors can wait, Mr. Hobbie," says the deacon, a smile on his face. "What'd ya say you come upstairs with me and help out with the storeroom." His blue eyes stare at me from across the bare, half-buffed floor. He still seems like a nice man. He's always seemed to accept me the way I am, even liking me—poking me in the ribs whenever I help gather up the hymnals, sometimes winking at me like we are pals.

"Okay," I say, not wanting to leave the fun buffer. "You'll be right back down here in a few minutes," the deacon tells me. "It shouldn't take long."

I follow him up the stairs and into the back portion of the Washburn Tabernacle. The building is old in some parts and new in others. There are lots of additions, most of which look like ranch-style homes that have been attached to the central Victorian house that serves as the sanctuary. There's always some kind of construction going on. It's a growing church, fanning itself out across the lots like plumage. It seems every week a new dead person has donated another parcel of land to the church council.

The red carpet is bouncy underneath my feet; parts of the floor in this area are patched and uneven. The deacon stops in front of me and says with a large, toothy grin, "My shoelace is untied." He fixes his eyes on me like he's giving a commandment, then holds out his foot as if he were Cinderella, waiting for me to act. We stand there for several moments; I'm confused. The church is humming a godly quietness. The blue eyes scan my face, accusing me of something I've yet to do.

"Your face is a mark of sin, son," says the deacon in a voice that contradicts his eyes. I can feel embarrassment making my face even more ugly, hot, and red. The deacon still holds his foot out, keeping his eyes on me. "Tie my shoe, son. Good deeds unto others are the path to heaven. Don't do it too tight."

I bend down and pick up the flat laces. His shoes are black brogues with scuffs healed over, the polish grimy across the toes. His weight shifts and I feel a hand on my cheek, brushing it gently. "You're an ugly boy for now, but you'll grow out of it." He sighs and sucks in. "Listen to me, do what I say and you'll grow." He retracts his hand as I secure the knot, pulling the tips of the laces so the bow is centered; I want to do a good job for him. He tousles my hair as I start to stand; then his hand is flat on my head, pushing me down so that my knees, which hurt, are planted into the floor. There's a leak in the ceiling and a bucket on the floor to catch the rain. A stale odor of water-damaged hymnals is strong in the storage room, decrepit and musty. A peach-colored curtain hangs over a window behind him, letting in a strange light. The sound of a zipper coming down rips inside my ears. I try and stand again, but his fingers are like a crown on my hair, circling my head. His breath comes out in halting puffs.

"Do you want to grow out if it?" Something other than his hand is on my cheek now, something warm. I don't answer. I don't even know what he means. His body smells like the men my dad drinks with, a mix of aftershave over body odor, smoky, too. He pushes his penis into my mouth and I gag. He tells me it's okay, all boys are bad, but that *my* sin shows all over my face. I try and pull away, but his hand on my head holds me hard, as if he were palming a basketball. He bucks and my eyes water. Then he moves away and back into the peach light taking over the room. A door is closed and he is gone.

I pull myself up from my knees by grabbing one of the bookshelves, and spit, and spit, and spit. I scrub my mouth with the sleeve of my shirt. The floor squeaks and groans as I leave the room and run down the stairs.

Back downstairs, the basement is even colder. My eyes are wet and it's hard to see. Roth's office is silent. The buffer stands where I left it, the cord lying like an asp on the dirty floor. I could get a pan of water from the canteen and dip the three prongs of the plug in it, shock myself to death, I think. The deacon said I was ugly but would grow out of it; my face, the mark of sin, is to blame. What else could explain why he made me do it? I stumble toward the buffer and climb on. I switch it to the lowest speed and let the machine idle; it's not able to turn at all, the buffer just stutters under my weight. One more notch up and it begins to turn, another click, and another and I'm feeling all the power under me. I accidentally slip and get caught up in the cord and my feet are trapped. Finally I leap off the buffer and fall down in a tangle. I stand and see that my Adidas sneakers are untied.

I bend to lace them and feel a lurch in my midsection. I puke up two hunks of hot dog right next to the buffer. I know I'm crying but can't hear it. Acrid saliva drips from my mouth as I get on all fours. Nothing will come up now, but my body won't quit trying.

Roth's office door creaks open and footsteps come closer and closer, purposeful on the solid floor. Something dark comes up as I heave once more with a force that seems to burn my rib cage. The inside of my mouth is bitter. I rock back on my knees and look up. Roth bends down and puts his hand on my back.

"Goodness. You're not feeling well, are you?" He lifts me up by the arm and walks me like a wounded solider to his office. He eases me into a chair in front of his desk, retrieves his wastebasket, and puts it at my feet. "Try and hit it if you feel sick again." He walks behind his desk and sits down, offers me Kleenex from a macramé cozy.

"You okay there?" he says, as I dry heave again into the trash. I shake my head, sputtering. Roth is wearing a tweed jacket with no tie, a white, crisp shirt underneath. "I'm going to go clean up the floor out there. You sit tight. It's Hobbie, right?" I nod. "You sit here and don't hold it back if you feel you've got to vomit." He stops briefly by my chair, puts a hand on my shoulder, and gives a quick, tight squeeze.

Outside, rain patters against the windows. Alone in the office I try and put all the pieces together in my head, but it's no use, I'm a jangle of thoughts. When I bend at the waist to spit into the trashcan, I can feel my legs shuddering.

Roth returns, drying his hands; he must've washed them after cleaning up my mess. They're red as he scrubs a rough paper towel over them, then says, "Pardon me" and tosses the wad into the trashcan. He returns to his chair behind the desk and says nothing else.

He straightens papers and performs a few more rounds of rapid 10-key calculations, scratching down figures with a sharp pencil. It grows darker outside, and the heat in his office kicks on and blows down on my head.

Finally Roth picks up his car keys from a spot on his orderly desk and takes me by the arm. We leave the church. The drizzle has made the air look foggy. Roth opens the car door and helps me inside. His car is neat and pine-scented. A holder that separates coins is well stocked and flawlessly arranged. It takes a while for the defroster to clear the window, and in the silence Roth reaches over to make certain the strap of my seat belt is snug. Circles emerge through the condensation on the windshield, the heat making them grow bigger every second. Roth puts the car in gear and backs up. In the passenger's side mirror, the lights in the church blur in the rain as we slowly move away. It's the only thing I can see.

The time in the car with Roth felt like it would go on forever. For years I associated foggy car windows with the abuse. I'd be warming up the car in Minneapolis, just sitting in the parking lot, hating the idea of going into the bank for another day of tellering, and as the defroster kicked on and the window cleared, I could swear I smelled the deacon, him sitting in the back seat, his creepy hands about to grab my shoulders. It all comes back in a rush of images, just like the floor buffer has triggered it now.

The memory of the deacon compels me to sit up more, heal myself. Terry is still conked out, the snore now more pronounced. I try very carefully not to wake him as I open yet another of Kari's letters. The lined paper is completely blank, but there's a photo. I recognize it immediately. The Polaroid is of Kari's cousin's baby, who died shortly after his birth. The little body is covered with at least 10 large birthmarks. Kari brought the picture home with her the year we were separated during high school and she was living with her grandmother in Colorado. I remember feeling for the tiny fella, his skin also marred and abnormal.

From then on she'd kept the photo stuck to various things through high school and college: a veneered dresser, the visor in her Beetle Bug, the scrapbook she kept with the roses and movie tickets I'd bought her. One night, she held the picture as we sat in my rusty car and talked in the cold air. "You should've seen him. He was so tiny and sick," she said. "He reminded me of you with all those sad spots." She sniffled and I hugged her, and we ended up kissing and promising each other we'd stay together the rest of our lives. Kari had gained her first new pounds while she was in Colorado, her legs and butt then growing more and more round as the months passed after she was home. Roth told her it was just the way her mother was built, that she was a beautiful girl and I was one lucky guy to get the chance to accompany her to the prom. I was in complete agreement.

Once we started living together after college Kari kept the photo hidden away. I'd find it tucked into a book I was reading or spot it in a keepsake box she hid under the bed, perfumed sachets covering it. Why, then, had she sent it to me in a blank letter with no explanation?

I sit in the bed staring at the wall. I can feel my face thumping again with blood. There's a complimentary comb and hand-held mirror along with several bottles of body wash, lotion, too, on the swivel table, courtesy of the hospital's Hospitality Committee. I pick up the mirror and take a deep breath. Back in my early twenties I went through a period Kari called my vamp-years, where I draped a towel over the medicine cabinet mirror after a shower so I wouldn't have to see my face. But still, I couldn't stop myself from picking. Late at night or after a day working at one of the myriad banks we tellered in, I'd sneak to the bathroom and survey my face, take my time deciding which quadrant to begin with. I'd use a special needle and kept a box of Kleenex nearby as I squeezed and dug into the sores on my face, going after the most apparent whiteheads first and then digging into anything that looked remotely inflamed. I'd spend hours at the sink, an entire box of tissue stained with blood, piled in a heap on the floor, my face as hideous as a killer's. I'd bend to pick up the balled-up tissue and make all kinds of promises to myself about not doing it again, but it never really worked.

I adjust the mirror to examine the stitched-up bear cut. It's an awful-looking thing, longer than I'd expected and by the way the torn skin is puckered up and pulled together, the edges revealing thick lips of skin, much deeper, too. I think of the surgeon again, how he would've had to push the needle through acne to suture me up.

All at once it occurs to me that Terry and I are survivors of a bear attack, a black bear attack at that, not a very common thing, and certainly not something I would've thought either one of us could've managed alone. I can't believe we were not killed, eaten up and found days later in the backyard, ripped open like the bags of trash. If we can survive a bear attack, maybe we can take on anything. The notion gives me some energy, makes me think of a life with other possibilities, new strength.

Terry flips onto his side and I worry his cut will hurt, but by the way he shifts into a deeper gear of snoring, I decide he's fine. I take the Polaroid and insert it into the envelope just as Roth fake-coughs at the door and walks confidently into the room. He has a look on his face of both disappointment and concern. Terry wakes up and slowly moves onto his hind end; we're both sore. He growls at Roth, a new, braver part of his personality emerging. They lock each other in a gaze, as if neither has ever seen such a strange creature in all their lives.

six   It's hard to imagine that enough time has passed that Kari's and my favorite heavy-metal songs are now fodder for sappy Muzak. I've chosen the radio button from the control arm on the hospital bed and am now being fully assaulted by a piped-in song called "Round-n-Round" by Ratt. One of the things that Roth disapproves of, besides our living together and not getting married, is our passion for heavy-metal music. After Colorado, when we were in the 10th grade and the tabernacle had found a new pastor, the elders felt they needed to bring themselves up to speed with the world of teenagers, which meant they booked a local Christian heavy-metal band called Beloved Crucifixion to perform at a dance. Later, when we were getting associate degrees at the community college, Kari and I discovered a band named Stryper, and we played their album, "To Hell With the Devil," over and over, first on the turntable and then the CD version. After that, we stuck with secular heavy metal. I can still see Kari in a pair of tight Lee jeans, her thighs bulging at the seams, neck doused with Gloria Vanderbilt perfume, as we waited in the car in the parking lot after a concert, letting the mob of traffic dissipate as we kissed and held hands, just like we were on a date, even though we lived together and were working at our first banking jobs.

It's hard to imagine we're even the same people from back then, as I wait for the nurse to discharge me. Roth is gone, having stayed for less than 10 minutes. He chatted a bit then clammed up again, not like the day before, but so very much like his personality, hot then cold. I reluctantly allowed him to take Terry with him and now I regret it, but the dog couldn't stay in the hospital. Roth has always been able to get me to agree to things I don't want. Kari hasn't ever reminded me of him, but now, with the stupid letters and forced restrictions, I realize they may have more in common than I'd ever thought.

I've been allowed to dress and put on my shoes. A nurse-in-training removed the bandage on my shoulder and arm, nothing under the gauze except for a few red scratches. While I wait for the official paperwork and my after-care instructions, I pull out the picture of the mottled baby boy. Kari never told me the name of her cousin or why the child died. The whole idea of him, his skin, the Polaroid, the way he's always been a part of our lives in the migrating photograph, seems odd to me for the first time. People define themselves by their tragedies, by the artifacts of some horrible event, which become more and more mundane as they move from apartment to house, from the '80s to the '90s and on into a brand-new century. It could be a curl of hair glued to a prayer card or a keepsake urn full of a twin brother's ashes—all of them morph and blend until they turn into just another knick-knack or mantel display. That's how the photograph of the baby boy seemed yesterday, normal and as familiar as our cheap silverware, but now, now the picture feels peculiar in my hand, as if it might leave a stain on my fingers that will give me away somehow.

My nurse comes in and smiles widely. "I heard your dog got up here to see you." Her smile fades some, and she winks. "What I don't see I can't report." She stands at the end of the bed and flips through her clipboard, initialing lines and scribbling the date. She reminds me of the men who work at quick lube joints, trying to rush through the requirements to get me out soon enough so I might fill out a customer-care card with high marks.

As I watch her scrawling on the paper, ponytail jiggling, I feel a sense of accomplishment that I've not picked at my face for a while, but there's another edge to the thought, too, a cut going in a different direction. I feel the energy of the past couple days building and need a release. All I can think about is getting home and spending time in front of the mirror, de-stressing by digging in.

"There you go, Mr. Hobbie," says the nurse, ripping the sheet of paper off. "Of course, you know, rabies in bears is rare, but they'll need to catch it to make sure it wasn't infected, until then, if you have any symptoms of fever, confusion, or rapid breathing you should come in right away."

In the wheelchair I clutch the letters from Kari like a granny would her purse. Before long, I am sitting under the portico, looking out into the snow-free parking lot. The attendant stands at my side. I envy his clear face, the small pores and smooth cheeks, what I wouldn't give to have been in the world with that flawless mug.

"Who's picking you up?" he asks. I can feel my ugly face reddening more than its usual. I've not made arrangements, haven't even thought about how I'd get back to my rented house. I can only manage, "Don't know."

From behind us, a voice calls me. "Mr. Hobbie," I hear, as the attendant wheels me around. The game warden is exiting the automatic doors, strutting up to us like a sergeant.

He takes a breath as he stands before me. "Glad I caught you," he says, much less formal than I thought he'd be. "I need to update you on the bear in question." The melting snow drips from the roof and splats near my feet. The game warden wheels me toward a bench and I feel absurd. Like most people, I walk with my legs not my face. He sits down and offers me a cigarette. He puffs and squints through the smoke. "This bother you?" I shake my head no. For a moment he basks in the rush of nicotine, then gets down to business. "We've tried traps, dart guns, and a pit full of hamburger, but your bear keeps eluding us. We know he's still alive because I took a shot at him myself, tried to drug him, but he took off right when I pulled the trigger." He blows smoke away from me, but the cold breeze sends it back. "Sorry," he says, waving his hand to clear the air. He assures me that bears rarely carry rabies but that the CDC requires all cases of animal attacks to be checked. He stands up and drops the cigarette to the cement, mashing it with his dirty shoes.

He coughs and wheels me back to the portico, where the attendant is now standing with his hands in his pockets. "Anyway," the warden says, "he'll turn up soon, I can assure you. If he's willing to attack he's pretty hungry. Black bears don't normally harm humans." He doesn't say goodbye and starts to walk away. He turns back and says, "Oh, you can't go back to the house. The Department of Natural Resources contacted the owner, and we've sealed it off for now, the other houses in that area, too." He rubs his chin and pats his pocket for the cigarettes. "You'll have to make other arrangements." He disappears into the sea of cars in the parking lot.

The attendant says, "I guess we should roll you back in to the nurses' station." Birds are swooping down from the sky, landing long enough to dip their shiny black beaks into a pool of ice-cold water a yard in front of me. I resign myself to having to go back inside and figure out how to get home, or rather, someplace else, maybe a hotel.

I could charge the room on our credit card, run it up even more; it's the way I've been paying for most things in the last six months, then barely making the minimum monthly payment.

The kid whisks me off and we glide through the automatic doors to the nurses' station. "Mr. Hobbie needs a ride," the attendant says.

The tall nurse behind the station shakes her head no. "Nope. His father-in-law is picking him up."

I wheel myself to the waiting area and look at the television. The anchors on a national morning show exchange good-natured ribbing regarding a new diet their guest is proposing. It sinks in that I will have to ask Roth if I can stay with him until the bear is found. He won't be in a good mood, after having been here once already to take Terry home. I change my mind and decide I'll simply ask him to drop me off at the Holiday Inn Express; after all, how long could it take to capture a starving black bear? The cast on the news program starts a new segment about illegal immigrants.

I begin to nod off but then jerk awake when I see Roth walking through the doors. He's wearing a pair of shorts and a sweatshirt. It's obvious he has just come from exercising somewhere. He's got to be cold. He spots me, and smiles with such happiness that he appears deranged, as if it might be him I should be concerned about having rabies. I imagine white froth dripping from his mouth and onto his fancy running shoes.

"Why they got you sitting out here like a senior citizen, son?" He pats my shoulder and steps back, the sweat on his shirt making a large dark spot over his entire chest. He sniffs and says, "Well, let's get going. I'm double-parked out there. I've got your room all made up."

I look up at him, puzzled. "What?" Roth asks.

"I thought I'd stay at the Holiday Inn. Do you have Terry with you?"

Roth snorts in disbelief. "We talked about all this yesterday. You don't remember?" He adjusts his shorts like a gym teacher, pulling at his crotch, unaware and unembarrassed. Before I can answer he has a hold of the wheelchair. I can't see him, but he says towering over me, "Besides, somebody's got to watch you. You might have rabies. I might just have to shoot you to put you out of your misery." I should just tell him no and stand up for myself, insist that I am going back to the house in the mountains, call the game warden and do the same. But I just can't bring myself to go back to that house, and besides, whether I want to admit it or not, staying with Roth feels like going home, and maybe while I'm there I can find out just how much he actually hears from his daughter. He laughs as we exit into the cold air. He says, "You don't need that thing. A good brisk walk to the car will do ya some good." As I stand up from the wheelchair, Roth tries to support me, but his grip is so tight on my arm I wince. "Excuse me for trying to help," he says in a whine. He walks briskly ahead, miffed.

seven   I'm wearing a golf shirt and the same jeans I had on when the bear attacked. The shirt is Roth's. I have no money on me, not even my wallet—all of it's still at the cordoned-off house. Terry is asleep in the laundry room, tuckered out. As we sit down to eat at his small kitchen table, my common-law father-in-law asks if I'd like to pray. He looks at me with benevolence and a serenity that implies he'll wait forever for me to answer. The skillet cheeseburgers and oven fries in front of us steam next to a paper plate of sliced apples. Roth likes to get all of his food groups.

"No," I say, "I'd prefer if you said it." I want to tell him his church and the deacon ruined religion for us, that he should know better than to ask me to say grace.

"All right then, I'll do the honors." Roth clasps his hands and uses his strong voice to bless our food. "And, Lord, please let the good men of the Georgia DNR find the bear and keep our Kari safe and healthy, giving her strength to overcome her weakness. Amen."

"Amen," I say softly.

He puts a cheeseburger on my plate and is already munching on an apple wedge. I ask him, looking down at my food, afraid my face will make him gag in mid-chew, "So, does she ever write you?"

He seems to bristle at the question, rearranging himself in the hard chair. Roth holds a forefinger out to show me he'll answer after he swallows a manly bite of burger. He takes a long drink of milk.

"No. I've not heard from her much."

I eat a fry and remember the time he told me I shouldn't eat so much fast food. He didn't point to my face, but used a quick glance to tell me it might help.

Roth looks uneasy, as if the food has given him indigestion. With his heart problems in the past, I don't think he should be eating anything that's fried.

"Does that mean you've heard from her some?" I ask, chewing slowly, hand up to my mouth for politeness.

Roth picks up his plate and walks to the stove. "Son, I said I haven't heard from her. Enough." He proceeds to scrape some of the fries on his plate back onto the baking pan. He returns and sits down, the tabletop shaking as he rests his elbows next to his plate and takes another macho bite.

With ketchup on his lips, his eyes follow some movement behind me near the floor. He says, "There's your boy."

I turn to see Terry standing a few feet away, head hung low, still sleepy but brought out of his snoring by the waft of hamburger grease. "Is it okay?" I ask, holding up a torn-off bite of sandwich.

"Sure," Roth says, warm again, smiling.

I reach down and hold the hamburger near my ankle. Terry sniffs the air and acts like he's not interested, but I know that his tummy is growling for it. He meanders toward me, the bandage on his back fresh, meaning Roth had to have changed it. Terry gives my fingers a kiss and takes the bite gingerly into his mouth. A gentleman, he doesn't gulp it down, but instead steps back a few inches and sits slowly, chewing bit by bit, turning his head slightly. When he's finished he lets out a burp.

Roth looks to me with surprise. "I guess that means the boy likes it, huh?"

"Kari should know he's been hurt," I say. Roth gets up and walks to the sink and turns on the garbage disposal, agitated. "Damn, son, just call her at the clinic and get on with it." Terry remains seated and watches as Roth bunches up his shoulders and gives me an exaggerated expression, mouth open, eyes wide, palms upturned and open, all of it to indicate that it's not that difficult to do. When Terry agrees with a yap, I offer him another bite of hamburger.

Roth has gotten up early to work out, a new piece of advice his doctor has instructed will keep his bad cholesterol from killing him. It's the second day I've been staying at his house, and it's strange to be here without Kari, but as I look around the living room, I realize she's everywhere. There are pictures of her driving a go-cart as a kid, riding a horse at a carnival, and a whole collage of her and Roth at various stages of her youth, his, too. Kari's mother is in a few, her eyes so much like Kari's. In one, her mother holds Kari in the tub, bubbles covering everything. In the shots of Roth in his youth, he looks enormous, biceps bulging, his hefty head cocked, perfect skin. I recognize a trio of pictures taken just shortly before the deacon got to us. Kari is standing with her hands on her hips, a bleary smile plastered on her face, the deacon's hairy arm tucked like a viper around her waist. It's a photo of the youth group trip we'd gone on. The group had volunteered for a mission working on a house for a needy family in a rough part of Pittsburgh. Kari told me the deacon made her do things that night while the rest of us finished sanding the trim in the kitchen. He'd asked Kari to go with him to the KFC in town to grab a few buckets of chicken, and on the way back he pulled the car off the road and pounced on her. He'd snuck a drumstick while driving, lips greasy. Over the years, she'd even joked about it if we had the munchies after a concert. "Gross, don't pull in there. I'll gag on Original Recipe, Hob." We'd laugh and I'd honk the horn as we drove on to Burger King.

The wall of photographs is depressing. I abort the living room and go peek at Terry asleep on the tile floor in the laundry room. For a while I just watch him, and before long I'm remembering Kari chasing him around our apartment as he growled at a squeaky toy she honked over and over. Kari would giggle, her beautiful face lit up, and then hold Terry in her lap as she caught her breath.

I walk into the kitchen absentmindedly and see a note stuck under the salt and pepper shakers. On it, Roth has told me that I can use his second car, a low-mileage Toyota, and that there's cereal in the cabinet. He ends with: "Here's the phone number. Call her."

I sit down at the table and hold the cordless phone in my hand. I've got a great excuse to call—a bear attack, how could it be any better? Kari would want to know we're okay, even though she doesn't know we've had any reason not to be. I imagine her saying, "No way, Hobbie. You guys were in a bear attack! No way!" She'd make lots of gasps and empathetic ooohs and aaahs. The idea of her reaction gives me the power to punch the numbers.

The phone doesn't even ring and I'm unprepared when a very southern voice asks, "Center for Healthy Living, how may I direct your call today?"

I sit stupidly and can't speak.

"Hello," she says.

"May I please speak with Kari Francis, please?"

The woman says, "Please hold." An easy listening station croons softly in the background. In a flash the operator is back on the line. "I'm sorry, sir, she's not available; would you like her voice mail?"

I'd forgotten they had their own message system. "Yes, please."

The line clicks and I hear Kari's recorded voice say, "Kari Francis." It sounds like she's saying her own name during a roll call.

After the beep sounds, I can't imagine leaving a message this way about the bear injuries. Finally I say, "Hi. I know I'm not supposed to try and reach you, but I…I, I just wanted to hear your voice. I miss you." I can't think of what else to say and record dead air. "I'm at your dad's if you want to talk. I love you."

I put the phone down and walk to the laundry room. When I open the door, Terry looks up and I tell him, "Come on. Let's go for a ride." He stands up slowly and follows me to the garage.

The space is tidy and smells of a lawnmower: gas and oil and clippings. I put Terry in the passenger seat of the Toyota and realize

I don't have the car keys. I move quickly back inside the house to search. I am about to look in a basket above the refrigerator when I notice Roth has put the keys on a hook. For some reason I still want to look in the basket. I pull it down and paw through a stack of utility bills. Under an unopened package of batteries is another stack of letters with rubber bands around them. I see Kari's handwriting immediately, a rush of heat overtaking my face.

I hear Terry bark in the garage. I don't know how soon Roth will be home. I pull out a letter dated nearly six months ago. Kari's weight is printed at the corner of the page just like the ones she's sent me.

I skim like a thief looking for a combination to a safe. There's not much there, only rudimentary comments about the staff, surroundings, and schedule. The letter Kari sent me from around the same time is very similar. I rush to fold the letter back up and put it away, reach for one at the front of the stack. It's dated just over a week ago and is also missing her weight.

She has printed: "Dad, I'm tired of the past. I want to find out what's so wrong with it. That's exactly what's *wrong* with me."

Terry begins barking incessantly; he's really becoming a new dog. The noise has put me further on edge. Why would Roth lie about the letters? Is it a private, family code thing with him, an attempt to keep Kari's newly found willingness to change and seek out the truth at bay? It scares me, too, of course, makes me wonder how I'll fit into her new slimmed-down life view, but still, I can't see why lying to me about his contact with her makes any sense.

I think I hear Roth opening the garage door and hurry to get everything back as it was. Terry is quiet now, and I walk to the front room to see if Roth is indeed out there. He isn't. It's drizzling, too warm here for more snow. I watch out the glass as the street shines black with rain. The letters Roth lied about make me want to snoop some more.

I find another photo in a frame near the fireplace. It's of Kari and me at the Sadie Hawkins dance in 10th grade. She looks soft and beautiful, chubby but ever so clear-faced and radiant, a delicate corsage wrapped around her white wrist. It was a pale day lily. She has on a deep green dress that made her dark eyes shimmer as black as the pavement on the street. I'm sporting a mock turtleneck over which I've decided to pull off a Don Johnson get-up, jacket sleeves pushed to the elbow, hair high and sprayed stiff. I look ridiculous. We are sitting in some kind of flimsy sleigh with a cutout cupid the size of a cat supposedly manning the reins. My face is strange look-ing, the large bump distorting everything, lending the impression of a gourd. Even with the photographer giving us plenty of space, you can see several ripe whiteheads on my nose and cheeks. Kari is wear-ing stockings and they make her calves look vulnerable, all dressed up but with nowhere to go but to a dance with a pizza face. I clutch the photo and pull it to my chest, embarrassed for us both. Terry yelps and I place the photo back beside a Falcons paperweight and a bowl of licorice gumdrops.

In the garage I am pleased to see Terry wagging his tail, standing with his front paws on the dash, eager for me to crawl in. I sit behind the wheel and start the car, press the garage door opener on the visor. While I wait for it to rise, I look at the stitches in my face in the rear-view mirror. The area looks inflamed and puffy, which reminds me to go back inside once more to swallow an antibiotic. When I come back into the garage, Roth is just getting out of his car, the garage door wide open and tailpipe fumes heavy in the air.

"Where you going?" he asks, a hint of suspicion in his voice.

"I thought we'd go for a drive, Terry and me, that is."

Roth nods and says, "Did you eat? There was a whole box of shredded wheat in there." He's sopping wet, sweat clinging to his brow.

"Not hungry," I say, wishing I could find the strength to accuse him right out about lying to me about the letters. His smile returns and he says in a chipper voice, "Let me back up so you can get out. I thought we could eat Chinese tonight." With that he jogs back to his car.

I back up slowly to show Roth I am a responsible man. He's waiting on me to make the turn past him so he can take the garage space. Rain is falling harder now and the whole taupe and white neighborhood is gleaming in wetness; it drips from the bare azalea bushes and runs in little rivulets toward the nicely painted storm drains.

Roth waves as I take off for the four-way stop. The traffic is dense, but I don't care. We head out with no destination in mind. It feels good to get away from Roth, think about why he's lied to me, while I listen to the radio turned up most of the way. I've always liked driving in the rain, the tempo of the windshield wipers, the way the water turns silver as it spreads across the glass. We pass several subdivisions that look identical to Roth's, and then the landscape changes and breaks into antebellum homes, large white mansions with sturdy columns. The slate roofs shine black from the rain. Terry turns onto his side and makes a strange noise, kind of a prolonged, gurgling exhale. His small body begins to convulse as if in a dream but then picks up in intensity, and before long it's clear he's having a seizure. I slow down and pull off the road. With Terry in my lap, I talk to him. "It's going to be okay, Ter. It's okay." I stroke his small head and look up to assess the road. Terry continues to shake and gurgle, sweet eyes rolled back, the whites exposed. With him still on my lap, I lurch back into traffic and around the other cars, many of them blowing their horns. I've got no idea where I'm going, but this is suburban Atlanta, and every strip mall has a grocery store and the requisite retail chains, surely there's a vet nearby. I floor it as Terry shivers in my lap.

eight   The sonogram makes me think of when Reagan was shot. The screen is black and white, tinged with a sickly olive green. I'm worried about Terry, but my mind is distracted with the memory of the attempted assassination. We were in the seventh grade, and Kari was still just a girl from the neighborhood to me. But the following Monday in social studies class with an ancient teacher named Ms. Rodder, we discussed our reactions to the shooting. It was the first time I'd heard Kari speak. Her voice was high and much more energetic than the topic demanded. She told the class that she and her dad were on a camping trip when it happened and that they listened to the news reports on a radio by a roaring fire.

In seventh grade, Kari Francis was neither skinny nor overweight, but average, and always getting into trouble for having a wad of Bubble Yum in her mouth. As for me, my face had already turned by then, grotesque and cursed. I hated being called on, or for any attention to be brought my way. I didn't share my thoughts in class. Our television set at home was used and didn't hold a picture well, flickering constantly as Hinckley was pinned to the wall by the Secret Service. And the screen where Terry is having his inguinal wall inspected looks just like our old TV set and since all things lead back to Kari, I'm still thinking about the tight Calvin Klein jeans she wore that day when the vet's assistant says, "Please hold him down while I take another look."

Terry has recovered some but is still out of it, glassy-eyed and shivering. As he tries to reach my hand to lick it, I am acutely aware that I'm 37, that the images of Hinckley and Reagan are more than two decades old. The bear encounter has shaken something in me, and I find each moment odd, like how you feel after a dream, trying to decipher what is real and what was fantasy. Right at this moment I'm holding down Kari Francis' pet while she's hundreds of miles away finding out how to consume massive amounts of protein. If someone had told me this back in seventh grade, that this would be my future, I'd have thought they were doped. That I'm now staying with her father, that he lies about being in touch with her, is surreal, yet homey, as if I knew this was how it would all turn out, but amazed that it did all the same. I focus all my energy on helping Terry.

The vet assistant shuts off the machine and removes her latex gloves. She pets Terry as he stands on a stainless steel platform. She smiles quickly, politely, and says, "You said on the form he was attacked recently?" She keeps her eyes on Terry. "That's what the bandages are for?"

"Correct," I say, sounding more like I'm being recorded in a court deposition. "A bear." The woman doesn't seem as impressed as I thought she would.

She asks, pointing to my face, "Is that how you got cut, too?"

"Yep," I say, trying to sound more informal. "Up north in the mountains, near the North Carolina border." I reach to pet Terry and add, "I'm down here staying with my father-in-law for a while."

"Well," she says, "I'll give the results to Dr. Madson. He'll be with you in a few minutes." She washes her hands at the sink and dries them off with paper towel. "Just have a seat and keep Terry calm." She leaves, and Terry and I sit quietly in a chair. I can see the cold day in late March again, the television set faltering and the interviews with the shooter's classmates, Reagan tumbling into the limo.

The vet comes in quicker than I thought he would and I am caught off guard. Another assistant whisks Terry away while we talk. The vet's a quiet man, which makes me feel more at ease. He keeps his head down when he explains that Terry's seizure was most likely caused from the attack, a type of post-traumatic syndrome. It shouldn't be permanent. He looks up from behind his large glasses, and I notice he, too, has had a severe bout of acne, his face pocked like the surface of a golf ball, but only in tiny sections. His "active area" is all gone, no redness or infection, devoid of inflammation, just a face with a past now.

"The thing is, and the vet that saw him after the attack should've done this, we've got to keep him for observation. Rabies is rare in black bears, but state law requires we keep him here until they examine the bear that attacked y'all." The last word is the only sound that indicates he's originally from the South; like his zits, the accent is gone, no longer raw and open. I covet his face as he scribbles on paper. I'd take that face over mine any day. He looks at me as if to offer some advice but stops short. It's comforting to see a guy who has healed his face but still wears the aura of a boy once teased relentlessly.

"Here," he says, "this is our phone number and contact information. I can assure you this is a very nice place and he'll be treated well." I take the paper and tuck it into my pocket. I nod, not sure what to say. "You can have a few moments with him if you like before he gets admitted and processed."

"Thank you," I say finally, feeling a sense of fellowship.

As we walk into the empty hallway together, a wall of manila files separating us from the front desk, he asks, "You getting treatment for that?"

I shrug. "They stitched it up and gave me antibiotics."

The vet stops and looks me in the eye. "You should try something else. They can really do wonders these days with a combination of drugs and laser resurfacing." He turns rapidly and walks to another patient's room and slips inside. I'm left not exactly sure which part of my face he was talking about.

At the front desk after waiting for 10 minutes in the waiting area, I get to tell Terry goodbye, which chokes me up. He wags his tail inside a small crate, and as he heads off to be quarantined, I ask the front desk lady how much I owe, hoping to goodness they'll allow me to be billed. The woman looks through the vet's paperwork and acts surprised. "Oh, well, the doctor has written that you are not to be charged." For once, it's my face that gets me a break, a comped vet visit from a fellow pizza face.

nine I've held off as long as I can. The incessant urge to mess with my face is cranking up my energy. Once, about four years ago, Kari and I enrolled in a human improvement course offered by the employee assistance program at the Regents Credit Union where we worked. The sessions were held one night a week at the offices of a psychologist who wore her hair in a buzz cut. She was an older woman with a no-nonsense take on human behavior. She said in a gravelly voice, "The two of you have childhood disasters that cause you to overeat," pointing at Kari, then motioning toward me, "and for you to pick at your face." Five minutes into the session she said, "Make the changes, that is, quit doing those things, and come to terms with whatever it is that hurt you and move on." For the rest of the session we talked about the books we'd read and we left. We saw her once more, but she told us we didn't need her until we chose to live differently.

As I pull the car into the driveway I'm hoping Roth is gone again. I don't have the energy to explain where Terry is, and I certainly don't want to go out for Chinese food with him. To my relief, he is not around. Another note on the table says he has gone to the church to check on a few things. After all that went on at the tabernacle in Pennsylvania, Roth worked handyman jobs before moving here, to Atlanta, where he started once again keeping the books at a church. He's hid out in churches like we've tried to drop out by moving from suburb to suburb, skipping from job to job. His new church is an enormous Presbyterian congregation, a mega-church; it has acres of parking lot and a structure that includes an indoor basketball court, bookstore, café, and enough breakout rooms to accommodate the spectrum of generations that attends. There's a teenager wing, toddler day care, senior citizen complex, and a marriage and family section that boasts everything from money management to weight-loss seminars.

Roth's house is still and cold; he hasn't turned on the heat, something Kari always complained about. "My dad is as cheap as they come. He'd reuse toilet paper if he could." I pick up the phone and try to reach Kari once more. I am edgy and my face is oily. The same operator as before comes on, or at least this one's been trained to sound identical, helpful, and benign, just like the one from before. I'm given Kari's voice mail again, but I hang up when I hear the rote voice she uses to state her name.

I want to pull down Kari's letters to her father from the basket on top of the fridge and read every one, but I know my mind is too wired to do anything that requires focus. I rummage through a drawer in the hallway and find a sewing kit. In the bathroom I lock the door and set a box of tissues on the sink. In the medicine cabinet, I find a bottle of rubbing alcohol and open it up, sniff it. This is a ritual I'm intimately familiar with. I push the bangs away from my forehead and inspect the skin. I squeeze four obvious whiteheads and dab them clean with a tissue dampened with the alcohol. It stings. The stitches over the bear cut are starting to sink in, relax over the wound. By the looks of it, the scar will extend from under my right eye to the center of my cheek; it's not that deep or long, but I enjoy that it's there. Maybe the scar will look heroic and cancel out the other stuff on my face.

I focus on the side of my face that wasn't mauled. There are two large boils, one above the other, and I push down and squeeze as hard as I can. Clear liquid eases out of the top one, and I do the same thing to the other one. For 10 minutes I become lost in repeating the process over and over, applying enough pressure that my eyes water. But I can't get any release. The vent fan in Roth's bathroom sounds like a jet, loud and annoying. I pick up the sewing needle and begin to dig inside the torn skin. If I could just excavate what's causing the sore, everything would be okay. I wipe blood away with tissue after tissue, digging further into the opening. I know I should stop, that what I'm doing is counterproductive and sick, but the energy is still rising in me and I've never stopped midway through. In the mirror I can see that my fingertips are sticky with blood. I rinse them only to start again. Water mixed with red drips from my face and onto the countertop, creating pinkish ovals over the light gray laminate. I apply more pressure and step back from the sink, lost in the heady mixture of control, in the hope for relief. I can feel the tension burning in my neck from craning in the mirror.

I've hit the point of satisfaction and my face looks even more awful, if that's possible. The stitched-up side is taut and raised, while the side I've been picking looks as though four or five vipers have bitten me, leaving their venom in packets under the skin and their fang marks all over.

I am about to begin the cleanup process, wipe down everything with alcohol, when the handle on the other door turns. I've forgotten to lock it. "Just a second," I say, but not soon enough. Roth has burst in accidentally, obviously not used to having a roommate.

"What the hell?" he says, as I stand before him with a needle between my thumb and forefinger, blood on my face and hands, used tissues on the sink and floor, red dimes blotted all over them. I am in shock, can't get the words out. Shame flushes my face, and I feel as if I've been caught masturbating.

"Son," Roth says, real pity in his voice, "what in the world are you doing?"

"I'm sorry. I thought you wouldn't mind." It's a lame answer and Roth knows it.

"Hell, no, I don't mind, by all means, abuse yourself right here in the toilet." Roth shakes his head and turns to leave.

"I'm sorry," I say. "Terry had a seizure and they quarantined him and I can't get in touch with Kari."

Roth stops as I toss the needle in the pile of tissue and rinse my hands in the sink. He turns toward me, hand grasping the doorknob so tightly it could turn to dust. "Hobbie, make some changes, son. Doesn't matter what they are, just get to living differently, you understand?"

Something rises in me; I want Roth to see me differently, stronger and more capable than he thinks. "Have you gotten any letters from Kari?"

Roth looks me up and down and rubs his chin. He's wearing a denim shirt and pleated pants and smells like Ivory soap, a trace of spicy cologne. "You didn't hear a word I said, did you?" he says, using his softer voice again.

"Have you?" I say again. I gather up the tissues from the floor and ball them together, as Roth watches me. "Just let me watch you do it, Hob," Kari would say. "I let you see me feed my fat face." We'd laugh, but I'd whine and tell her it would make me feel weird to have her watch me pick. If she'd come home now, I'd gladly let her watch, keep her glued to me anyway I could.

"I've already told you I've not heard much from her," Roth says. "Now get cleaned up, we're going out for Chinese and then over to the church to hear a new evangelist speak." His tone is direct and firm, as if I'm a teenager all over again. He doesn't ask about Terry, and when I look up, a wad of tissues matted in my hand, he's gone, the door closed. In the mirror I spot a zit I've missed and drop the tissues again to the floor. With my hands shaking, I squeeze softly and it pops forcefully onto the mirror. It feels good to release it.

ten We're waiting for the main preacher to take the stage. A woman plays the organ professionally; she's been recorded on all kinds of gospel albums, Roth said. He was uncomfortable with me during the Chinese buffet, but at least now the music playing over the expensive speaker system provides us a real excuse for not talking. I am a pipsqueak sitting next to him. He takes up a large part of the pew. The back of the pew in front of us, like all the others, has the King James version of the Bible stored digitally in an e-reader format. There's a stylus to choose which book, chapter, and verse you want to read. Roth fiddles with his as the organ music subsides. A slight smile sticks to his face as he uses the stylus to poke at the menu items, clearly fascinated. I'm glad he's busy and there's music playing so we can regain our balance, not that we had much to begin with, but still.

I sit in the pew wondering whether Roth saw the General Tso's chicken the way I did. At the Chinese buffet, the chicken, red and crackled, oily in the crevices, looked like my face. Did Roth think it looked like that, too? He asked a few questions about Terry and quizzed me about the hospital and the game warden and the rabies test, but other than that, we ate in silence. The restaurant was empty except for a young couple arguing, the woman holding a baby on her lap, while outside it rained and the evening dusk fell earlier than usual.

Roth shifts in the pew and glances at me with an expression of gleeful disbelief, the e-reader in his lap like a plate of food; he's careful not to drop it. I lean over to whisper in his ear. "Thanks for dinner," I manage, as the organ climbs higher and higher, as loud as some of the heavy-metal concerts Kari and I've attended. Roth shrugs his shoulders.

I can't imagine staying at his house much longer. It's been two days and we're lost in how to act around one another. The fact that he walked in during my macabre facial didn't help. He goes back to the computerized Bible and I sit tense in the pew. I don't like it here. It's a good thing I've already performed my stress reliever, or I'd be using the car keys to go at my face, scraping the skin off just to have something to do other than sit in silence. He was this way while we watched "M*A*S*H" together when Kari and I were in high school; he'd get focused on setting up our TV trays, engrossed in the show, and almost overfill our glasses with milk. Roth is so into the e-reader that he doesn't even flinch at the sound of the microphone's high-pitch feedback. Someone moves quickly onto the stage to fix it.

A woman sitting across the aisle keeps staring at me and getting caught, even though I'm not trying to; in fact, I'm only killing time when I glance her way, but I keep busting her. I think she's eyeing the cut on my cheek. It feels good to have something else for onlookers to gawk at other than my regular mucked-up features. The organ music is at a fever pitch as the pews continue to fill up. The men are wearing polo shirts and khakis, the women, dark slacks and light blouses, uniforms to indicate the informality of the evening service. Their pamphlet reads: "Come dressed casually, but worship Him formally."

Roth reluctantly puts his toy away and takes out his billfold. He pulls a $10 bill free and hands it to me. "What's this for?" I say, the music deafening.

He leans into me with his bulk and heat and commands, "For the plate. Here it comes." He points to the front of the church, and I can see that throughout the pews, trays with deep-red lining are being passed down the rows in rapid exchange.

"No, thanks," I say, waving off the bill he still holds limply at my shoulder. I don't want him to think I need a handout to tithe, and I'm not certain whether his gesture is simply a way to make me feel better, since I have no money of my own at the moment.

"Take it." Rather than escalating the situation I take the $10 and say thank you. The offering plates continue to circulate as everyone stands and begins to sing. It's a hymn I don't know, but it's clear the origin is from Psalms; there's lots of still water imagery and the chorus contains the phrase "green pastures."

The song ends abruptly as a young man in his late twenties approaches the elaborate pulpit. He sports a neatly trimmed beard and the clothes of a golfer. The stage is magnificent. There are hordes of fresh flowers and gigantic stained-glass windows behind him. There have to be more than a thousand people in attendance, maybe more, and this is a weeknight service.

The young preacher stands before the assembled masses and

stares out into the stage lights. It's an effective opener, the silent treatment. He adjusts his glasses as Roth rubs his rough hands together as if he were cold, but it's easy to see that the movement comes from sheer expectation. At the Chinese restaurant he told me, "Listen up tonight, this guy just might have something to say to you."

The preacher begins with a question, "How many of you tonight feel ugly inside?" No one stirs or raises their hand or even looks around; the parishioners are like cement statues in the high-tech, 30-foot-long oak pews. So am I. I can feel Roth shift his weight, but I'm not certain if it's to look in my direction. My eyes stay glued on the wide expanse of stage. A baby starts crying and the preacher says, "Not you, baby girl, you're still beautiful inside and out!"

He holds the crowd with more silence. He turns a circle and says slowly into the microphone, "Because I used to feel ugly myself, that is, until I started my very own personal walk with the Son of Man himself, Jesus Christ." The deacon who molested us would sometimes preach, and when he did, it was as if Jesus condoned his sin and gave him a special hour on Sunday mornings in Pittsburgh to show how little we meant to God. Kari and I would hold hands as we sat and listened in the pews at the Washburn Tabernacle, Roth just two rows over, and we'd squeeze tighter and tighter while the deacon spit out his lame words, smiling, just like he did at other times when he wanted something. By the end of the service our hands would be so sweaty and numb we couldn't feel anything. Roth would spot us as he walked toward the car and without looking say, "Get in. Let's go have breakfast now."

When the preacher says, "Now please take out the Bible in front of you," Roth looks as though he might explode with joy. He smiles and grabs the e-book. The woman across the aisle shoots another furtive look my way, then begins using her stylus to tap out her commands to the Bible. The preacher clears his throat and says, "Perhaps the most pertinent part of the gospel regarding the outward appearance, the beauty, if you will, of the physical self comes when Jesus takes Peter, James, and John up to the mountain to pray."

The e-book lights up, yellow crosses swirling around the passage Roth is supposed to go to. Roth leans closer to me, holding the stylus like a child clutching the top of a fat pencil. "I already knew that," he says, grinning.

The preacher takes a sip of water from a bottle, the kind they sell in the gift shop with the church logo printed on it. "For those of you new here tonight, thanks to space-age technology, the book and verse you are to go to should be right there on your screen." He chuckles. "Samantha, my wife, says I wouldn't be able to deliver a sermon without these computers." He makes a grand sweeping gesture across the interior of the church as if to indicate the scope of the digital Bibles, but instead it seems as though he's pointing to us, that we're the computers.

Roth scoots closer and tilts the LCD screen so I can see, too. "You see, up there on the mount," the preacher says, "the three apostles see for the first time really, the true beauty and nature of our Lord Jesus Christ. Before, they'd been viewing him with worldly eyes and because Jesus loved them so, he allowed them to witness his transfiguration. They get to see his beauty from every angle, from his insides to his out, from the top of his head to the interior of his precious, messiah soul." Roth nods in agreement. No doubt, he could quote nearly any passage he'd like.

The sermon goes on for 20 more minutes, the preacher cracking more Samantha-my-straight-shooting-wife gags, and it pays off; the crowd laughs at all the right moments. As he closes, a plea is made for all those interested in finding their inner beauty to come forward and get saved, to claim Jesus Christ as their very own personal savior. "There's a real babe or hunk inside every one of you out there," he says. Lots of people march forward and stand before the stage, waiting to get their time with the preacher.

The woman who's been staring at me all night gets brave. She looks right at me across the aisle and holds the gaze. Maybe she doesn't mean to imply I'd have to be ugly on the inside if my outsides are in such a jumble, but that's what it feels like. And she's got someone seconding it as well. Roth nudges me in the ribs and asks, "You need to get saved again?" But it doesn't feel like a question, really. "Well?" he says.

"No, Roth. The first time was enough." I want to tell him to whip out that Bible again and query it regarding lying about your daughter's letters, but instead the finale music starts up for those of us who won't be getting nice and pretty on the inside. We file out of the pew and down the long aisle toward the amphitheater's many exits. It's a true coliseum. Person after person approaches Roth and shakes his hand, as though he were their pastor.

Just as we are about to put on our coats, I decide to pray for Terry and Kari. It's been a long time, but with my eyes closed, pretending as if I am rubbing my nasal passage, I chant in my head that they be kept safe. I can hear Roth telling people hello and offering up good-natured ribs.

I say a silent amen, as Roth tells a couple, "He's my son-in-law. We like to do things together, just the fellas. Even had a nice Chinese dinner earlier." He laughs and pats the man on the back and kisses the woman. The couple nod at me and look away as soon as they lay eyes on my face. To my knowledge, Roth has never been ashamed of me, and I am touched by his willingness to claim me, even after the bathroom incident. I pray again to thank God for Roth and to ask that he be granted forgiveness for all his lying. I ask also that we won't be living together much longer.

eleven   Roth sent Kari away after the abuse, thinking the distance would make things better. But she's so kind, so forgiving, that she's always regarded the year with her grandmother in Colorado as a saving grace, a way to get her balance back, even if it felt like being apart was killing us. On the day she left, Roth and I still went to Wednesday night service at the tabernacle. During the ride, we didn't talk, and Roth seemed as if he couldn't breathe; he kept inhaling deeply through his nose, pounding the steering wheel as he drove erratically, sometimes honking at people or mumbling.

It seems to me that most of us have several reasons for everything we do, not just one compact, neat motivation, but rather a messy tangle, tripping us up as we go. For Roth looking back on it, he was trying to figure out why he'd sent Kari away, using the drive to church as a kind of purification period. But it wouldn't take, and he ended up even more upset than when he started. Several times he looked over at me and tried to smile, but all I could think about was our last kiss, the way Kari collapsed into my arms.

We had stood hugging on the sidewalk, a breeze edging her hair to the side. She touched my face and I sobbed. Roth was standing nearby, and I may be wrong, but it sounded like he was crying, too. I felt incapable of comforting Kari, and the truth is, I was thinking of myself. Without Kari, who would I be? She'd become my mirror, telling me daily that I was okay, a worthy person. Back then, as teenagers, all I could think of as she got in the car with the aunt who would drive her to Colorado Springs was how lonely I'd be; it still bothers me that I didn't have the capacity to be more understanding.

Roth said it was time for Kari to go. He hugged us both quickly, and took a deep breath, as he and I stood watching her. Kari got into the station wagon, her face pink, eyes red. She was in the back seat, trying to smile, waving at us through a dusty window. Someone in the neighborhood was cooking out, and the smell of lighter fluid and smoky charcoal filled the air. Roth and I stood there until the car disappeared. He said, "Come on, if you don't mind, I could use some help in the backyard." As we burnt leaves the little piles emitted an acrid smoke that made our eyes itch; it began to drizzle, a perfect cover for our melancholy.

At the church service at the tabernacle that night, the air smelled rotten to me, as if the baptismal tank had soured. Afterward, Roth and I went out to eat. Both of us kept looking around, half expecting to see Kari exit the bathroom in the Pizza Hut, her glossy hair hanging loosely around her beaming face. Roth prayed before we nibbled on the large pepperoni, but then we couldn't find anything to talk about. I was mad at him for sending away my girlfriend and only barely able to comprehend his loss. We sat there a long time, slurping on our ice pellets, refilling the big maroon glasses with root beer. I fell asleep in the car as he drove me home, and I didn't see him again for a while. When I did, he was upbeat, chipper to the point of delusion. I couldn't get used to his fake smile, the way he tried so hard to find the positive in everything. That's what his whistling in the bathroom at his house reminds me of now, and really, his intense periods of optimism since back then are similar; it seems to me he uses them to forget the negative and convince himself the world is the way it is because of some great plan. For the third time I try and reach Kari and only get her voice mail. Either the operator gave me the wrong extension or their system is down because Kari's voice announcing herself is gone, only a buzz followed by a click and the beep that indicates when to begin speaking. I sit in the kitchen and move my jaw, the stiffness over my cheek an interesting sensation, tight and painful, irresistible. I imagine the bear loose in the woods, some of my skin under its nails. Roth is in the shower, steam curling out from underneath the door. I don't know how he stands it so hot.

I've learned by being with Roth for four days that he takes as long in the bathroom as his daughter does. He likes to scrub himself squeaky clean, leaving redness to prove it. Roth walks around in his towel and sits rudely when wearing a bathrobe and frequently irons his shirt wearing only underwear. He's not like the men of my generation who shave their torsos, buy expensive grooming products, and try to get their waists to look like only slightly larger versions of their female counterparts.

With Roth holed up in the bathroom, I can safely rummage through his Kari letters again. He doesn't know it, but I am leaving today, whether my own house is okay to return to or not. I've got to get away, think through the best plan to reach Kari. Hopefully, he'll allow me to borrow his second car and I can pick up Terry on the way back to north Georgia.

I take a swig of coffee and eye the basket on top of the fridge. Outside, the sun is bright, reflecting off the glass tabletop on the patio. Starlings fall from the sky toward a birdfeeder Roth set up under an oak sapling; clusters of birds fight over food. Beyond, I see that all manner of vehicles are stalled in yet another traffic jam at the exit out of Roth's subdivision. Atlanta is a clogged mess, so much so that situations like this, when residents are stuck on their own streets inside complexes such as New Magnolia Cliff and Peachford Farms, are the norm.

I move my jaw, stretching the tight skin, as I double-check to make certain Roth is still in the shower. I pull the basket off the fridge and listen again for Roth; the shower is still blasting away, the air inside the house moist from his steam. I move the large pack of batteries and sort through the other stuff—a carton of long matchsticks, two flashlights, and a couple of old issues of "Outdoorsmen"—but the bundle of Kari's letters is gone. Is Roth on to me? It seems unlikely that they'd be moved unless he knew I'd looked at them, but it's also possible that he relocated them on intuition, suspecting I'd have a penchant for snooping. After all, I did ask him outright if he'd gotten letters from his daughter, and he did deny it.

I'm on the hunt. They're not in any of the drawers or cabinets. The garage is cold when I slip in to look around there as well. Roth has neatly stowed all of his tools; everything is in its place. The hand tools on the corkboard wall above the table are framed by painted outlines to indicate where each one goes. Several mason jars hold sharpened pencils, rulers, and long dowels. I flip open toolboxes and yank out the drawers under the table, but the letters are nowhere to be found. He's hidden them, just like he did Kari after the abuse. It angers me, makes me want to pull him from the shower and drag him around the house until he shows me where the letters are. Just then, I hear a loud thud. Going back inside, I listen. The shower's still running, but I hear a low gurgling, followed by a loud gasp. I run to the bathroom door.

"Roth, are you okay in there?" I shout, hand on the doorknob. I don't want to barge in like he did to me. I knock. Nothing. I pound on the door. "Roth, can you hear me?" I demand. Bursting in, I find Roth naked on the tile floor, one leg still in the shower. The steam is so dense it's like fog or smoke. Roth's eyelids are fluttering rapidly. He grabs hold of my T-shirt and pulls me toward him. His throat is burbling, the whites of his eyes showing, and I can't help but think of Terry.

I cradle Roth's big head in my arm and lift him toward me, even though it doesn't move him much closer. "Hold on, Roth," I say. His legs kick lightly. I grab a stack of bath towels and place them over his hairy body. I can't remember the rules of moving a person or not, so I tell him again, "Hold on. I'm going to call 911." I sprint down the hall and find the cordless and punch in the numbers hard. The operator assures me an ambulance is on the way. "Hurry," I say. "Please, I think he's dying!"

I have to force myself to go back in the bathroom; I take a deep breath as if the steam really is smoke and I don't want to die of inhalation. Roth is shivering; at least he's moving. The shower is still running, and as I reach in to shut it off, the lukewarm water splashes on my forearms. I find another stack of towels and spread each one over his body, then rush into his bedroom to retrieve the duck comforter from his bed.

When I return, Roth has flopped onto his side and he's vomiting. My hands are shaking as I gently roll him even further onto the tile, remembering in a rush of Health Class rules and Phys. Ed. lectures that he could choke and die on his own puke if he's anywhere near being on his back.

I spread the comforter over his pink-and-white body and sit down next to him. Stroking his forehead, I tell him it's going to be all right, though I'm not certain that's true; I'm listening to my words echo in the sweaty bathroom just as much to calm myself as to give Roth comfort. He's quiet now, not moving, and I don't want to see his face and catch a glimpse of pain or fear. It's strange to be the one afraid to look at someone's face.

In the distance the sirens howl, and as if on cue a neighbor's dog chimes in. The sirens hurry closer with every second, and when the noise seems just a block or so away, I decide to stand and make sure the front door is open. When I make myself look back over my shoulder at him, he's lying in a peaceful pose, bluish lips closed, an expression of content around his resting eyes. Lying that way, he looks like a huge boy taking a nap. The paramedics pound on the front door. I rub my hands over my face, and out of habit look in the mirror; it's only a glance as I run to the door, but it's enough to make me want to change.

twelve St. Francis Hospital is newly built and has every type of specialty doctor there is. The place is high-tech and overly decorated. Still, it's a scary place, full of those sterile smells and the worried faces of huddled families. The fear of Roth dying reminds me of how long I've known him. In the waiting room, I think of one of Kari's and my first dates. Kari and I were at the end of our eighth-grade year and we'd been kissing on her porch for a little while when the front door opened. Roth was holding a Bible and had on an Adidas T-shirt. He said, "You kids shouldn't be getting so serious at your age." He told me goodnight and pulled Kari inside the house, but after that he loosened up. Just a little while later Kari would be sent away to her grandmother's, and after that, when she came home, it seemed as though Roth needed me around to help with her. Kari would go from being happy one second to cranky and sad the next; I understood it, even felt the same way, and I always figured that was one of the reasons Roth let me hang around. And I sure didn't mind; I needed them as well after all the deacon had put me through. I wanted to be with Kari and her dad as much as I could. My own father was rarely home, working construction jobs wherever they took him, while my mother drank and watched rerun after rerun on TV, occasionally recognizing I might need a meal. For the most part I stayed at Kari's house until well after dinner, sometimes watching the Johnny Carson show with Roth on Fridays. He would laugh a deep bass when a monkey pooped in Johnny's hair or Doc Severson played a practical joke on an unsuspecting Johnny. Roth and I would share dry roasted peanuts as Kari got ready for bed in the bathroom. When she'd come out in her PJs he'd say, "Well, son, let me give you a ride home. It's late."

In the waiting room I can easily picture those days when Roth would take us fishing or to the wobbly roller coasters of a strip mall fair, or to a Pirates game. All the while, he'd come in and out of his moods, sometimes teasing us about our tight jeans or our heavy-metal music and sometimes sitting as silent as a stone behind the wheel as we drove through the dark streets of Pittsburgh on our way home from seeing "Jaws" in 3-D.

Poor Roth. As I wait for the nurse to come out and let me know how he's doing, I put my hands in the pockets of the same pants I'd worn to the church service, a pair Roth had loaned me, that is way too big. I touch a bill with my fingers. Pulling it out quickly, I am instantly ashamed. The collection plates stalled when the service started and I didn't remember to drop the money Roth had given me in the identical ones by the doors on the way out. I hold the $10 bill and turn it over, looking for something, I don't know what.

In fewer than five days I've been in two hospitals. The irony of Roth and I switching caretaker roles is not lost on me. A nurse appears and beckons me to follow. I can think only about how I prayed in the church that Roth and I wouldn't have to live together for long. At the moment, I'm ugly on the inside and the out.

thirteen   There are crickets thrumming. It's daylight, a breezy afternoon in fall, the kind where you can hear the wind starting your way, rustling tree leaves a few blocks down and climbing like a slow wave toward where you stand, rushing over your face as it moves on. It's 1985 and Kari has been home from her grandmother's in Colorado for more than a year, and we're having a picnic near the reservoir. We are talking about getting out of Pennsylvania. The sun is high in the sky, warmer than we thought it would be. Kari has gained weight rapidly but hasn't yet started not to care. When she's around me she tugs her sweatshirt over her butt and makes efforts to keep the lighting just right when we touch. Our physical passion is awkward and often sad, two abused kids trying to find a way to leave the disgusting parts of our bodies behind.

We shuck off our sweaters and spread out on the blanket, shielding our eyes from the glare. Kari picks up a handful of pine needles and begins pushing them into my hair; it's not a new thing, she's made me up this way before, "Prince Pine," she calls me when she's through. We're just 17. She sits up and asks me to do the same. She gets on her knees and continues to work on me like a hair stylist. "How many kids do you want?" she asks.

"I don't know," I say. "How many do you want?"

"A lot and none." She's now applying pieces of soft birch bark, like snakeskin, anywhere it will stay; I tilt my head to balance it. Most of the bark falls off as soon as she puts them in place. Her fingertips trail over my pimply face. I imagine a video sped up real fast of a flower growing then dying, like the one we viewed in our biology class the day before. My face builds up with infection, erupts, heals, and starts all over again at supersonic speed.

"You want lots of kids and none at all? You want them both?" I ask, closing one eye as she tries to place more bark over my temple.

"Yep. If I could, I'd have them sometimes, maybe six or seven of them, and then have them all leave for a month and come back the next." She bites her lip and brushes some bark from my shoulder.

"I don't get it. Why would you have them leave?"

She chuckles and leans back on her knees to inspect her work. "It's just a game. You know, like would you eat curdled road-kill guts for a million dollars, like that."

"Gross."

Kari nods in agreement. "So, how many do you want, Hobbie, Prince of Pine, Bark Boy?" she asks, softly pushing my long hair behind my ear.

"One. That would be enough for me," I say, and Kari falls away, sitting farther back on her knees. Instantly, she's become somber and desperate looking, big eyes blinking fast. She opens her purse and wordlessly pulls out her compact. Like Roth, she's started to use silence to retreat from the world. She clicks open the face powder and tells me to look, holding up the mirror. In the sun I catch a glimpse of the pine needles sticking out in all directions from my oily hair. Kari says in a monotone voice, "I was afraid you'd say that."

fourteen Roth lies in the hospital bed with a tube up his broad nose and an IV in his muscular arm. His hair is combed back; one of the nurses must've done it. He's asleep or in a coma or dead, I don't know, because the nurse who retrieved me has passed me off to another one. The new nurse is quiet and waits for me to look at her before she gives me the scoop.

"He's resting. The doctor will be in shortly to talk with you. Mr. Francis had a moderate stroke. For tonight, we'll have to keep an eye on him. It's important that he rest, then tomorrow we'll slowly bring him off the medicine and evaluate his progress." She bows her head and walks out of the room, leaving me alone with Roth, his skin greenish under the hospital lighting. I sit and watch him from a chair in the corner as his chest climbs and fades, lifts again. My eyes are heavy and they begin to falter and blink lazily, as if I were lying on a raft in a pool rather than watching my common-law wife's dad tinkering with the afterlife. I fight the drowsiness and win momentarily. Out in the hallway a couple of young nurses giggle and stop near the door to Roth's room to gossip.

"I know, Sherry, you're not telling me something I don't know. The guy is F-I-N-E, fine." They walk on, their voices trailing off. The respirator is the sandman; its rhythmic percolation sends me right back into sleepiness. The room is warm and I close my eyes.

I dream about Roth when he was young, about the story of him leaving home. Most of it is stuff I've heard Kari or her grandmother talk about when she was still alive. In my dream Roth is young and formidable, his saggy bulk turned back in time to when his chest was like a barrel and his peers feared his temper. He's in a park in Pittsburgh, close to where he grew up. It's a hot summer day and the tall trees stand stone-still in the sky, no breeze whatsoever. Roth is telling his mother good-bye, a picnic he put together himself clutched in his right hand, swinging, as they walk toward a bench. Kari's grandmother is telling him he should hurry up, the bus to Indiana will be leaving soon. He's on his way to Bible school in Anderson, not far from Indianapolis. Roth smiles at her, his short, perfect teeth like hers. His father is just weeks dead, a massive heart attack during his break at the steel mill. Roth's taking the Greyhound to Indiana with his father's life insurance, a portion that his mother demanded he use to chase his passion. Roth lusts after being a man of God, a pulpit thumper who incites the crowd like Elvis minus the pelvis, a preacher who can marry but still live a holy life. At the age of 13 he made his first appearance on the church stage of a visiting evangelist. Roth was "called," his mother would say later, and before she knew it, her only son was behind the podium delivering a short sermon on the Pearly Gates.

In my dream, Roth holds his mother's hand as she sits on the bench. He waits until she's comfortable, then opens the basket, takes out the sandwiches wrapped in wax paper, and leaves the cold pint of heavy milk and two apples for later. His mother smiles and pats his leg. Pigeons peck nearby, dragging around bread crust. When Roth and his mother move their mouths, no sound comes out, but they are all smiles and cheer, their faces perfectly smooth. Before long, they vanish from the bench, and the broad, unblemished plat of green grass stretching on forever is empty, no people or birds or benches or even trees now, until a small boy descends from the whistling sky and stands staring. He turns around and his back is covered in birthmarks; he does a complete 360 and begins to rise back into the blue, blue sky. He waves as the scene switches to Roth boarding the bus, waving, too. It's odd—there are no fumes spewing from the end of the bus as it disappears down a long highway.

"Sir, sir, wake up, sir." The nurse is pulling on my sleeve and gently shaking my shoulder. I open my eyes wide to get right in the real world. She has a look of concern on her face.

"You should have someone look at that, sir." She points to my face and I'm too sleepy and out of it to realize she's talking about the cut, not the *acne vulgaris*. I am afraid like so many other times in my life (during hair cuts, ordering food, getting a DMV picture taken, listening to a story at a party when someone moves in close) that several pimples have ripened like magic and are at that very moment about to squirt someone in the face, land on their chin like rice or larvae.

"You've got to keep an eye on that. It's fairly deep and there's some infection there. That's to be expected, but with your skin prone to microbes, it would be best to keep it clean." I'm slightly offended. Over the years, well-meaning school nurses, church mothers, PTA leaders, bank supervisors (especially a woman named Marge in Indy at the Bank of the Midwest) have all thought the only reason I look the way I do is because I am unclean. They didn't come out and say it (well, Marge did), but it's always implied. "Dear, if you'd only wash your face more often I'm sure all that would clear up." But to hear trained professionals using words like "microbes," that's a different story.

"Okay," I tell her and stand up from the chair with guilt. "What about Roth?" I point to him in the white bed, silver rails to keep him from falling out, just like a child's bed.

"As I said before, he's resting now. Tomorrow we will know more, how serious the situation is."

"The doctor didn't come in," I say.

"He will, but maybe not until tomorrow. It's been a busy night," she says, taking Roth's pulse.

I am exhausted and sit back down in the chair.

"You can't sleep here, sir," she says. "Visiting hours begin again in the morning at 10 a.m."

I stand back up and follow her out of the room. "By the way, we've called the next of kin, his daughter's house, but the phone line is disconnected."

"That was our old apartment in Conyers. Kari—she's in Durham right now."

The nurse nods and smiles at me, warm and gracious, and I wonder whether she's thinking Kari has left me and her father behind, took off for good. "Well," she says, "the other number, the one in Pittsburgh worked."

"What?" I ask, confused.

"The number there worked. She's coming down to see him."

"Who?" I ask.

The nurse motions me to follow her to the station. She opens Roth's chart. "Mr. Francis has been here before, you know, for his heart condition. His paperwork lists a..." The nurse uses her forefinger to trace across the paper and stop at a name and number. "A Sally Francis in Pittsburgh. She's listed alongside his daughter, Kari."

I stand under the humming lights, the computer screen blinking with green text, and try and fathom what she's just said. Sally Francis is Kari's mother.

My brother in skin, the vet who's found a cure, tells me I can take Terry home. "He's fine. The wound on his back will need to be cleaned and cared for until it's healed, but the stitches will simply dissolve. No need to bring him back unless something should change."

"Where is he?" I ask, looking around.

"Follow me." We walk through a maze of cages and steel tables, past a crate of blind kittens and into the back where a nice pen is clean and filled with curly woodchips. Terry is snuggled into a ball, one ear flipped over, as vulnerable as a child. He wakes up immediately and begins wagging his tail and padding his front feet in excitement. I can't wait to get my hands on him.

"Looks like someone is ready to go home," says the vet, a smile around his eyes. I reach into the pen and pick Terry up. He gives me kisses on my neck and I have to pull him away to keep his tongue from licking my face.

"Good luck," says the vet and he offers his hand. We shake as I try to hold Terry. "Thanks so much. Thanks, doc."

"No problem. And call me Simon." He smiles and walks away. Terry is a bundle of energy in my arms, moving quickly, licking me, and making little grunts of uncontainable pleasure. When we exit the doors and walk outside, Roth's car that I've borrowed is next to the building where I'd parked in a giddy hurry. Terry and I get in, and before I know it, we're headed back to the house in the mountains. Bear or no bear, I've got to get my wallet and extra clothes, something I should have done earlier. If I'm going to care for Roth and meet Kari's mother for the first time I need to feel put together.

fifteen On the drive toward the Georgia mountains Terry is zonked out. His excitement to see me is matched only by his fervent desire to get some real good, noisy shut-eye under my careful watch. Perhaps lately, since we've been apart, he hasn't gotten much rest, confused by the bear attack, the separation, and most of all, by where Kari is, the woman who used to hand-feed him potato chips and put him in the bath with her.

I look for the exit off the highway, and it occurs to me in a panic that I really have to get in touch with Kari. Roth's condition is still up in the air; I don't know if he's on the verge of death or seriously disabled, but either way, he needs his daughter and I'm the only one at the moment who can go and get her. The idea of seeing her, holding her, and taking in her changes, maybe even spending a night together—all of it sets my heart racing and I notice my foot has pressed down the gas pedal to the tune of 85 mph. I've zoomed right past the exit and now will have to drive another few miles to turn around.

Finally I steer the car over the knoll in the narrow road leading to the house. It's been only a week and a half, and yet the scenery looks different. There's no snow in sight and the trees hang low and gray, leafless, the grass beneath them brown, scruffy looking. I can feel myself tighten, the scary scene of the bear vivid in my head, the hungry, desperate noises it made. The house sits closed up and dark, as if it, too, were recoiling from the memory of the bear. I pull the car up to the driveway, look around in all directions. Sweat gathers behind my neck. I'm starting to doubt my capacity to leave the car, go inside, and get my things. I grip the steering wheel and putter forward ever so slowly, the brakes groaning. The noise wakes Terry; he perks his ears, or what passes for a perk for him, a minor shifting of his long, loopy dangles. He gets to his feet and begins barking madly.

I'm afraid he'll collapse into another seizure or incite the bear lurking hungrily in the wiry brambles surrounding the house. "Shhhh." I say. "Terry, lay down. Lay down. Shhhh." He cocks his head momentarily, then rips right back into another fiery fit of yapping. "No, Terry, no," I command, showing him I mean business by pointing my finger at his flustered chest. Finally, he becomes still, nervous, climbing into my lap and regaining his breath. I edge the car as close to the front entrance as possible. The front tire slips off the cement drive and eases into the moist turf. I've not called the landlord or the game warden, so I have no idea what the progress has been on the bear situation—if they've caught it or not. Terry doesn't have rabies, but a part of me is not certain about myself. I look in the rearview mirror and see the same old rutted and potholed face that I've had since puberty, with a new twist, a red cut in the shape of a hook. I'd sort of hoped the mirror would reveal a crazed man with a frothy mouth, so wild from the rabies that I'd become unafraid of the bear, people's stares, and the lifetime I assume I have left to stand behind a teller's window in another suburb, in another generic chain of banks: Countryside, CityWide, Neighborhood Nations.

The front door is less than 10 feet away. I can't decide if leaving Terry in the car to shiver and bark is best or if bringing him inside is the way to go, exposing his scent to the outdoors in the process, and the bear's excellent sense of smell. But I can't handle the thought of poor Terry alone in the car, and I picture the bear shoving against the door, climbing on top, pawing and scraping at the windshield. I tuck him into my sweatshirt, step from the car, and make a break for it. I clutch Terry too hard and he whimpers as we take the steps two at a time.

In my rush to make it to the door I've forgotten the keys to the house, lying on a separate ring in the back of Roth's car. "Crap," I say, and Terry burrows deeper into me, scratching my stomach some. I jog us back to the car and grab the keys. I unlock the door and slam it behind us; it shakes the entryway. I put Terry down. He peers up at me with a look of shy terror. I pick him up again and go to the bedroom to gather clothes, my wallet, and then to the bathroom for toiletries; all the while Terry is tucked under my arm like a carry-on bag.

I survey the place and maybe it's because I've been away, but I see as if for the first time all the items Kari and I have accumulated over the 20 years of living together: a big television, DVDs, CDs, all types of books, magazines, tapes, wall hangings, computer games, and the list goes on. The items we've dragged from place to place have changed with our ages, sure, the heavy-metal posters of our youth, the outdated clothing, burnt pans, and chipped knick-knacks. But that's it. Our lives together don't show much more than a few tables full of junk that could be sold at a garage sale in half a day, Terry is the only thing we've got together that really matters, and I let him get attacked by a bear.

I close the house door and sprint hunched over toward the car, Terry in the crook of my arm. We're just about to get in when I hear a horn toot. Looking up, I see it's the mailman at the end of the drive. He waves and shouts as if we're old friends. And the truth is, he's the nearest person I've got to a friend; the man saved my life or at least close to it. Kari and I have never had friends of our own, not during middle and high school, when we made each other our only confidants. As adults, the normal friendships never materialized either, as we moved from city to city, never in one place long enough to develop euchre partners or hook up with another couple to take trips with. Our hiding out meant that all of our time and energy was spent with each other; having friends is not something we know how to do.

I find myself excited to see the mailman as I back the car up, the engine making a tapped-out whining purr. I pull the emergency brake and step right out, some new courage bolstering me since he's present. The mailman says, "Dude, I thought you just gave up and weren't coming back." For some reason we embrace; he initiates it, that kind of chest knocking young men do, along with an elaborate handshake I mess up fairly well.

"Oh," I say. "Yeah, I went to stay in Atlanta with a friend until, you know," and I point to my face. I can't tell if he knows what I'm talking about.

"Well, hell yes, dude. You had to crash someplace 'til they got the bear right?"

"Do you mean they captured him?"

He holds up a finger and runs to my mailbox, flips it open, and scuffs his way back to me holding a stack of letters and advertising fliers. "Thought we'd have to find a forwarding address for you. But I think there's a letter in here from Georgia Parks Service, dude." He hands them to me, and I'm so anxious about the status of the bear I skip over several letters from Kari, rummaging through until I see the official Georgia state seal on the return address corner of the envelope. I rip it open as Terry yaps in the car.

"Cool," says the mailman. "I see that your pooch is fine, too. That's great, man." He offers a thumbs-up as I tear open the letter. It's crisp and terse and to the point. It reads that the bear has been "eliminated" and "tested" and that it's not been found to be a carrier of rabies. A cc has been sent to my landlord, the hospital, and the Secretary of the Interior of Georgia. I fold up the letter.

"Well," the mailman says, "I guess I better get the mail delivered, dude."

"Right," I say.

It makes me sad to know the bear had to be killed, but by the way Terry is standing on the armrest inside the car and panting happily, he doesn't feel the same way.

sixteen It's good to have my own stuff, to wear my own clothes. I feed Terry, who is famished, and take a hot shower. It's odd and seems sort of sacrilegious to be bathing in the very spot where Roth fell into a stroke, but there's only one bathroom in his house and I've got to get clean. I have plans before I go back to the hospital: read new Kari letters, quit being a wuss and demand to talk to her, doctor my face some, clean up the wound, and get rid of any whiteheads.

Terry sleeps like a handi-vac by the dishwasher, his bloated, bullet-shaped body spread for the entire world to see. I open the first of three Kari letters and think how strange it is to be somewhat in control: Kari has no idea I'm no longer at the house in the mountains. I may not be able to get in touch with her, but the same is sort of inversely true as well.

I sip coffee from a mug that reads: Christ Is Your Savior, Check Your Behavior! The first letter is completely blank. I mean nothing, no weight printed anywhere, not even a stray scribble or a funny face Kari likes to draw. It pisses me off. I rip open the next letter and it says simply: "This is how I feel. (Please see tomorrow's letter)." It takes a second, but I figure out I've opened them randomly. The last letter is actually the first and it reads: "I've gained weight and hate myself. This has been a waste of time. I'm leaving. Take the picture of 'my cousin's baby' and show it to my dad. Ask him who it is."

I'm tired of this game, sick of playing along; I've not thrown away any of her letters, but these I ball up and toss to the floor. How am I supposed to show a picture to a man in a coma? And why does she want me to ask Roth who it is? She's told me only a thousand times it's her cousin's baby.

But something begins to form in my mind—it's Kari's quotation marks that have me putting the pieces together, her time away, the weight. The thought takes me back to the last time we really tried to have a baby of our own. It was a cold December morning in Indianapolis, 1990. Kari and I had moved again and started teller jobs at the bank where I met Marge, the worst supervisor I'd ever had. Kari's weight had climbed to more than 200 pounds and my face was riddled with scabs and spots that ranged from pinheads to quarters, all of them ugly and tender. Kari sat on the toilet of our bathroom in her underwear, lid down, as we waited on the test results. We'd been actively trying for almost two years and it wasn't working. Kari told me to sit down; she got up so I could be on the toilet.

"Purse your lips," she ordered.

"Why?"

"So I can get the foundation spread around your laugh lines."

"I have laugh lines?" I asked. Kari stood barefoot on the tile floor, using a large makeup brush, swirling it in powder. She'd just come out of the shower and was wearing only her bra and panties.

"Yep, all people do," she said, glancing down at me. "Close your eyes and purse your lips and throw your head back, Hobbie." I'd been her life-size doll for years by now. She knew I'd participate without complaint, that I'd pretend for her, put on a show, and not question the tricks of the trade. "You look dead," she said as she brushed her hip against me, my head slung back just like she'd commanded.

"That's morbid," I said. "Why are you such a morbid person, Kari Louise Francis?"

"It's the company I keep, I guess." She applied the powder over the surface of my bumpy face. She smelled like Ivory soap and the fruity shampoo she'd just used; her hair was still wet and long, sticking to her back.

Sex had become easier over the years; we'd been able to partially leave behind whatever jagged remnants were leftover from the deacon's hands. We'd become focused; our lovemaking had a purpose, to bring forth a positive sign, a pregnancy, and finally a child together. "Faith" if it was a girl and "Michael" if it was a boy. We'd play heavy-metal ballads and light candles when we made love. Whitesnake, Bon Jovi, and all the others we had stacked in a compact disc tower next to the television. Kari liked the songs to be turned up high so we couldn't hear the bedsprings chirp. "My big butt's going to break the bed," she'd say, to which I always responded, "So, my face is gonna crack the mirror."

For the next 10 minutes or so Kari applied make-up to my t-zone in an effort to hide my blemishes. That's what she called them.

"I don't have blemishes. I've got craters, pizza toppings, super-duper pimple-zillas," I said.

She smiled and kept brushing, the soft bristles soothing, tickling my cheeks. We tried to forget about the test sitting on the edge of the sink, the folded-out instructions like a map on the floor.

"If we have a baby," I said, "will you tell your mom?"

Kari's pressure on the brush increased and the tickle sensation was gone, replaced by a movement that felt like she was painting a wall, solid force, the metal ring at the base of the bristles coming slightly in contact with my skin. She was silent for a moment, feigning concentration. Finally, she stopped and told me I could quit pursing. "Nope. I wouldn't. The baby doesn't need all its grandparents. Roth and at least your mom will do." Kari had talked with her mother on the phone on birthdays, sometimes at Christmas, too, and there had been cards at graduation. She even sent a card to us along with a cheap glassware set, thinking we'd gotten married instead of shacking up, but their contact was stiff and full of unsaid things, a time bomb. Sally Francis liked to remain positive, and Kari did, too, so it was kind of like listening to the polite conversation of acquaintances. In many ways, the two women are very much alike, so they are a volatile mix, even on the phone.

The television in the living room was blasting, as Bernard Shaw yelled out his report on the Gulf War. "That TV is so loud." Kari said. "Do you mind?"

I got up from the toilet. "Wait, look in the mirror first," she said, grabbing my arm. I looked, Kari standing at my side, soft mound of belly wide over her white panties. She's about a foot shorter than me. "Geez, look how fat I am," she said. She jiggled her thighs. I thought they were sexy and smooth, and said so. Kari shook her head.

"You're beautiful," I said. Kari shrugged. I turned her toward me and we kissed, a slow one. She smiled as she withdrew and said, "Autumn Glow looks good on you. It's Maybelline."

She tilted her shoulder toward the living room. "Do you mind?" she asked.

I went and turned the television off and inserted a John Mellencamp CD, poking the button until Lonely Ole' Night started. I turned up the CD and moved quickly back to the bathroom.

Kari sat on the edge of the tub, her hair now pulled back in a tight ponytail, giving her face a severe look. She'd put on a T-shirt and held the pregnancy test dipstick between her knees. "It's negative," she said. I sat down beside her on the tub and took her hand. "Someday," she said, "I'll have to tell you why God won't let me have our baby." She ducked her head into my neck and began to bawl.

seventeen At the hospital I tiptoe into the room and see two nurses working around the bed. They are shuffling bedding, maneuvering tubing, and generally working to straighten things up. I can't tell if Roth is still in the bed or not. I freeze; I've never seen how a hospital room is dismantled and re-configured for the next patient, but this activity has all the markings of how it might be done. I clear my throat to let them know I've arrived.

The nurse closest to me turns on her white shoes and spots me in the yellow light from the hallway. "Oh, look who's here, Mr. Francis.

It's your son-in-law." She steps to the side and reveals Roth sitting up in the bed with the tube still dangling from his nose. But a rosy complexion spreads over his cheeks and his hair has been recently combed. I walk quickly to him and see that his mouth is drooped. Roth smiles, but only the left side of his lips, upper and lower, curl, giving him a cartoonish grin. Before I can even say anything he begins to cry, nothing sobby or snotty or even audible, but his head palsies from side to side as he reaches for my hand, pulls it to his new, crooked face. He's changed, a lot.

"I'll leave you two alone," says the nurse, smoothing her loose-fitting uniform. "The doctor will see you shortly to fill you in." When her footfalls have quieted, the whines and clicks from all the machines around Roth's head provide a strange accompaniment to his muffled hurt. I think of our time in the pew together just two days before and wish I could take back my annoyance with him. Whatever indecision Roth's emotional makeup has shown us in the past, his ups and downs seem like long-ago history. He clutches my hand against his warm face, and I think, though I cannot be certain, that he's dipped his mouth and made a slight kissing sound to the back of my hand.

"How are you feeling, Roth?" I say, finally.

He looks up at me. His eyes have dark circles under them and they're watery and puffy. He opens his mouth and a low groan comes out, a soulful wail that cuts me to the core.

"What?" I ask, uncomfortable, praying once again, asking please God that the nurse come stomping in and demand that he not use his precious energy needed for recuperation on an obviously face-infected nincompoop, that my face was, in fact, putting all the patients in danger of a truly wicked and persistent staph infection. But there's nothing but the wheeze of Roth's breathing and his continued guttural. And suddenly, I recall that my stomach was nervous earlier not just to see Roth and be in the unfamiliar role of familial support, but that today was indeed the day I would also meet Sally Francis for the first time, another person who would need to make up her mind about my face, my character. My nerves had been on edge when I dropped Terry off at the vet, this time to board him so I could be at the hospital more. Simon, the face-healed, pock-reduced vet himself had greeted me. "Sorry to hear about Roth's stroke. Give him my best."

I was shocked he already knew about it. Had he sensed it? Who better than a man with vanishing facial Braille of his own to read my face like a prophet?

It turned out he wasn't so intuitive. "I live just down the street," Simon said. "In the same subdivision. Roth is a popular man—he's got more people who turn to him for advice than anyone I know."

I nodded.

"What are you going to do?" Simon asked.

I shook my head, handed over Terry, who seemed excited to see the vet again so soon.

"Listen," Simon said. "I don't know what your plans are and maybe I'm out of line saying this, but I can help you. If you're looking for a job, I could use a bookkeeper. Not much different from being a bank teller." Simon seemed to know quite a bit about me. I imagined Roth telling him about my face, thinking the vet could help me.

"I don't know, but thanks for the offer. I'm just going to stay at the hospital as much as I can."

Simon patted me on the back. "Terry will be in good hands, and please tell Roth we all wish him well."

....

When Roth finally quiets down, his attempts at speech quelled for the moment, I can't help thinking that maybe Kari and I've been wrong, maybe you can hide out in the suburbs, and strip malls, the drive-thrus and mammoth bookstores only if you will yourself into anonymity. Simon sure seemed to be a true neighbor to Roth right in the middle of suburban Atlanta.

As I stroke Roth's hand and try and focus, the intern comes in and clears her throat. She stands at the end of the bed and addresses Roth. "Mr. Francis," she croons, a little too loudly, her voice cracking under the strain. "Do you mind if I let your son-in-law know what's happened?"

Roth nods. The intern turns to me and begins. "Mr. Francis has suffered a mild to moderate stroke, which as you can tell has left some of his body paralyzed and his speech impacted." Roth has his eyes closed as if in prayer, and in all likelihood that's exactly what he's doing.

The intern continues. "At this point, we'll monitor his vitals and watch him for a day or so, but then he'll be free to go. You all will need to make a decision as a family about rehabilitation." With that, she slips from the room before Roth can even open his eyes. I notice he's fallen asleep, snoring almost exactly like Terry. I am thankful he can rest. My heart jumps when I hear from the hall, "Yes, ma'am, Mr. Francis is right in here. Please follow me." I can hear a throaty, thick voice say, "Please, call me Sally."

PART II

one Sally is remarkable. It's hard to believe she's the same age as Roth, mid-sixties. Her face is wrinkle-free and her dark eyes remind me of Kari's: clear and youthful, some pain behind them for sure, but the wideness offering up optimism. Also, Sally is dressed like a younger woman—not trashy, which I half expected—but modern, wearing a nice peasant blouse and a pair of black pants that are neither too tight nor baggy, flattering. She's a large woman, which is to say she's not heavy, but rather full-figured. Her colored hair is pulled to the back of her head in an amber bun. Her makeup is thorough but not overdone, and she wears jewelry that seems to go well enough. If I'd met her on the street, I'd say she was in her mid-forties. I think of Dolly Parton's face for some reason. When she walks into the hospital room, Roth is still asleep. She glances around—maybe looking for Kari—her eyes going past me, then over me again, before finally settling her inspection in my direction. This is the worst part of having a face like mine, when strangers have to decide whether they'll see me as something more than a demolished face.

Sally smiles and sets a large bag on a chair. She offers her hand and quietly says, "Hello. I'm Sally Francis. I used to be married to Roth." She motions toward his bed with a dip of her head and makes a face to indicate her empathy; she truly seems to care when she looks at Roth lying hooked up to hoses. She steps in closer to me, still holding my hand, and I can smell her sweet perfume, but not too candied, floral, too.

"And you are?" she says, giving me a cue to showcase my manners, but not meanly; in fact, Sally is looking at me with fond eyes, a gentle look that her daughter has definitely inherited. My head is swimming, not knowing how to explain who I am or how I will answer the inevitable question of where the daughter she abandoned is. My face feels like it's about to burst into flames; it's oilier, too.

"Oh, sorry, Mrs. Francis," I say. "My name is Hobbie."

She pops a smile and swats at my arm, then embraces me in a big, warm hug as she squeezes me. "Sweetheart, I know who you are. I've heard about you a thousand times from Roth."

They talk? On a regular basis?

She steps back and takes me in, placing her hands on either side of her face; it feels like I'm naked. "You are a slender thing, I'll tell you that. Wish I was your size." Sally straightens her blouse and pushes a strand of hair off her brow; she's still smiling. "Is Kari in the bathroom? Or didn't she want to see me? The last time I saw her you were at work, in Minneapolis I think it was. I was passing through on a bus tour. She wasn't thrilled to see me then, but of course that's my doing, not hers."

I instantly like Sally. Like Kari, she cuts through it all, fessing up. She bears the cross of leaving Roth and Kari. Plain and simple. I'm about to answer her when Roth twists slightly in the bed. As soon as he catches a glimpse of Sally, he tries to sit up straighter.

"Oh, my," Sally says, and pats her heart. Her thick high heels clunk on the tile as she walks to Roth's bedside and sits down.

Roth seems not accustomed to his new face, how it works or why it feels so leaden on one side. He tries to look chipper, but his cheek and lips and the eye on the left won't allow it.

"Oh, Rothie," she says, running her hand all over his face. Roth is crying again. I begin to creep away to give them some time alone, maybe even slip into the bathroom at the waiting area to pick my face, but Sally catches my movement.

"Where are you going, hon?" she asks, her voice a dulcet, controlled hush. She doesn't wait for me to answer. "No, sit down here with us. Roth needs all of us right now."

I stand dumbfounded and looking quite inert, I am sure. "It's all right," she says. "Come on." She pats an empty chair next to her. I finally manage to sit down. Roth is nodding his head.

I've got to get a hold of Kari as soon as humanly possible. Since the phone calls haven't worked, I imagine sending her a telegram, a carrier pigeon, or a helium balloon with an attached note: "Come to Atlanta, your dad had a stroke and Sally is a nice lady! I want to see you! PS: There was kind of a bear attack. PSS: Why do you want me to show the picture of your cousin's dead baby to Roth? PSSS: I think I know why, and I'm hurt you've not trusted me enough to tell me."

Roth begins a kind of muffled cry, which sounds like his face is buried in a pillow. "I know," says Sally, now almost engulfing Roth's head in her ample bosom, leaning over the bed railing and cradling him. "Let it all out. Come on, that's it."

I feel a presence behind us at the door, and I turn quickly in the chair with a vivid picture of Kari in my head but am disappointed. In the doorway, a slim man with a wiry mustache and a full head of black hair is standing with his hands in his front pockets, staring through a pair of large eyeglasses, the frames held together with duct tape. Sally turns in the chair and speaks over her shoulder, as if she has been expecting the guy to show up all along. "Donny, get back in the car. I'll be down when I'm down." The little guy does as he's told and drags off like a third-grader meandering down a hall, his tennis shoes chirping.

"Donny. He's always wanting me there beside him every minute," Sally explains. "I took him in to try and help out. We started out dating, but things have kind of changed between us. He's a sweet guy, but not my type. I'm just trying to let him down easy you know, not hurt him. He's had too much of that in his life. It's a long story. Sorry." She offers no other explanation and goes back to comforting Roth, kissing his hand.

He smiles through his tears, mouth warped, one eye runny and red, and makes some words I can't understand. Sally laughs. "Oh, Roth, that's so sweet," she says, tickling his cheek. She turns to me and clues me in, "He said, 'Who wouldn't?'"

Nights lying in bed with Kari, her energy for being silly high, we'd play the mind-reading game. You know, think of a color, a number between one and 50, a state, etc. In fact, on more than one occasion playing this game was exactly how we got from one sprawled city to the next; Dallas-Ft. Worth became our home this way. We were surprisingly good at it—together that is. And sometimes, Kari would guess the color or number so quickly it would leave me wondering whether she could truly read my mind. Anyway, as Sally picks little pieces of fuzz from Roth's hair, snickering and showing them to him as if they were slivers of gold, I close my eyes and send Kari a message. "I need you. I need you. I need you." I've got my eyes so tightly closed it's kind of blurry when I open them and Sally says, "Now, where is Kari and what happened to your face?"

two "Well, I think you look like Richard Belzer and he's handsome, hon." Her compliment builds me up; after all, the actor clearly had an acne problem at some point. Sally taps my knee and winks, "You're a cutie, don't let anyone tell you any different." We're in the snack area together. Back in the room, the nurse came in and ushered us out; we were told Roth needed his rest. Now we're waiting for the doctor to discuss Roth's condition, which worries me.

"So the bear was just really, really hungry then?" she asks, handing me a little bag of chips from the machine.

"Right," I say, shrugging. It's hard to believe a woman like Sally wouldn't have gobbled up motherhood like pudding; she's caring, intuitive, and nurturing. She's already told me that her leaving Kari and Roth way back when was a mistake, as breezily as if it were old news—her fault, but nevertheless, ancient history. But I know that it doesn't feel that way for Kari. It dawns on me that Sally has been so absent from Kari's life that she probably doesn't know about the deacon and the abuse, or Kari living in Colorado Springs with her grandmother 20 years ago. It's difficult to get a handle on how chummy she and Roth have been since we've been hopping around from bank to bank for 15 years.

"So what about that guy?" I ask, reminding her of the man who stood at Roth's door, wanting her attention.

"Donny, oh, he'll be fine. Between you and me, I've just about had it with him, to be honest. He's a good man, but a little on the needy side. And sometimes he drinks too much, smokes too much, and stands around too much. We met on one of the Catholic bus tours I take." I nod, though I don't exactly know to what I'm agreeing.

Sally is ravenous; she eats her barbecue corn trumpets in a flash, licking her rosy lips to get every morsel and tosses it over my head into a trashcan.

"Why do you keep looking at my face, sweetie?"

I feel busted; I've been doing what I hate other people doing. "I was just noticing how young you look, that's all."

She bats her eyes, reminding me of Kari. "Honey, like I said before, if Kari's getting some work done at a weight-loss clinic, then good for her. Modern medicine is there to be used." I can easily see why Roth and Donny would want her around a lot. She makes you feel comfortable, special really, as if she's thinking only about how she can help you become a better man.

"How did you and Roth meet?" I ask, knowing some of the story from Kari.

Sally grins as if what she's about to tell me is the core of who she is. "Let me get a cup of coffee." She gets another cup from the snack bar and sits back down. She takes a sip from the paper cup and begins.

"Roth got off the bus in Indiana in 1959 with a brand new King James Bible." Sally kind of chuckles. "He was on his way to the Bible college in Anderson. When he got off the bus, with that duffle bag slung over his broad shoulder, he was not hard on the eyes, I'll tell you. Strong, you know, really built well.

"It was a cloudy afternoon, dark along the horizon. There was a storm a few counties over. I was in town with my father. He'd taken a job that was kind of like a circus caller, signing men up to work on a duck farm. He'd shout, 'Come work at one of the finest duck farms in the world. Culver Ducks!' My job was to get the men's attention, make them stop dead in their tracks and listen to my father's pitch.

"When Roth walked by, I said, 'Are you or are you not going to fill out an application?' My dad was a decent man, drank too much, but he knew the score, knew what would get men's attention. He had me wear a short skirt and a white blouse that highlighted my assets." Sally actually glances down at her large bosom. "Anyway, the sky over the city kept getting darker and the wind was really blowing hard. We got paid for each application a man filled out, and since the storm was coming, I wanted to make sure Roth filled one out.

"I took his hand. 'My name is Rebecca Means,' I told him, 'but people call me Sally because I sound like my Aunt Sally.' We were the same age, just out of high school.

"I asked him what his name was." Sally laughs some more. "Roth said, you know, like he was being graded on his manners, 'Roth Francis, ma'am.' I'm from Pittsburgh. On my way to Bible school in Anderson.'" Sally pauses. Maybe she's just now realizing what Roth's dream had been, to become a fine, upstanding pastor of a church. "I told him, 'You can get a hundred dollar signing bonus if you agree to work at Culver for a year.' But he told me again, 'I'm going to Bible school, ma'am.'" Sally looks at her watch, takes a big drink of coffee.

"Well, it started to storm, hard. And it just felt so natural to hold hands and sprint toward an old warehouse. Of course, I initiated it. Roth was too proper. The next day, the paper had a story about how an inch of rain fell every hour for six hours and that the tornado touched down three times before leaving the city. We ran down the steps to the basement and ended up in an old boiler room." Sally widens her eyes, "It was so quiet down there, you wouldn't think a tornado was right outside. Anyway, there was something between us, some kind of very strong attraction. Roth was shy, but you'd be surprised how nature can change that. Roth dug out these old canvas tarps, and we spread them on the floor like we were playing house. We fell into that rough bedding and lost ourselves. God, it was really something else, I tell you, Hobbie. That storm changed our lives. We were meant to be together, but you know, I've learned something, even at my age." Sally looks up to the ceiling, as if the thought is above her head. "Roth and I were made for each other, but our love was too intense for us. We needed time to learn how to handle it. The truth is, I'm scared of it. But Roth needs me now, and I know he'd do the same for me if the tables were turned."

I love the story, the romance of it, and I want to tell her so, but suddenly she looks past me and whispers, "Here comes the doctor." I finish off my chips and swallow hard to make certain if I have to speak I don't have a bubble in my throat. The doctor, about Roth's age, with a shiny scalp and a tie that seems like it might be giving him high blood pressure, asks us to follow him. We trod down a hall past supply rooms and small offices until we arrive at a conference room. It's uncomfortable to watch him pull out a ring of keys and fiddle with them until he finds the right one and lets us in. It's as though we're about to meet with the janitor to discuss Roth. The room smells stale and unused, the lighting above flickering as he says, "Please, sit down."

He pulls out a chair and almost flops into it. He seems exhausted as he looks up and catches a glimpse of my face. He performs a doubletake and asks, "What happened to your face, son?"

Sally pipes up. "He's kinda like Grizzly Adams only for the Georgia mountains. A bear attacked him and his dog, Terry, and this young man fought him off barehanded."

The doctor actually looks impressed. He sits up more and seems to leave his fatigue under the conference table. "Really?" He seems to survey my scar, not my acne, actually zones in on it, checking the wound out. He says, "Well, I'll be damned. I have a weekender up near Taccoa Falls; where'd this happen?" He looks at me with the respect he might've given one of his Korean War buddies.

"I think it's near there, the house that is. It's a rental, so I'm not all that familiar with the area, but around the state line."

"Oh, sure, sure," says the doc, again looking at me like I might have more to me than what's on the outside, a deep well of courage beneath the surface, the vein running past the ugly face and down into a mighty reservoir of gumption.

The doctor seems to be contemplating that very idea when Sally speaks up. "So, Doctor . . . ?"

"Oh, yes, Dr. Causster," he says, the tiredness around his eyes coming back, shoulders slumped.

Sally nods toward him. "So, Dr. Causster, how is Roth? What can we expect?"

He flings off his stethoscope as if it's bugging him; it hits the table hard and one might assume he's mad about us asking, but his voice is sympathetic and controlled when he answers.

"Mr. Francis suffered a mild to moderate stroke that has, as you certainly have perceived, paralyzed his left side. Strokes work in that manner, so his is a completely normal post-incident response. That is, his speech and gait will be impacted. The question is, when and in what fashion will he recover. Where will he be taken care of?" He looks first at Sally and then to me as if one of us could answer the question he's posed.

Sally seems a tiny bit offended. "Well, Dr. Causster, we of course do not want Roth to have to get his care in a nursing home. We'll take him back to his residence and provide the care there." I back up Sally, nodding hard. I am thankful that she's here; the warmth of gratitude is a nice feeling.

"That's what I thought," the doctor says, clearly pleased, as if he couldn't imagine we'd come to any other conclusion. "The good news is you can take him home today. If he chooses to follow any of the routine rehabilitation courses, you can help Mr. Francis schedule those within the week. Strokes are odd incidents and some people prefer just to get on with their lives in a diminished capacity, or rather accept life at his or her new participation level and find ways to support that. And don't be surprised if this event causes some emotional differences in him. Many, many stroke patients find themselves with a whole host of new feelings. You see, coming close to death *and* having a brain-altering episode can produce a kind of robust change in one's view of the world."

Sally nods, but seems as if she's not so certain about what the doc is saying. I realize this must be very sad for her. She and Roth have a history, one that has produced a child, and their bond is clearly deep, even if they've been apart for a long time. I can't help but think whether this might be the same predicament Kari and I'll find ourselves in 30 years. I'll be lying in a hospital bed, face healed over but still distorted, dying of loneliness and sepsis, Kari having been gone for years but still in contact, the stacks and stacks of her letters crammed into my bedroom back at the Y where I live as I now hold her slim hand and die.

The doctor gets up and offers his hand to Sally, then to me. "Good luck with the face," he says, shaking my hand. "I'll have to watch out for bears at my cabin up there, I guess."

"Right," I say, instantly worried that my face has festered since this morning, not the stitched area, but the acne. Once the doctor has left, Sally picks up right back where she left off.

"We were married just one month after the tornado went through downtown Indianapolis and plowed into the farmland to the north, uprooting trees, overturning combines and tractors, ripping barns to shreds." She stops for a moment. "Is this boring to you?"

"No, not at all," I say. "I find it romantic, actually."

Sally pats my hand. "Kari's got good taste, I'll tell you that much. Anyhow, in Roth's mind he'd committed a lustful act and the only way to make it right was to marry me, and make me a dutiful preacher's wife, even if he hadn't taken the first class at Bible school. We were so much in love, and got married in Pittsburgh so that his mother could attend, along with her sisters, and a whole church full of cousins.

"We moved back to Pittsburgh and rented a house near a church called the tabernacle, as you know. Roth took a job there doing the books because he thought it would give him a chance to preach. The pastor at the church was sickly, and Roth thought if he could help out around the place, he'd be able to convince the preacher that he could handle the pulpit, but it never really happened. The pastor had some kind of brain disease that made him forget almost everything, and before long the congregation installed his son as the pastor. To be honest, I was nagging Roth to move, to get out of Pittsburgh before it was too late. I'd tell him, 'Come on, let's go down to Florida and lie on the beach. There's just as many churches there as in Arm-Pitt.'" Sally winks at me, proud of her old joke. "I never really liked it there, but Roth hated that I teased him about his city and called it that. He felt he was close to taking the stage at the tabernacle and didn't want to leave. Looking back, I was really immature, and leaving him and

Kari like I ended up doing was so childish, but I really felt like I'd die there if I didn't leave. I can't explain it any other way."

Sally pats my hand. "I wanted to see the world, you know, make my mark on it. I thought I could model—big gals like me could do that back then—but in the end, I got knocked down a few times and had to make do." She pauses. "I got remarried to a man who worked for an oil company, and we lived pretty well until he died in 1987. After that, I became a paralegal."

Sally shakes her head and emerges from the story. "How's that for a condensed version?"

I don't know what to say; my mouth is dry.

We sit and talk some more, about Kari and how pretty she is, and for some reason I think of the day we practiced walking down a grassy strip to receive our high school diplomas, and how we hung out afterward in my junky car, talking. For some reason, Kari started talking about her mother and how she'd left. "She took off when I was just a year old. I wonder if she knows what a shitty thing that is to do to a kid."

I didn't know what to say. I sat silent, tempted to pull down the car visor and squeeze a gleaming pearl on my nose. Instead, I reached over and patted her thigh. She didn't seem to notice. Finally she said, "I wonder if I'd be less fucked up."

Sally stands, ending our conversation. Her brow is creased, and she appears to be in deep thought. She flashes me a hopeful look, as if just remembering where she misplaced something. "I'll be right back. I've got to go to the car and get my rosary and prayer book. I'd like to pray over Roth before we take him home." She notices that I'm taken aback by her seemingly genuine religious convictions, particularly in light of what she's just told me about how she had to run away from life with Roth and the tabernacle.

"Oh, I'm not really Catholic, I've just found over the years that some of the rituals help me cope better. You know, something a little bit more tangible to hold onto." She smiles and pats my arm. She pauses as she holds the doorknob. "You know, I just realized, you're the same boy after all these years, aren't you?" She's holding her breath and then lets out an audible sigh. I've not answered when she says, "Isn't that something. And you two are in love. I can see that." Sally opens the door and walks out. I feel lost and found all at once.

three It's 1985 and the movie "Mask" has been out a couple of weeks. Kari and I have one more year of high school and our plans are to hit the road as quickly as possible, leave Pittsburgh and the Washburn Tabernacle and the deacon as far behind as possible. We are basking in being back together after her yearlong stay in Colorado. Everything— holding hands, eating together, kissing—all of it seems brand new, and the possibilities of our lives together, looming just out of our reach, somewhere around June of '86, are enough to keep us moving forward, positive and energized. As we pay for the movie tickets, I realize some people are staring at us. Seeing the movie, this particular one, has been a conversation Kari and I have had over and over. Some reviewers have mentioned that Rocky Dennis' story is one about any teenage kid who's suffered the ridicule of his peers, that the movie is ultimately about what's on the inside versus what's on the out. And while we've wanted to see the movie together, there's been a lot of talk between us about when to see it, the timing. I didn't want to be seen buying the tickets while some schoolmate decided to nickname me "Rocky," the name of the kid in the movie, or "Mask."

Of course, my face isn't as strange looking as Rocky's; his was deformed, caused by a disease that made him look like he'd been mauled. But I can see myself in it, the roughness and coarse layers. I can also see how lucky I was to have Kari, someone to love me for me, and Kari didn't even have to be blind to see it like the girl in the movie who falls for Rocky.

The theater's cold as we munch popcorn. I'm glad that it's dark and that when we leave it will be dark outside, too. As we hold hands, I can feel Kari's heartbeat in her wrist. She's started wearing very long, very loose sweatshirts since coming back from her grandmother's, and the sleeves of the one she has on now are bunched up so that she looks like the Michelin Tire Man. All through the movie, we hold hands and kiss. The ending is so sad that we both wait until the theater has cleared so people don't see our red eyes.

In the car heading to her house we can't quit talking about the movie—how we are outsiders, too, that we see all the silliness behind the cliques at school, the expensive designer clothes Brooke Shields tries to sell us, the way owning this or that kind of car is such a crock. Our pontificating is inane self-help philosophy, but to us, right then, it was the foundation of our future. There's something in the air inside the car that is pulling us closer together. Looking back on it now, Kari and I were as fated by "Mask" at the Carmike 8 Plaza as Sally and Roth were by the tornado.

"We just have to steer clear of assholes like the deacon," says Kari.

"Exactly," I chime. We're holding hands and sitting up straight, the dark road out before us. The centerline is bright and straight.

Kari leans over and kisses my cheek, nuzzles my shoulder. She says, "We're going to be great together, Hobbie. Just you wait and see." I steer the car like it's my destiny, taking the turns with confidence.

When we get to the house, Roth is gone to a church convention in Philly that he's been planning for months. He's grown accustomed to not living the life of a pastor in exchange for the life of a well-loved church member.

Inside the house, Kari and I fix a romantic meal. The kitchen smells of ripe tomatoes and dried oregano, as we stir a big pot of sauce and boil water for pasta. Together we cut onions, tear lettuce, and swab sliced French bread with a fresh garlic and butter mixture. It's fun pretending we are grown up and living in our own place, although when we do move away we'll begin eating fast food regularly and forego the preparation of our own meals in whatever generic suburb we're tellering in. But for now, we are putting the final touches on our plates and heading for the living room to watch a night full of MTV, staying up later for "Headbangers Ball. "

Our plates are cleaned and stowed, the kitchen wiped down, and all traces of our activity washed away with a spray bottle of 409 and paper towel. We shut off the lights and stroll down the carpeted hallway to Kari's bedroom, and without turning on the light climb into bed together, slipping off our clothes underneath the covers, kissing lightly. Everything is right and easy, not like before, after Kari just returned from Colorado and we seemed to have lost any use for words, me driving us around for hours, Kari just tired and slumped over in the seat, crying. I had no idea how to comfort her, so I'd turn up the music and drive and drive, the stoplights taking forever to turn green.

Under the covers Kari's body feels padded. Her hips are wider than when she left and they feel good to run my hands over. There is more of her, but I like it, a lot. Slowly, we find each other, entwine and make mistakes, laugh some, sweat and burn and pant before lying next to each other holding hands. Later, when we're in our mid-twenties, we'll call this night the "first time," but neither of us is sure. It seemed we'd already consummated our love by confiding in each other about the deacon. Afterward, Kari turns quiet and asks if I'll get a photo album from her closet. Shy, I pull my jeans back on and retrieve it. She turns on the bedside lamp and opens the front; it's made of burlap with a "Holly Hobbie" character ironed on the cover. I've not seen it before.

In the rose-colored light, Kari shows me the first page, Polaroids under a sheet of crisp plastic. She peels the plastic back and shows it to me. It's a picture of a baby.

"See, he was so little and had all those birthmarks on him." I nod. Her cousin's baby, she says. Kari sniffles and replaces the picture, takes another from the gluey cardboard; it makes a scratching sound as it comes off.

"This is him right after he was born." This picture is one of those narrow, grainy 35mm shots; next to it is a series of matte-finished square photos, obviously taken with a different camera. Kari snuggles up closer to me. "Please put it back in the closet, will you?" she asks. I smooth down the plastic and close the album.

Back in bed we press our bodies together and listen to the quiet house settling. It will be the first night we stay together. Kari's hands are cold, and she puts them anywhere on my body that she can find warmth. We doze, drift in and out of sleep, and wake early in the morning, the sunlight filtering through the blinds, casting a yellow glow on the carpet. She tells me, "You snore, you know that?" And she laughs and tickles me and I can't find a single flaw about her sleeping habits. I'm worried, though, that my face has birthed another litter of whiteheads overnight. I'm on my side, Kari wrapped around my back, when she says in a monotone voice, "That was a sad, good movie last night, wasn't it?"

"Uh, huh."

"Those pictures were sad, too, weren't they? That he died at birth?" She blows warm air onto my neck. Kari holds onto me as if she might be falling backwards off a cliff; I can feel the sharpness of her nails in my rib cage. She says, "Rocky, I love you."

"I love you, too, Kari, but please don't call me that."

"Okay, Hobbie. He was the tiniest little thing, wasn't he?"

I should have known then that her cousin's baby was really hers, but I didn't. I was too caught up in our love. I expect the best of Kari. That I would receive one of those same photos in a letter from her at a weight-loss clinic 20 years later with instructions to show it to her father and ask who's it was—if that would've been said to me as we cuddled under her blankets and talked about "Mask," I would've thought the notion just as absurd as why such a beautiful girl had allowed me to make love to her poorly.

four   "I'm not sitting in the back," Donny announces. He says it without a trace of anger or disgust; it's simply a statement, a preference he likely thinks won't be accommodated.

Sally ignores him as she assists Roth from the hospital wheelchair and into the middle row of her brand new minivan. I notice that Roth is more ephemeral, less substantial now. His entire body seems to collapse in upon itself. Is it possible that a stroke can diminish bulk overnight? His shoulders, although still much broader than mine, seem sucked in, as if he's involuntarily protecting his best physical feature by hiding it. Roth needs the whole middle seat to stretch out his legs, keep clots from forming, per the doctor's instructions, and that leaves Sally and me up front. I quickly offer to turn over the passenger seat to Donny.

"No, no, no," Sally says. "Donny, be a dear and just sit that scrawny rear end of yours in the back. We'll be at the house in no time."

Donny chews his bubble gum loudly, snaps it, and lets out an exhale as he gets in. "It's hot back here," he whines. Sally ignores him. He blows another bubble and pops it so it sounds like distant gunfire.

Once we're all in the van, I look back at Roth, who seems to be smiling too much; his face appears a tad demonic. He mumbles a series of guttural sounds, some of which I make out. He's said something about the day, the sun to be exact. It occurs to me that maybe understanding him now won't be nearly as difficult as when we were kids in some ways; back then he rode the highs and lows of his mood like a daredevil, mumbling at times, clear spoken at others. I look to Sally.

"He said the sun is pretty, that it's a very pretty day," she says, nodding, a look of contentment on her face, as if to say this isn't going to be so hard to manage. Donny's pouting in the back seat. I turn to look at Roth again, his skin bluish, dry patches around his forehead and mouth.

Donny looks at me, wad of gum in his mouth, and says, "What the fuck happened to your face, kid?"

Sally brakes then speeds up as she steers the van through a yellow light. "Donny, for God's sake, you're a visitor here, a guest, you don't just go and ask a question like that so rudely." Her face is showing some heat, bangs dampened. Roth is shaking his head, a small grin on his face, but he's definitely not pleased; he makes a pfffft! sound.

"What? What did I say?" asks Donny, a grown man acting like he's 7. "I didn't mean the pimples and shit."

Before Sally can answer or Roth can force out some distasteful sound, I pipe up. "It was an accident, nothing really, a bear was hungry and our dog and me got in the way."

"Holy shit," says Donny, intrigued.

Sally actually pulls the van off the road where slow-moving congestion is creating all types of red and orange lights in the dark gray evening, flashing around us on all sides like little controlled pockets of fire. "Donny," she says, putting the van in park. "Now, I'll put you on the first bus out of here if you keep using that language."

Donny tries to protest but she shushes him. He sulks down further in his seat and mumbles something.

Sally holds her cupped hand to her ear and says, "What was that?"

I've made eye contact with Roth, who seems to find the whole situation amusing. I can't help but hold back a smile, too.

Donny says, "Nothing," but it might have been something else.

Sally's not convinced, she continues cupping her ear and saying, "What was that? What?"

Donny kicks the space in front of him as if he's in a child safety seat. Roth turns to give him a sidelong look. Donny finally speaks up. "I said I'm hungry. I'm hungry, Sally. Hungry." It sounds so absurd, so babyish, that when Roth spits out a loud guffaw, followed by a hysterical wheeze, and Sally cackles a round of high-pitched giggles, I lose it, too, and we all laugh and laugh inside the minivan, the traffic outside not moving at all, while Donny tries his damndest to keep a grin from crossing his mopey face.

five Donny is fitting a metal handrail on the wall next to the toilet in Roth's bathroom. He's able to get the first rail affixed in no time, as his little eyes squint at the work and he takes gulps of coffee from a mug. As it turns out, he's quite talented in the areas of building and repair. While Roth sleeps in his bedroom and Sally works on dinner, Donny and I have made a run to Loew's and returned with a whole back seat full of mobility devices, braces, supports, and handrails that are supposed to make Roth's new life, his changed body, work to its full potential. Sally paid for it all, giving Donny a wad of cash, which I wouldn't have advised, given that as it also turns out, Donny's never far from trouble, his official record dotted and lined with police misunderstandings and petty grievances. But Sally would know better than I what Donny is and isn't capable of.

"Hold it still, will you," he tells me, slurping his coffee as I steady the handrail and he uses the power screwdriver to attach it to the wall. He sits with his legs crossed on the floor in front of the toilet. The smell of ground beef simmering, taco mix just added, wafts into the bathroom. I hold the rail in place and look over at the shower floor where Roth became another person. I'm still staring at the spot when Donny whines, "Come on, line up the holes, man. I want to eat." I could smack the little punk, although you don't really think of a punk being just 10 years away from membership in the AARP. "Sorry," I say, lifting the handrail to fit over the predrilled holes in the wall. Donny, in just a few seconds, has the thing attached so well it seems it could take the weight of several people.

Sally is humming in the kitchen, loudly; in fact, we've made no attempt to stay quiet while Roth sleeps for the first time back in his own bed. But for some reason, I decide to whisper now. "That seems really solid."

Donny looks at me and follows suit. "Yeah," he whispers. "I think it'll hold the old man pretty good."

The doorbell rings and I'm glad to get a reprieve from having to play Donny's sidekick, his little helper.

"Can you get that, Hobbie?" Sally calls.

I can't imagine Roth could sleep through the ruckus, but he does. At the foyer, barefoot, I answer the door, pulling it open wide. "Hi," says Simon, the vet, who is also Roth's neighbor, I remember. He's holding Terry. In the rush to get Roth home, I'd forgotten to pick him up. Terry wiggles and wags his tail, trying to jump from Simon's arms into mine.

"I saw the car in the drive and figured you'd want to see your little buddy. You did say you were going to get him today, and I thought I'd save you the trip. Like I said, I live just down the block," Simon says.

"Thanks so much," I say, chuckling as Terry climbs my chest, planting slick kisses on my forehead.

Simon laughs. "Wow, that's quite a greeting. Really, he's a good boy. The women in the office have taken to him." Simon's smile falls and he steps forward. "How's Roth doing?"

"Why don't you come in?" I say. "He's asleep, but we're about to wake him for tacos."

Simon shakes his head. "No, I don't want to be a bother. I just wanted to see if there's anything I can do."

"Why don't you have dinner with us?"

"No, I couldn't, besides, my wife and son are ordering Chinese for us tonight."

"Okay, well, maybe some other time," I say, trying to contain the bundle of love that is Terry.

"Listen, Terry here may continue to have seizures for a while. If you notice anything irregular about his behavior, don't hesitate to bring him in. I can't find any abnormal brain functioning on the CAT scan, but something in his chemistry caused the seizure, and I can't guarantee it won't happen again. At first I thought it was just from the bear attack, but I'm not so certain." In this light, I can see the pockmarks on Simon's face better than before; I can tell there are some sections that are not filled in, but he has no active acne. I'm intrigued.

"Well, I better get home," Simon says. "Enjoy those tacos!" He jogs down the front path to his car. I hold Terry and wave as Simon drives away. The subdivision is peppered with all kinds of light—security lights clicking on as the dusk turns to dark; the lamps inside the split-level ranches emanating yellow, blue glows from TVs, warming the thin drapes moving slightly from the heating vents. I close the door as a strong, cold wind blows in our faces, Terry's ear flopping over, then back down. Sally gives a strident call that dinner is in fact served. Donny's drill is making short little blasts.

The spread is impressive: grated cheddar cheese, steaming soft and hard taco shells, shredded lettuce, diced tomatoes, and no less than five bowls of condiments: guacamole, sour cream, salsa, cilantro, and some type of black bean sauce. Sally's smiling broadly next to the entire display, her face cheery and slightly pink.

She spots Terry and almost rips him from my arms. "Oh my, this must be your little dog. He wasn't much of anything when I visited in Minneapolis. Just a handful then." She strokes his ears and tickles his belly. Terry loves it and sighs as if this was what he's needed all day. Sally puts him down and says, "Let's get Roth up and out here for dinner, okay?" Terry looks at her as though she's taken away his life support and then slowly meanders under the table where he'll wait for the morsels to drop.

Donny stumbles into the dining room. He shoves past us and sits at the head of the table.

"Have you washed your hands, Donny?" Sally asks, already knowing the answer.

"No," he says, disappointed she's caught him. But he doesn't move, just remains planted in the chair.

"Are you serious, Donny? Get your butt up and go wash—what are you, 10?" Donny scoots back quickly from the table and points at me.

"Has he washed his hands?" he demands. Sally just shakes her head and takes me by the arm as we walk to the back of the house to get Roth up.

Roth's bedroom is dark except for a night light on the wall opposite the bed. He's breathing lightly and moving his feet some under the covers. Sally sits on the bed as I stand back.

"Roth," she says. "It's suppertime. Come on. Let's get up." She brushes his hair back and rests her hand on his cheek.

Donny yells from the dining room. "I've washed them. Can I eat now?"

Sally acts like she doesn't hear him. Roth opens his eyes and squints, his mouth sagging, a strand of saliva hanging from the corner. Sally wipes it off with her bare hand, as if it were merely dew on a flower.

"Come on, wake up and we'll have a nice Mexican supper," she croons.

Roth tries to purse his lips but they won't cooperate; they sort of blubber and slip into a loose pile on the left side. He shudders and lets out a cry. It's hard to watch and my throat tightens.

Sally coos, "Oh, I know, I know Rothie, just let it out and then we'll eat real good."

Roth struggles to reach his hand over her back, but then pats her softly, tenderly. Sally moves further into his weak embrace and for a while that's all there is, the two of them holding each other awkwardly. I can hear Donny hitting a spoon on the condiment bowls.

"Come here, Hobbie," Sally says, looking over at where I still stand at the edge of the room. I step forward once, then again, and finally I'm at his bedside.

"Help me get Roth up," Sally asks. Roth lets loose of her and she looks down at him with teary eyes, smiling. She lowers her mouth to his forehead and plants a kiss right above the bridge of his nose. "You still like tacos?" she asks. Roth nods.

With some effort we get him out of bed and propped up on the walker I was instructed to buy at the drugstore on our trip to Loew's. He is shaky at first but gets the hang of it pretty quickly. He pushes it down the hall and over the smooth carpet, Sally and I trailing behind him as if we're in some type of wedding rehearsal.

Donny is sitting at the table, a white dime of sour cream on his chin. Roth pushes his walker toward the wall and then sits down clumsily. *I'm going to whip this*, that's what his eyes say. He has a lipstick print on his forehead where Sally kissed him.

Sally and I sit down, too, and finally it's Donny who speaks up, frowning. "I'm a guest. I shouldn't have to say grace." Sally shakes her head. "Donny, have you ever said grace before a meal?" she says, smiling some.

"Grace," says Donny. "See, I just said grace before a meal." He's proud of his joke and sits up straighter. It's so stupid that it's funny, and we laugh like we did in the van coming home, kind of like a family.

six Once, five years ago, Kari and I decided to forgo the suburbs. We moved to Cincinnati and found a rental downtown and jobs at First International Trust Bank, right in the heart of the city. We thought it would be good to try something new, see whether we could survive without the aid of strip malls and mammoth anchor stores, but it was short-lived for two reasons. One, the manager wouldn't let me work the drive-thru; he made me man the more visible front-teller position and I hated it. Kari was right for the most part, that people don't really look at the teller's face when they do their banking, but the computers at the downtown FIT branch were notoriously sluggish, which gave customers a few slow-motion minutes to look up from their checkbooks and give my face a good once-over. That was the first reason.

The second was that we never actually did anything downtown. We tried. More than once we walked to a play or meandered to a Chinese take-out place that served piping hot egg rolls, and we even got in the habit of going on evening strolls together. But something happened that drove us back to the impersonal sprawl of the suburbs. One night Kari said, "You know, we're becoming known here in the city. I can just hear people saying: 'That couple, you know, he's got that face, and oh, you do, too, know, she's a rotund woman.' That's what people say, they know us here."

"But don't you think people have said that in the other places we've lived?" I asked.

"Yep, but here it's *expected* that we be accepted, become part of the quirky, newly restored downtown district. The hip people like us living here because we contribute to its strange charm. Here we're lovable freaks. In the suburbs we're just an anonymous joke." It was true. When we lived in all the other suburbs no one knew who we were; they didn't invite us to their parties to show how accepting they were.

They may have laughed behind our backs, but we didn't know it, and even if they did they'd never be able to use our names to make fun of us. We never knew our neighbors, and they didn't bother to get to know us. And although we thought we wanted something more personal, it turned out just like Kari said. In downtown Cincinnati we had names attached to my wrecked face and Kari's heft. We hated it, and when people began to greet us by name, we wanted out.

So we started taking drives from our apartment downtown to the malls and sprawled shopping centers in the suburbs. We'd drive almost an hour just to get away from our community. Sometimes, we'd shop at a Best Buy, finding deals on previously viewed DVDs until lunch time, then drive across the interstate to a Cracker Barrel, taking some time to make fun of the old-timey illusion the food chain sold. After eating, we'd get back in the car and cross the interstate again to the shopping center to hang out for the rest of the day in a Barnes and Noble, reading and drinking coffee, eating pastries, and flipping through magazines. "How do these places make money? Nobody ever buys anything," Kari would say, sipping her $5 coffee. I'd point at it and she'd say, "Oh, yeah, right. The coffee."

By nightfall we'd be back in our apartment downtown, tired from the long drive, and ready to watch whatever DVD we'd snagged. We'd fall asleep with the smell of fast food in our hair. The time we spent there, a six-month lease, had the worst impact on my skin and Kari's weight. She gained 50 new pounds, and I picked my face with greater brutality, making it a bloody mess. That was when she started to waddle rather than walk, her ankles swollen and calves indistinct and tight looking. And my face looked like it had been shot with a pellet gun over and over. Kari ate KitKat bars and King Size Snickers like they were appetizers. She'd still eat a super-size combo from McDonalds, one for lunch and another for dinner. It was as if she were challenging herself, trying to reach an all-time high. At our job, she had to have a special chair to sit in, an orthopedic one, because the swelling in her feet was excruciating, but in the end, the manager forbid the chair, saying the ADA didn't cover fat people. Kari, to my surprise, said, "She's right. I'm just a fat woman, my own fault. I shouldn't get the same treatment people with cerebral palsy or quadriplegics get."

Finally, when the lease on our place was up, we headed to the Minneapolis suburbs. We lived next to a Nations Bank branch with a drive-thru, and a 24-hour Wal-Mart right behind the apartment complex. By far, that was the best place we ever had to hide.

seven   A few days pass while Roth gets used to his walker and learns how to communicate as best he can, using a slightly garbled, yet discernable speech pattern. Donny, with my help, finished installing the handrails, most of them in the bathroom, but some, too, along the hallway, in the kitchen below the countertop, and one at the front door and another in the garage. Even if Donny did whine a lot about the work, and wanted Sally to kiss his thumb if the hammer fell the wrong way, all and all he did a good job and provided Roth with a home that would accelerate his recovery by offering a manageable way to get around.

Each day, I leave Kari a message in her voice mail at the Center for Healthy Living in Durham, but she never returns the calls. Finally, I leave a long message about Roth. "Look, Kar, I didn't want to have to tell you this, this way." I pause, waiting for her to pick up, which is stupid on my part; it's obviously an electronic message center, not a blinking answering machine she's screening me on, my voice echoing while she stands by and just listens. "Roth had a stroke. He's home and doing okay, but the thing is . . . he's impaired, I guess the word is. And Kari, your mom came to help. Kari? Call me. I'm at your dad's." I hang up and don't remember to tell her about Terry and me, but then, once I've thought about it, I'm glad I didn't.

I suppose I could leave Roth's house and go back to my life in the mountains at that house, but Roth needs me and the truth is I feel like Sally might be able to help me get Kari back, which is stupid, I know, since they are estranged, but still, something makes me think that staying around Roth and Sally during this whole new family set-up will make all the difference. So I'm happy to stretch out each night on the fold-out couch in Roth's study, my small collection of things I've brought from the rental house aligned neatly on the shelves of the closet. I know I'm facing another restless night of sleep, if I can get any at all. I've been dreaming vividly of the bear. Everyone else occupies three separate bedrooms, even though Donny asked several times why he couldn't sleep with Sally in her room.

It's evening, after dinner. Sally has prepared a toothsome Italian—or "Eye-towel-yun," as she pronounces it—dish, a casserole with Vienna sausage, mushrooms, and onions in a tangy tomato sauce, with big lasagna noodles along with corkscrew pasta, too. Delicious. The garlic bread is warm and filling. Roth wears his napkin like a child, but Donny, of course, acts like one, asking for seconds before he's even finished his first serving. "I got dibs," he says, pointing a fork at the casserole.

After, we sit in the living room with our stomachs full, the entire group politely burping, mouths closed, even Donny, which surprises me. I would think he'd let one rip, belch the ABCs or something. The television is off. I'm trying to decide whether this is the right time to let them know I can't reach Kari. Roth has asked for her, of course, and I've postponed having to let him know I've failed. I'm just about to speak when Donny pipes up. "Can we watch re-runs of 'M*A*S*H' on cable?" he asks. Roth, looking sleepy but content, shrugs his shoulders.

"I thought we could all play a nice board game," Sally counters. "It would be good for everyone, get us thinking, using our noodles."

Donny becomes animated, "Yeah, good, good," he says.

Sally goes to the closet and brings back a worn Monopoly box, a hardly used Pictionary game and two checkerboards. She sets up the Pictionary game first. I assume she's chosen this game for Roth's sake, but even that might be a stretch for him.

"I'll play on Roth's team," she says.

Donny tries to get her to reconsider. "No, play on my team, babe. We can kill these two," he says. Terry wanders in from the laundry room, pieces of grayish-purple dryer lint stuck to his coat. His wound looks naked and obscene in the bare openness, the ceiling light accentuating it. Simon had promised his fur would cover it up in no time, but as he pads his body toward me, the wound looks improper, as if he's been the recipient of an ill-advised organ transplant. I remind myself to have mine looked at; I don't know when the stitches on my face are due out. As Sally sets up the game, my body feels drained but on edge, as if I've run a race and have been told I've got to do it all over again.

We gather around Roth. I pull the coffee table toward him, and Sally tells Donny to put the chairs in a semicircle. "Now remember, we've got Entenmann's tiramisu for dessert," Sally says. "Coffee, too, if anyone wants any, but decaf—it's too late for caffeine."

The house is too warm for my comfort, but Sally is cold natured and Roth seems to need the place oven-like now. He's wearing a pair of thick sweat pants and a nice cardigan over a black turtleneck. Sally's been dressing him some, but calls in Donny when it gets too private. "You shouldn't have to see a man who you've respected all these years in his birthday suit. It's better if someone he doesn't know does it," she explained.

Terry goes directly to Roth and snuggles in under his feet, lying so that he can rub up against Roth's wooly slippers, maybe using them to replace his missing hair. Sally shuffles the Pictionary cards like a pro; she fans them, collapses the deck, and arcs the cards into a spitting crisscross motion that seems self-propelled. She turns the split-deck with two fingers, and offers them to Donny for a cut. I know he's going to be a bad loser.

"Our team should get to start. I'm a guest." He's worn that out over the past few days, using the guest bit as reasoning for first dibs on everything from the shower to extra desserts.

Roth says with effort, "O---kay." He attempts a wink. If I'm picking up on it right, Roth actually likes Donny, which is strange to me. In his old body, the former Roth would have thought Donny petty and highly in need of Christ in his heart to make him grow up, which is not entirely what I'm thinking, but kind of; he does need something to help him mature, maybe a good ass kicking.

"I'll draw first on the paper," Donny tells me. He also wants to draw the card from the deck, but I do it and am so tired I read the thing so everyone can hear: "The Cat's in the Cradle and the Silver Spoon."

"You're not supposed to read it out loud," Donny sputters. "Gaw! Now we have to pass!" Before he gets too out of whack, Sally jumps in. "Oh, never mind that. Just draw. It's all just for fun anyway. We'll play like this, won't keep score."

Donny starts out with the cat, which ends up looking more like a lab rat. Next, he puts his baseball cap on backwards. He skips the cradle part and draws a spoon that looks exactly like a spade used for digging potatoes.

Roth provides a good-natured answer, "Cat shove....uull?" Sally laughs, throwing her head back. It's funny. Donny gets agitated.

"Yes, that must be it," Sally teases, "a cat shovel." She smacks her lips and pats Roth on the leg. Donny shakes his head, on the verge of a tantrum, and goes back to drawing a different size cat shovel on the crinkly paper, pausing a few times to get the thing to look more rounded. The heady scent of permanent markers fills the hot space around the coffee table. Roth's mouth drips a string of spit. He reaches up and wipes it away forcefully, the strand following his veiny hand back down to his side. The sight of it makes me want to look away, pretend it's not there. I've got to get used to it though; this is Roth now. I need to tell him about Kari, that his own daughter is listening to messages about his dire health situation but is more concerned about changing her own body to something different.

Terry yawns at Roth's feet. Donny is scribbling like mad, going from one failed spoon to another, never stopping to think he could draw a moon or cradle or that at this point the game isn't really a game. He's digging the marker into the paper; it begins to bunch up and tear. Sally says, "Now, Donny, take your time. It's okay, just think it out."

Donny turns to face us and throws the marker hard against the wall. His eyes are brimming with tears. He shouts, "Fuck this stupid game. You bastards aren't playing it right anyway!" He storms out of the room, hitching up his loose, dark jeans. Roth has a look of utter surprise on his face; his eyes remain staring at the space in front of the coffee table where Donny's small body had been. Slowly, he turns to Sally, arches his eyebrows. She begins to whisper something, then stops, looks over her shoulder to make certain he hasn't come back into the room. "It's his dyslexia," she says. "He's smart, but sometimes letters and numbers and stuff jump around on him. I'll go check on him in a bit, give him some time to save face." She stands and says, "Okay, who'd like dessert? Give me a hand, Hobbie, would you?"

From where we are in the kitchen, we can hear Donny in the guest bedroom drilling something. I'm not certain if he's actually installing anything for Roth or not, perhaps he's in there right now fastening the headboard to the wall with decking screws just to have something to do with his frustration. Sally doesn't seem to notice the noise. "How about getting me some plates down while I cut the tiramisu?" She holds a long silver knife, pausing before putting the tip into the brown-and-tan frosting. "Hobbie," she asks, "what's the story with Kari, is she coming home or not?" I feel myself freeze on the inside but keep going through the motions of getting down small plates from the cabinet, grabbing forks from a drawer.

"Sally," I say, ignoring her question, "do you know the child in this picture?" I pull out the photo Kari sent in the mail from my back pocket. Sally juts her head forward, then backs off, trying to see it without her glasses.

"No, hon, but he sure looks like a pitiful little thing. What are those spots on him?"

"Birthmarks," I say. "But you've never seen him before?"

"No, I can't say that I have." She goes back to slicing the cake and I tuck the picture into my back pocket again. The drilling in the next room stops, and a door opens. Sally is careful not to let her fingers touch each slice as she places them on the plates I hold out.

"I've left Kari a few messages," I tell her. "But I don't know if she's gotten them."

Sally's engrossed in her serving duties. "Well, I'm sure she'll call you back. You'll talk soon." She lifts her fingers away from the knife's edge and places the last slice on a plate.

"Actually, we probably won't. I've not talked to her in six months. I just get letters from her."

Sally looks up, some cleavage exposed as she leans over the cake to cut it; I think of Playtex. "What? Why not? Why haven't you?" She seems shocked and intrigued.

"That's the way she wanted it," I say, now wanting to back off, but at the same time wanting to share, make our love story as interesting as hers and Roth's.

"Good Lord, that's quite an experiment of love, isn't it?"

I pick up two plates and so does Sally, and we stand facing each other like third-shift servers in an Applebee's. I shrug. Maybe Sally sees the no-communication stint as strangely romantic. Or maybe she's even proud of her daughter—it's hard to tell.

I'm right behind her on our way back to the living room when she stops short just inside the arched doorway. "Oh, my goodness," she says.

I step to the side and see that Roth is standing next to the bookcase with no pants on; the sweats he's been wearing were too loose and have fallen off, apparently. His rear end is smaller than I would have imagined and is flour-white. Sally and I watch as he paws at the books and other items on the shelves, searching for something, I assume. He looks over his shoulder at us standing there with slices of cake and then turns back to his task, choosing to ignore us. He moves to a shelf that holds a stack of photo albums. Terry glances up, eyelids heavy, and it may sound unbelievable, but he, too, gives the sight of a half-naked Roth a second look, as if to say, "I believe I see the moon." I half expect him to howl.

Donny walks in and fixes on the dessert plates we're still holding. "Yum, yummy," he says as he nearly gallops toward Sally. He takes a plate and starts eating, unaware, apparently of Roth. Sally and I are frozen, still staring at Roth. I start to move toward him to help, but Sally gently holds me back. "Let him be, Hobbie. He needs some room to make mistakes." It seems like a sound idea, but it also feels a tweak or two off, like we're watching a person who's just fallen on ice, but not going over to help.

Roth finally finds what he's looking for, an album that looks familiar. He makes his way back to his chair and flops down.

Donny takes another bite of tiramisu and says with his mouth full, "What'd you say this was?" He finally notices us staring at Roth and turns to see himself. "Damn," he says with a mouth full of cake, "I thought you said this guy was a preacher once."

It's then that I finally realize Roth is holding the burlap photo album from the night Kari and I saw "Mask," the one she had me retrieve from her closet, the same one that held the picture I just showed Sally. Roth is determined as he flips through the album. I touch my fingers to the picture in my pants pocket and watch as he searches the pages, still naked from the waist down as he sits in his chair.

eight   "Seriously, is anyone gonna make him put his pants on? It's grossing me out," says Donny, shoving cake into his mouth. Roth's sweat pants lie in a bundle where they'd fallen next to his chair, where he sits and fumbles with the photo album, apparently determined to find something. Terry stands, yawns, and takes a couple steps before settling back down into Roth's clothes as if it were a nest made especially for him.

"Donny, go eat your cake in the kitchen if you don't like it," Sally says.

"I don't," Donny answers, and lumbers out of the room.

Sally goes to Roth and kneels down next to his chair. "Honey," she says, "what are you looking for?" She tries to discreetly cover his midsection with a throw pillow.

Roth doesn't answer but looks up and stops rifling through the pages. His eyes well. He puts his bluish, shaky hand to his mouth. He looks at me and his upper body begins to shudder, just like his hand, as if he were cold. I can feel myself beginning to chill, too. I'm not even standing next to him, yet it's as though we're locked in an embrace, something like burden and relief holding us together.

Sally looks at Roth, then at me, and back to Roth again. "What is it?" she says, rubbing his forearm, trying to warm him up. "Honey," she says, "if you're embarrassed about dropping your drawers, don't worry about that. See, even Terry's okay with it." She points to Terry curled into the Russell Athletics, his eyes twittering in dream as he hiccups.

Roth bows his head and cries into the photo album. Sally doesn't seem shocked—he's experiencing the emotional wax and wane the doctor warned us about. She lifts his chin and speaks slowly and sincerely to him. "Roth, we're here for you, no matter what, okay?" Her nails look like little ovals off the hood of a red Corvette against his pale chin.

I take the photo of the baby out of my pocket and cup it in my palm. My throat hurts.

Roth rubs his hand over his face and clears his throat, trying to regain his composure.

He struggles to hand the photo album to Sally. His turtleneck is long and provides the coverage he needs, except that a jut of very pale hip is showing. Roth points at the photo album.

"What?" asks Sally. "Do you want me to look at this?" Roth nods. She flips open the cover. The "Holly Hobbie" iron-on patch is worn and peeling off. I can envision Kari and I holding hands at "Mask," all those years ago, planning our future in the car ride home, being together in her warm bed. I miss her and I hate her. Roth sniffs hard, and we look at each other, knowing what's coming. Sally flips to the first page and says, "Well, I think the baby in these pictures is the same as that one you showed me in there, Hobbie." Roth looks to me, a deflated relief in his chest.

He works hard at telling Sally, "Go to . . . ba . . . ck." She turns the bulky album over and flips open the back cover. She picks up a bundle of letters wrapped tightly with two rubber bands. Roth shoots me a look. His speech may be tough to follow and he's certainly different, but his mind is sharp. His eyes tell me: "Here are the letters. I hid them from you after you found them above the refrigerator. I've lied in the past, but let's fix this together. You ready?"

Sally says, "What are these, hon?" She slips the rubber bands off and tilts her head, trying to read the addresses. I move the coffee table with the Pictionary paraphernalia out of the way and pull a chair closer to Roth, the picture still in my hand. My jeaned knee touches his white, bare one. He's locked in a gaze with me. *Do you know? You do, don't you?*

Sally says, "Well, these are all from Kari." She smiles and her lips make a little parting smack as she sorts through the letters. She picks one up and shows it to me. "This one's to you, but it's not been opened. Postmarked about a week ago." Roth apologizes with his eyes: *Sorry, I was scared.* Donny yells in from the kitchen, "Can I have more cake, please?"

I take the picture of the baby that I've been holding and show it to Roth. Roth licks his lips and reaches for the photo and then passes it to Sally. He takes my hand and squeezes it. Up close, I can see how much the stroke has changed the muscles in his face; it's all falling on the left side: eye socket, the corner of the mouth, his saggy cheek.

Sally says, "Well, now you two have got me curious. Who is this baby and why do you both have pictures of it?" She shuts the photo album and looks at the picture closely, squinting. Roth uses his head to indicate I should answer her question. "That's Kari's son," I finally say. The words hang in the air, and I can feel my whole body embrace the truth.

nine

Dear Hobbie:

I know it may seem weird to get a letter from me that's longer than my three-digit weight but here it is, right in your hands.

Durham is a lot like all the other places we've lived, but of course, I haven't really been living here, just existing, trying to find what's underneath all the years of hiding. I've lived in a small room for six months now. It has a single bed with one of those old granny kind of bedspreads, you know the kind, like the one we had for a while in Minnie. It's thin and cream colored and has fringe on it, barely enough to make a sheet. I don't know why I'm writing so much about the bedding. I guess it's because I've been foolish and haven't talked with you in so long, which I miss, honey, I do. But I can't think much about all that or I won't do what I've got to.

The other day, during weigh-in, a woman who brags about making over 200K a year as a PR consultant for some right wing political group, smarted off to me and I had to punch her right in the nose. It was wrong, but she's so egotistical. You would think being just under 300 pounds would make her less so, but…. Anyway, I was put on probation and reminded by the team of doctors that this is a voluntary weight loss inpatient program and that I could leave or be told to leave at anytime. I guess it doesn't matter, I mean, I am leaving here, soon.

Do you remember the time we hopped that train senior year? How could you forget, right? Well, I've been thinking about that a whole lot lately, the way you smelled so good (Polo cologne) and the wind in our clothes and how it was chilly after a while even though it was summertime. When they'd blow the horn at all the little towns even though it was desolate at the crossing, and they'd still pull the rope on the tiny bell even though there was no way it could be heard over that elephant horn, that makes me sad to remember. I wish I knew why. Things like that, and you know this the best, really get me down. One doctor here said I was not a good candidate for depression medication because I'm not depressed. I'm just cynical. He said in a joking way, "Cynicism doesn't count, Ms. Kari, you've got to be clinically depressed."

I tried calling the house yesterday but you were not there, which I guess I knew since you'd be at work at that time. I hope your tellering job is going well. I'm sorry for a lot of things. To have made you haul me around all over the country, for getting us stuck in teller jobs, for making us so isolated, for making you hide with me. I know, it's not all me, but still, I want you to know I set you free. I've hogged you for too long. Just like my eating, I've really kind of devoured you, too, kept you all to myself. You're a kind and gentle person and beautiful. I want you to know that, Hobbie, to really know it.

It's almost lights out here and I don't want to have to argue with the peer police here (that's what we call the newly skinnied who patrol and counsel and badger us). Even though I've gained some pounds back, I bet you wouldn't recognize me if we passed on the street. Remember how we used to tell each other stories? How we'd say, what kind of story do you want: scary or sexy or just stupid? Well, that's how I'm going to end this, with a story like that, about how different I am so that you'd have a hard time picking out your common-law wife in a morgue (late-thirties, slightly obese, dark hair, birthmark on her inner thigh, Caucasian). Don't get freaked out, I'm just talking. Well, here it goes, a story like old times:

You are driving a convertible Beetle Bug you just bought in a deserted town. It's autumn and you're wearing a rugged sweater that covers your throat. On the radio you're playing Quiet Riot, *Cum on Feel the Noize*. It's kind of a stupid song now that you're older, but still, it makes you feel "possible" again. Your slacks are tweed and baggy. And yes, you have on that cologne, lime and spice. You've just left your job in a converted loft space that has brick and wood floors and pipes and ventilation that's coolly exposed. Let's just say you're doing what you always dreamed you would; we don't know what that is, neither of us, just something more than what we've done. Anyway, you pull your car over and step out. The leaves on all the trees lining this street are perfectly red and orange and golden, but are not falling, they're not falling off at all, just rustling up there in perfect colors. You lean on the car and wait for a woman you don't know, but have a strong feeling you're supposed to; it's destiny, soul-mate stuff.

You see her walking toward you down the sidewalk as the sun begins to leave the sky, turning it pink. Her heels hit the cement with demure pertness as she comes your way. She's wearing some kind of perfume that only you can detect. She stops before you, looks at you with your hands shoved in your pant pockets, and smiles. Her long wool skirt and high heel boots drive you crazy. You want to run your hands over her stockings. The two of you clasp hands and begin to dance, a slow, sweet waltz that's in sync with the end of the day, but it's only the start.

Love,

Kari

PS: I love you, but I'm going to find my son, which is weird to say, because really, I've always thought of him as ours.

ten   It's early morning. Sally and Donny are still asleep, in separate rooms though. I can't quite figure out what their relationship is, or was, maybe that's the operative word. Clearly Sally is trying to set some new boundaries with him, help Donny see that a friendship is what they have now. The night was long and irritating; for all the hope I have, there's a well of hurt, too, a sense of betrayal that Roth and Kari hadn't trusted me with their secret. I can't absorb that she's lied to me, told me over and over that the baby in the picture died. It's kept me awake most of the night, and I'm feeling so worn out, running on no more than a few hours of sleep. I have to do something about it; the dreams I'm still having where that bear attacks me are vivid and strange, terrifying. In some of them, Terry doesn't make it, and I wake up with a painful thrumming in my head, on the verge of tears. I've got a severe crick in my neck from sleeping on the foldout in the den where Roth's bookcases are full of biblical titles.

I've gotten up early to get the chance to talk with Roth without Sally's assistance and in the absence of her baby Donny's petulance. I set two steaming bowls of Cream of Wheat on the kitchen table and tiptoe to the back of the house, past the two guest bedrooms that Donny and Sally are snoring in; Terry's got nothing on these two. I creep into Roth's bedroom, and I'm shocked to see that he's awake and struggling with putting on a shirt and tie. Of course, he's bottomless, his penis hiding in a thick nest of hair. I avert my eyes and whisper, "What are you doing, Roth?" He's trying very hard to flop the end of the tie up through a space he's created for the knot. It's not working; he's using his good side to make it swing upward. He's leaning against the wall, the walker nearby.

Roth doesn't answer me but holds out the tie and lowers his head. I remove the tie from his neck and loop it around mine; it's the only way I can tie a tie. "How about you put on some pants while I do this?" I say.

Roth glowers at me and manages, "I can't . . . do . . . it . . . by . . . myself." I instantly feel stupid for suggesting it.

I take a pair of black cotton pleated pants from the closet and hold them up. They've been dry-cleaned, like all the clothes in his closet. Roth nods and wipes spit from his lips. As I'm about to bow down and help him into them, I realize he needs underwear, too. "Where do you keep your shorts?" I say. He doesn't answer and latches onto his walker. I'm in the middle of the room and he's coming at me with resolve, a John Wayne type of grit in his clenched teeth.

"What? What's wrong, Roth? I'm just trying to help."

He stumbles over a loose spot in the carpet. He rattles the walker as if it's a cage and forces the wheels ahead. I think I should go but he's between the door and me. He's pissed, I can see that, and I'm totally confused.

"Okay, okay, I'm sorry," I say, remembering what Sally said, that it's better for a stranger to assist him with things like this.

Roth reaches out and grabs my hand and tries to lift it to his face. He's gets madder when he can't seem to get my hand where he wants it.

"What? Do you have a fever?" I say, thinking he wants me to feel his forehead. He makes a "puh" sound and drops my loose arm.

"Listen, I'll just leave and come back a little later, okay?" I say.

He butts me with the walker. I think he's lost it, that the stroke has left him more impaired than I thought, a little crazy even. He's sweating and swallowing the extra saliva to try and speak. He picks up my hand again and brings it this time all the way to his face, pressing it as hard as he can into his cheekbone. His cheek is unshaven, the stubble like sandpaper across the back of my hand.

He says slowly and with effort, "It me!" He grunts and tries again, "It me!" I've no idea what he's trying to say. His eyes are on fire. I try to pull my hand away from him, but now that he's gotten a good hold of it, he's surprisingly strong. I think of his days when he curled weights and exercised. It seems like ages ago when he picked me up at the hospital in his workout clothes; the remains of that regimen are still somewhere inside him. He finally manages, "Hit me!" The eye unaffected by the stroke is wide, and his breath comes in short blasts. Finally, after a long moment of Roth gripping my hand harder, I reach up and peel his fingers from my hand, and he lets go, defeated. He says slowly, his mouth lax, "Please hit me," almost under his breath, his chest heaving.

"Why?"

He shakes his head and moves to sit down on the bed, backs up, and flops onto it. I hand him a throw from the bed and he covers himself, fumbling the afghan. He points toward the small desk in the corner of the bedroom and says slowly, "Please?"

"What?"

He manages to get out, exasperated, "Pa—purr." I retrieve a pad of legal paper and a pen. Roth takes the pen like he's thirsty and it's a glass of water. He's unsteady, and repositions the pen in his hand a couple times and scribbles as if checking to see whether the pen works. It's tough to watch, and I'm afraid this is only going to be another mundane task from his old life that now seems exotic and unwieldy in his new one. I sit down next to him on the bed, careful, as if my presence alone might ignite another round of self-hatred.

I study the side of his face where soft, loose skin clings in tiny folds under his ear. He's working the pen over the yellow paper with so much force that his writing sounds like a cat clawing a post. I think to simply ease the pen and paper away and help him get back in bed.

Painstakingly, he begins to print. Each letter takes several beats to form, the squiggly lines and slanted marks create the words he's looking for, and before long, he's moving with more confidence.

The sun has come up fully, and a strong, glimmering ray of light is shafted through the window and onto our feet. Roth's toes are white and hairy, the nails thick and ridged. Behind us, through the wall, Donny or Sally or both are up, flushing the toilet and coughing. Roth is reviewing his work and literally dotting his i's and crossing his t's. It's taken him nearly a half-hour, but it's done. Satisfied, he hands me the pad of paper, his eyes bleary and swollen, the throw over his legs like a shawl. He leans toward me and gives me a warm hug, points to the legal pad. The writing is tough to make out, but I manage.

"I'm a bad man. I want you to hit me. I knew about the deacon before he hurt you and Kari. I thought he wouldn't do that because I helped keep him out of trouble the first time. I'm a bad man, Hobbie. Forgive me. Help me see Kari. I want her to know it was all my fault. I used to know where her son was. Please, please, just hit me once."

I tear the page off and fold it up and put it in my pocket, buying some time unable to talk. Roth falls into me again and sobs, moves his hand all around my chest, trying to soothe us both.

There's a knock at door. "Roth," Sally says in a husky morning voice. "Hon, are you up?"

Roth looks at me and nods.

"We're just about done in here, Sally. Hold on, we'll be out," I call.

Sally says, "Oh, Hobbie. I didn't know you were in there, too. Okay." Her shadow moves away from the crack under the door.

I help push Roth up straight, balance him. Despite the two decades of silence and lying, I can't remember ever feeling more love for both Roth and Kari. I'm amazed at how clear and confidently I tell Roth, "Listen, you didn't do anything to us, he did. I'm not going to hit you." Roth closes his eyes as if my words either sting or relieve his eyes.

"Let's go get Kari," I say. "If she's still there in Durham. I don't know though, she may already be gone."

Roth nods with his eyes still closed. I put my hand to his face and pat it, and he struggles to do the same to me. It feels good to have him touch my ugly face, even though the stitches still hurt, kind of like a bee sting. We're stuck in that position, like two monks pardoning sins, when Donny doesn't bother to knock and busts in. He's holding a bowl of the Cream of Wheat I'd left on the kitchen table. "Sally said I had to ask you guys if I can eat—" He stops mid-sentence and stares. Finally after a long pause he speaks. "Hey," he says, "I'm supposed to dress him, that's what Sally said."

eleven It takes almost 40 minutes to drive to the vet's; traffic is awful. Terry looks out the window as if he, too, can't believe how slow it is.

Finally we make it to the office. Simon the vet says, "This fine gentleman seems like he's on the mend," his hand tickling Terry under the chin as we stand over him on the examining table. "He may still have some problems, but for now, just keep an eye on him." Simon runs a finger over the pink ridge of Terry's scar. "Looks like it's healing well."

Simon turns and washes his hands in the sink, steam rising. He rinses then dries his hands vigorously, tossing the paper towel into the trash. He turns and says: "So, you all are going to North Carolina, huh?"

"Right. Roth is anxious to see his daughter, Kari, now that he's feeling stronger. And of course that means Sally and her friend will also go along. He prefers to have Donny help him with dressing and everything." Simon nods his head.

"What are you going to do about your face, your stitches?" Simon asks. He stands with his hands in his pockets, rocking on the balls of his feet. "Because, you know, I could take those out right here if you want, save you a trip to the doctor's office, the visit fee, too." He places Terry in a little bed on the floor. Terry turns two circles and lies down, eyes already dopey.

"Climb up on the table here, Mr. Shepherd," says Simon, chuckling and winking, making sure I get the joke.

"No, you've mistaken me for someone else. It's Mr. Doberman," I say, playing along, a real sense of companionship starting in me. Simon's the "after picture" and I'm the "before," the ones on late night infomercials where '70s sitcom stars sell miracle pimple creams at $90 a pop. "Sorry," says Simon, shrugging his shoulders. "It's been a slow day, guess I'm kinda stir crazy."

I tilt my head as Simon pulls on a pair of rubber gloves, eyes squinted in concentration as he examines the wound.

"Of course, this is just one neighbor helping out another here. I don't make a practice of this. I'm sure you know the health department and the veterinary association would not look kindly on me for this. Mum's the word, Hobbie."

I haven't had a friend in years and to hear my name spoken by a guy whose face has weathered the storm makes me hopeful, in a strange way. Strange but good. "Right, I wouldn't tell a soul," I promise.

Simon gently touches either side of the wound, slightly splaying it, maybe checking for signs of infection. "Looks fine to me," he says, massaging the area a bit before stepping back. "Let me get a new pair of tweezers from the stock room and some scissors, too, and we'll have that all taken care of so you and Mr. Terry can hit the road new men." He leaves the room, the door closing slowly behind him.

Alone, I wonder how I must seem to Simon: I'm in a relationship with a woman sequestered in a fat camp, my face sports a deep bear wound, and I have a dog with seizures, not to mention that my sort-of father-in-law's home now houses not only Roth's ex-wife but her boyfriend, too.

Simon steps back in the room. "Here we go. We're good to go." I watch as Simon's pale hands fiddle with a pre-packaged set of scissors and tweezers; he pops the plastic seam as if they were a cutlery combo from a fast-food joint.

"We'll get the stitches out, and then we can see how your scar is going to look." Simon begins to lightly clip at the stitches, his wrist brushing my chin. His breathing is controlled as he performs the miniscule actions of freeing the thread from my cheek. I sneak a peek at his pockmarked face, in much better shape than mine, of course, but still showing the signs of *acne vulgaris*. I wonder what his high school days were like. Maybe guys in his 10th-grade PE class put pizza coupons on his locker, like they did to me.

Simon is quiet and focused. "There we go," he says. "Does that feel better? You should be able to feel that the skin has loosened. I've got them all snipped—now all we have to do is pluck them out." He smiles as he moves to the sink to drop the scissors into a disinfectant jar like barbers use.

"How did you get interested in being a vet?" I ask, trying for some small talk that might actually bring us closer to being friends. I could use a friend like Simon.

Simon smiles and returns to my face. "Well, that's pretty easy. I wanted to be a doctor, actually, and you'll find this kinda funny, I wanted to be a dermatologist, but a career counselor in college told me I shouldn't choose a profession based on some personal hurt, that it wouldn't serve me well." Simon pulls the first stitch out and drops it into a little kidney-shaped stainless steel container next to me. "He even told me I wouldn't be a very good advertisement." Simon laughs.

"One down, 20 to go," he says, then takes a deep breath and goes in again. "Don't think I'm taking my latent dreams out on you, though, I'm happy being a vet, and who knows, maybe the counselor was right, maybe I would have ended up being a bad skin doctor after all." Out in the hallway, there's a ruckus—a large sounding dog is barking. Phones are ringing, too, but Simon continues to methodically pull each stitch out. With some of them he has to pull a little harder to free them. I can feel the resistance in my skin, and think of a stubborn fishhook. "You almost waited too long to get these taken out, Hobbie, but the upside to that is the scar is already in good shape. It should heal real well."

The dog in the hallway must be wagging its thick tail against the wall, a rhythmic thumping. "Just one more," Simon says, his voice upbeat. In a few more minutes our interaction will be over. I search my mind for something else to say, but my mind is blank. Along with finding Kari, I'd like to have a friend, but I'm at a loss for how people go about making them.

"Well, that does it," Simon says, smiling and holding out the sil-

ver container for me to see the results. The stitches look like coarse
whiskers, as if I've been strop-shaved without cream. Simon moves
to the sink again and rinses everything with hot water and soap.

"You'll want to keep a thin film of Neosporin on that, but leave
it open, let the air get to it." Simon offers his hand. "Good luck on
your trip."

I shake his warm hand and try and find something that will make
us friends. Finally, I blurt out, "Kari had a son she's never known,
from a deacon who raped her. That's why we're going after her. He
did stuff to me, too. Roth used to work at the church. It was in Pittsburgh." I am breathless and embarrassed immediately, afraid that
Simon will think I'm crazy. But I add anyway, sensing the damage is
already done, "How'd you fix your face?"

He turns away from me and opens a cabinet above the sink, although I can tell he's not really looking for anything and is just looking for a way to make this whole scene less awkward. I'm certain I've
been too forward, blown any possibility of friendship by divulging
too much information, or "T.M.I.," as a woman at the last bank job
up north used to say.

I step down from the examining table. My cheek feels less tight
and yet bare, too, as if I'm forgetting something or dreaming that I
am, like my pants in a science class. It's been forever since something
felt different about my face, I realize. Simon's got a fresh roll of paper
towel, busies himself tearing the plastic off. I slip on my jean jacket
and adjust the collar, still embarrassed and a little queasy by my out-
burst. I should just get out of the office, I think, and quick, leaving my
stupid comments behind.

"Well, thanks again," I say. I stoop and pick up Terry. He doesn't
even open his eyes. I have one hand on the doorknob when Simon

finally speaks, not turning around. "You know, Hobbie, people can be cruel in their life and also do good things." He slips the new paper towel roll into place on the dispenser. "I guess what I'm saying is, there's redemption and damnation both. I've found having friends and family and a community, too, that it helps."

I don't know what to say, or whether I should say anything. Terry snores lightly, then stirs. Finally Simon turns, hand outstretched to shake mine. "Anyhow, I hope you all find Kari and her son." We shake hands again, hard. I still don't know what to say. Terry is waking up now, one eye cocked open and focused on Simon as if he's fascinated by what the doctor's saying, too.

Simon points to his face, his brow furrowed. "And this—my face finally getting to be half-normal looking, the worst of the acne gone for good—this didn't come from some magical cure," he says. "Time, and the care of a good doctor, and the willingness to take a risk—that's what fixed it, if you can call it that. There are even better treatment alternatives for acne now." He opens the door and sort of bows. "I'll see you when you get back. Give Roth my best."

I manage to stutter, "Thanks," and Terry licks Simon's hand as we make our way out.

twelve   It's late, almost 2 a.m. I've woken up, shivering after only an hour's rest. The bear dream this time was bloodier than normal and so ridiculous, but still terrifying. At the end, just before I woke up, I was removing stitches from the bear's cheek when suddenly his whole carcass, bones and organs, slipped out of the incision. I stood waist deep in the mess, whistling for Terry, calling for Kari. Stupid, but chilling.

Roth's house is quiet. I stumble toward the bathroom to pee. In the medicine cabinet there's a bottle of Tylenol PM, only four pills left. I take two with water and head to the kitchen, thinking food might help me sleep. I need rest if we're going to hit the road tomorrow; I try and calculate how little sleep I've had since the attack, but my mind's too shot to do the figuring. The cabinets are nearly bare, not much to eat as a bedtime snack, but I find a package of Milano cookies next to a bottle of Riesling wine. I sit down at the table and take a swig from the bottle. The wine is tart and warm. I eat a cookie, and then another, taking big gulps of the wine in between. My body begins to relax, shoulders falling. When the cookies are gone, I take the Riesling and retreat back to the study, where I've been sleeping on the foldout couch, Roth's volumes of Bible study books as company. In my bag, I dig around for some of the Kari letters I've brought with me. I find the one I want and take a long draw from the bottle and sit back reading in bed. Somehow this one seems it should be read at this particular moment; I don't know why, exactly. At least it's one from early on, longer, not curt.

Dear Hobbie,

It was about a month and a half after the deacon got you, or at least that's what we've figured out over and over. Remember how we'd stay up at night trying to figure out who he got, when and where? Kind of sick, but we were kids, what else could we do? We spent our time obsessing about him like other kids did with baseball cards, remembering the dates and places like RBIs or homeruns. We were weird.

Anyway, I know you know this story, but part of my therapy is to write out the worst thing that happened to me as

a kid; so I figured I'd send it to the best thing that happened
to me: you! Who knows, maybe this will help. It's supposed to
unleash me from my past, pardon myself, they say.

I was in the church with dad, helping him in his office.
Dad was punching his ten key again, trying hard to get
the books in order, I guess. I was filing the donation slips,
chomping on Bubble Yum, the gum that the deacon took from
me, the fucker. Dad had to run into town and do the night
deposit, and told me he'd be back in an hour. I ignored him,
really into the rock station on the clock radio. I've wished since
then so many times that he would have forgotten something
and come back that day—his wallet, anything.

I turned up the radio station and began to dance around
the office—it was a great song and you remember how much I
used to like to dance, don't you, Hobbie? You remember?

Man, this is hard to write. I hope you're not freaked out,
reading all this. I know you've heard it all before, but somehow,
seeing the words on this paper—it's kind of freaky. Seems like
yesterday. Anyhow, I looked up and saw the creepy deacon, his
shirt collar open more than normal, legs spread like an umpire,
as he sat in Dad's chair. It was like he just appeared there as I'd
been dancing, making no sound at all. What a perv!!!! I froze.
Even then I knew I was screwed, literally. I know, bad joke.
The therapist here says I use shocking humor to control how
people see me. Fuck him.

I can still see the deacon in my head, the way he ogled me
from that chair, how his eyes were so cold and sort of empty.
I should've beaten him unconscious right then and there. I
could've done it with the radio.

He knew I was scared; I think that's what turned him on even. He made some comment about how lucky Dad was to have his job, how it would be a shame if he somehow lost it. He licked his lips.

He got up from Dad's chair and put his hand on my shoulder. I think I saw smoke rising, you know, like dry ice or something, I swear. His hand was just like that—icy hot.

He ran his hand over my shoulder, and told me how sad it was that my mother had left us, and how he could understand, what with girls being so hard to train. That's just what he said, you know, "hard to train."

I remember the gum in my mouth seemed to dry up, lose its sugar. He bent down and whispered in my ear, "You need training," and I could smell the garlic he'd had for lunch. The deacon grabbed me by the wrist and yanked me up, pulling me out the door. It felt like my whole damn shoulder would pop out of its socket. I can still remember how his big mealy hand felt around my wrist.

I tried to twist away and he slapped me across the face; then I kicked him, but he only grinned. You know how it went—he told me if I kicked him again, he'd frame Dad for stealing the tithed money, and the whole time he was talking he kept that shit-eating grin on his face, like he was flirting or something.

Inside his office, he locked the door. He was so fucking big, like a big dumb rock, only he was like a rock that would roll right over you. I tried to make a move to get out of there but the asshole put his arm around my neck like he was going to break it and held me close to him.

He kept going on and on about this mission coming up to Haiti, where he was going to save the natives. He told me how the villagers were so hungry for God they stripped down to nothing and danced to get His attention. "Just like you were doing, Kari, dancing to get my attention, wanting me to see that you're hungry, too." He was unzipping his pants and I could feel his old nasty prick on me, pressing against my side. I prayed that I'd be able to vomit right then, but nothing come up.

That's when I started to cry, which is something I can't forgive myself for. I should've just laughed in his face, made a joke about his sub-standard dick.

He pushed me to the floor. The lighting flickered, like in a thunderstorm and the room turned on its side. On top of me, the deacon was all hot, stinky breath and deadly weight, his pants down, tearing at my top and covering my mouth, yanking at my jeans. I couldn't breathe.

It hurt like hell. I could smell my own blood and feel my insides tearing. I thought I'd pass out, but I held on. I didn't want that nasty jackass to get the best of me. His hairy chest smelled like a matted dog, which I shouldn't say because that's a put-down on dogs. I hope Terry is good, by the way. Don't forget to get that all-natural food for him. (That was kind of like an intermission, maybe the therapist is right, I joke when I want to be in control.)

Well, you know how it went. That day seemed to end it all: my life, the next day, going to the ninth grade, finding my mom, getting the graded English paper back on Wednesday, the plans for a sleepover with friends at my house—all of it faded to black. There was only this monster banging and panting, taking me bit-by-bit.

It occurs to me now that I know the real devil that those Washburn pastors all preached about; they didn't know shit. The real devil was right there on top of me with "666" on his greasy forehead, smiling as if he'd done me a favor.

If I'd had a gun I would've blown his pea brain out. After, he kissed me hard and I felt something come out of my mouth. The sicko took my gum.

He told me no one would believe me if I told. Then he went behind his desk and flipped on the lamp. In the creepy light I found my clothes and dressed. The deacon started to work as if I weren't there, as if nothing at all had just happened. As if my life wasn't going to be everything it was never supposed to be from that moment on. The bastard didn't even look up when I left.

Can you believe that shit? I was a stupid kid, Hobbie. I wish we'd done something to him, you know? We could've tied him up and stuck a crucifix up his butt. Then we could've drug him out before the congregation like a sacrifice, a horny old goat laid on the altar for all to see. He'd feel what we did, Hobbie. Mean and sick. Dying inside.

I've got to go for now. Give Terry a kiss. You should write out your story, too. I think it does kind of help. Love, K

The last bit of wine trickles down my throat like medicine. The way Kari told the story this time breaks my heart all over again. My hands tremble as I fold the letter. The Tylenol PM is in full effect, which is a good thing; anger is an insomniac's worst enemy. My legs are heavy, eyes so drowsy it feels like I'm passing out rather than going to sleep. This is the way to avoid the bear in my dreams, to put him to sleep, tranquilize the son of a bitch until all he can do is find someone else to sleep with.

thirteen   Roth wants to lead a prayer circle before we climb into Sally's minivan and hit the road. His speech is clearing, but his body is dragging more, as if some secret physics rule is at work on his stroke: *Symptoms are neither created nor destroyed.* Terry is in the van already fast asleep.

In the driveway Roth allows Sally to drape his neck with one of her rosaries. She's holding a Catholic prayer book, a large purse slung over her shoulder. Donny is smoking, waving the plumes away from his face. My scar feels exposed and tingly. The sleeping medicine has left my head in a woozy daze, and I can't tell if the hangover is from the wine or the Tylenol PM.

Roth bows his head and speaks slowly but much more clearly than even the day before. He's wearing a dark jacket with a white T-shirt underneath and an olive sweater over that, which does give him the appearance of a priest. "Dear God in Heaven . . . hear us, please," he begins. "The road . . . BEE-for us . . . is long, and we KNEE . . . duh, your help."

The day is clear and warmer, and the thought of snow at my rented house two weeks ago seems as plausible as Queen Anne's lace on Mars. "How about I drive for a couple hours and then we'll switch?" Sally says, looking directly to me, not at Donny. Maybe she doesn't trust him behind the wheel, or maybe he just doesn't like to drive.

"Sure," I say. "Sally?"

"What is it, hon?"

"Are you sure they said she was there, I mean, really there?"

"Yes," she says, trying to convince herself and me, too. "I called and said I was her mother, that I just had to see her. I said there'd been a family emergency, and the receptionist said she couldn't let me know if she was there or not, but she's a mother herself. She understood and more or less said Kari was still there." Sally flashes a quick, empathetic smile. "Don't worry, Hobbie. We'll just do our best. That's all we can do."

I climb through the van's sliding door and sit as Donny fumbles his way to the back, apparently knowing he'll get reprimanded if he tries to take Roth's front seat.

Roth takes a long look at his house, then smiles and waves to no one before Sally helps him into the passenger's side. He whispers something into Sally's ear that makes her giggle. She pats his arm and gives him a kiss on his cheek. If Donny minds, he doesn't show it; behind me I can hear him humming as he flips through a bass fishing magazine.

Once we're free of the subdivision and heading north on the bypass, Sally turns on the radio, cooing something to Roth. Sally is driving with her thigh and her left hand at nine o'clock. The other hand reaches across and holds hands with Roth, and sunlight glimmers off the windshield.

I'm lost in thought. I can't imagine seeing Kari, finally—what she'll look like now, how she'll respond to me, my face, Terry's marred little back. Will she hit her mother in the nose? Bawl at the sight of Roth's crippled body? Tell Donny to go fuck himself? I can't even think about her son, or what it might be like to meet him. The truth is I am nearly nauseated at the idea of seeing Kari after six months, but I'm also excited. It feels like we're speeding over the smoothest stretch of highway that ever existed, a sensation I'm sure will not last long. It never does.

PART III

....

one   After traveling on Interstate 85 north for well over six hours, stopping every 60 minutes to stretch and hit the restrooms, the exit for Durham is a sight for eight sore eyes. I've booked us in a place not far from the Center for Healthy Living; it's called the Millennium Hotel, one of those newly erected resorts just off the interstate. The area is home to a plethora of upscale restaurants all owned by the same franchise but differing only in their specialty: Mexican, Chinese, Italian, Southwest, and something called "Homestyle." An enormous Old Navy store, a flat and spacious Target, and a towering Borders surround the eateries. A series of supposedly quaint boutique stores takes up the rest of the space. I feel right at home.

I pilot the minivan under the portico and put it in park. My heart is pounding, thinking that Kari might be only a few miles away. It's beginning to turn to dusk and the sky is dark blue, a few twinkling stars overhead.

I leave the van and run inside to check us in. A roaring gas fireplace brightens the Lobby Bar, warms the hotel restaurant called Bel Gusto's. Here it's fake Italian and a faux fire, a picture-perfect setting begging for some reality. My face should do the trick, and Roth's crippled body will drive the point home, too. As soon as I pull out the credit card and hand it to the smiling blonde woman behind the counter, I realize the sleeping arrangements will be weird. I'll have to discuss it with Sally.

Back outside, a major scene is transpiring around the minivan. Next to a brass luggage carrier Donny is sulking. As Roth struggles to get out of the van on his own, Terry yaps from the back window.

"Hey," I say, now standing between Sally and Donny, as Roth rumbles up behind me. "What's going on?"

"I'm sorry, Hobbie," says Sally, her hair a little more frizzy than when we left Atlanta. "Donny's upset because I suggested he share a room with you so Roth and I can talk about our daughter."

A bellman steps forward and asks, "Will you all be needing the baggage carrier service?"

Donny pushes the brass support bar on the carrier and yells, "Fuck off, dipshit! We're trying to settle a family deal here, can't you see that?!" I guess Donny now considers himself part of the family. The bellman stares at something beyond Donny, apparently trained to ignore this kind of abuse.

"I do apologize," Sally says, shaking her head. The bellman merely bows and ushers the carrier back through the automatic doors and into the foyer where a sane family is glad to have his help.

Donny, meanwhile, has stormed off and is trying to unlatch the gate to the swimming pool area. I can see that there is a tarp covering it—it's closed for the winter.

"He's a lot like a little boy sometimes," Sally mutters. Beside me, Roth sighs. The three of us are alone now.

Sally lightly scratches her nose with a long, finely manicured nail. "Did you get us all checked in, honey?" she asks me. I nod. "Shall we get settled in then?" I don't answer. Standing so close to her, I am reminded of her substantial stature—both physically and emotionally. She's a planner, a thoughtful idealist, and a confident free spirit, but I'm surprised to find that I'm feeling something like bitterness toward her. Maybe it's the long drive or the effects of the Tylenol PM and the Riesling, but I've had enough. I can hear Kari's voice in my head, as if she's reading aloud the letter about her abuse to me. The thought of Kari being raped by the deacon, of him kissing her, so hard that he actually takes the bubblegum out of her mouth— I'm flooded with sadness, and anger. I take a deep breath and pull Sally by the arm, so that she's standing directly in front of me.

"Hey, hon, what is—" she begins, but I cut her off.

"Sally," I say, with a firmness I didn't know I possessed. "Why did you leave them? Kari needed you. So did Roth."

Sally flushes and pauses for a moment, sniffing, before she takes my hand. "Oh, hon, you're right to ask me that. I've wished a million times I'd not left." She tries to bring me into her in a hug, but I back up and lean against the van, crossing my arms in front of me.

Roth pushes his walker next to Sally, clearly as a show of support.

"Oh, don't give me that, Roth," I say, hearing the pettiness in my voice but unable to stop myself. "You had to have hated her for leaving. After all, if she'd been around, maybe all that happened wouldn't have. Happened, that is." The words have spilled so quickly from my mouth I can't seem to understand how language works anymore. I feel my heart pounding and my face flush. There's a long silence, then Roth has Sally in his arms and the walker knocks against the van, and behind me, I hear Terry bark softly. The van is still running and the fumes make me nauseated. My head hurts and I rub at my temples. When I look back up, Sally is cradling Roth's head against her chest. They are both crying—great, heaving sobs that make me look away. It's as if I'm not there, that's how tender their embrace is. Something in me—something that's still decent and respectful—tells me to look away. I stare at the ground, kick at a loose piece of asphalt. Roth and Sally have nearly a half-century of history together, and what they have and what they need is something that's apart from me. They are a rumpled bundle of two people who should've stayed together. I am a jerk for blurting out what I did. Maybe I'm no more a part of this family than Donny is.

Donny has come back from the pool area, a cigarette in his hand, eyes bleary from smoking. In that weird way he has of seeing only what he wants to see, kind of like a 4-year-old, he seems not to notice that Sally and Roth are holding onto each other for dear life. He leans against the van next to me and says, "Man, I wish it was summertime. They've got a diving board in there and a Jacuzzi. Shit." I wonder for not the first time if he might be a little slow or perhaps has some kind of a short-term memory malfunction. "If I had some cutoffs," he says, "I'd just sneak in under that tarp and swim anyway." He turns to the van and sees Terry. "Ruff, ruff," he says. "Good dog." I stare blankly, not sure what to say. For a few moments more we are all locked in place, the hotel receding into the dark silhouette of a tall pine grove, car headlights blinding us. Cars whiz by on the highway and it seems they are pointing at us. Whether they're pointing at a man barking at a dog or two old people crying like babies—or at me, as usual, with my pizza face, it's impossible to say. It feels good, in a way, to know that I've got company, that I'm not the only freak with the fingers pointed at him. I take a deep breath, let it out.

Donny laughs and elbows me in the ribs, and nods his head at Roth and Sally, who are now kissing. Just a small peck or two, but still, it's a kiss. "Looks like I better sleep in a room with you tonight after all." Apparently he's not upset anymore about how things are turning out, how Sally's starting to mend fences with her ex. Donny winks, and in spite of myself, I wink back, the scar on my cheek tight under the movement of my facial muscles. "Ruff, ruff, ruff," Donny says, chuckling. Sally and Roth hold each other still, swaying to the sound of the wind.

two It's 10 'til six when I wake up, the digits on the clock radio the color of lava. I lie in bed and listen to nothing. The curtains are pulled and I can't see my hand when I wave it before my eyes. I run my fingers over my face in the blackness. How many times have I done this same thing? Nights before going to bed, fiddling and touching and testing until I have to get up and go to the bathroom to release the pressure, the pus, the stress? I try and think if I've packed the tools I usually use on my face or if maybe there's a substitute in the hotel toiletries kit I could use.

My body is full of anxiety. I have to do something. I sit up when it occurs to me that I can change, right in this instant, make my anxiety work for me rather than against. Simon had said something about taking a risk, doing things differently. Maybe getting better is simply a decision every moment to do just that. I won't pick at my face, I think. I can choose that right here, at this precise moment.

Before I know it I'm out of the bed and pulling on my clothes, zipping up a jacket and quietly opening the door. The light from the hallway slants in and briefly stirs Donny, who is nestled deep under his covers in the bed next to mine. Before we went to bed he called the front desk for two more blankets and cranked up the heater. It was like sleeping on a rotisserie in a pitch-black abyss.

I take the MapQuest directions from my jean jacket and unfold the paper. I gather a deep breath. Outside the moon is full and gorgeous, a milky yellow, hanging in the sky like a platter. My feet tap the sidewalk as I walk out the parking lot and head down the street; I've pulled on the dress shoes I brought especially for Kari. She notices shoes. The car would've been the more logical choice, of course, but I'm looking for a romantic entrance. I want it to seem that I've run into Kari, like in a movie. Besides, in the car, I know that the urge to pick at my face in the mirror at stoplights would've been too strong to resist. I won't pick at my face, I think again, the phrase a chant in my head as I walk.

I make my way east on Pickett toward Sandy Creek Drive, about two blocks. A semi downshifts on the highway and it sounds to me like music, something dirgeful and poetic, gathering strength to make it out of the city and power on to a new place that will look just like this one, but maybe, just maybe, it will all work out for the better. There's always that chance.

As I pick up the pace and begin to slightly jog, I realize I'll have to merge myself onto the US-15 bypass. I chance it, knowing it's illegal but needing to get there any way I can, ready to accelerate my body to 65 mph if I have to. It turns out the bypass is relatively quiet at this hour. The soles of the dress shoes slip some as I jog, but before long I adjust my stride and get more confident, speeding up some, too. Some cars blow by, a few honk, but for the most part the jog is invigorating. I think of the cross-country team in high school, how I could place in the county competitions, running through the woods, dappled light like the strobe on a dance floor, emerging into a patch of open hummock, no one else around. Then, as I'd run over a bridge and make it toward the finish line, the stares at my face, and some jokes; crossing into a crowd—even as the winner—was the worst part of the race.

I pass a huge open area, murky in the early dawn. It's the rolling hills of the Duke University Golf Club. A solitary man drives a cart over a knoll and disappears forever. My legs feel good and burn with the rush. After a few minutes, I enter the area beneath an overpass and hear a noise up in the hollows, near the metalwork and under-pinnings. A man's voice shouts, apparently to someone else, "Better stay away from here, you bastard! This one's mine, asshole!" There's a rustling, and some loose gravel tumbles down the steep slant of concrete, as if an avalanche is starting. A sign reads: "Absolutely no sleeping in underpass. Urban campers will be prosecuted."

I take the Morris Road exit and kick up stones as I slow down and tromp along the shoulder, running my hand over the railing. It's almost morning now, things coming alive, lights clicking on, and buildings taking shape. Some birds explode from a section of dried grass, tak-ing flight and curling to the left in a scattered flock, black apostrophes against the bluing horizon. I'm so close I can hardly contain bursting into a full sprint. Maybe we could live in Durham, I think, somewhere near the center in case Kari still needs the support. Jobs would be easy to get—there are always tons of banks in college towns.

Durham has the dubious title of "the weight loss capital of the world," and right now it seems everyone who's in town to drop pounds is out in force, walking quickly up and down the sidewalks, some of them right up the center of the still-quiet streets. I wonder whether they're from the Center for Healthy Living. In one of Kari's letters she called this the "herd slowly stampeding the track." More and more people dressed in what have to be extra-extra-large clothes are taking to the sidewalks; I have to dodge a whole group of large men at one point.

I take a left onto Campus Walk Avenue and stop. A sign points me in the direction of the center. I run my fingers through my hair and curse myself for not having brushed my teeth. A reunion with foul breath and a bear scar is not romantic.

All I have to do is take those steps, let my feet carry me forward. Overhead a plane drones through the dim sky. Its red lights blink, winking at me, telling me to move ahead, go for it. My lungs ache from the cold morning air, and finally I walk up to the front doors. I push a button and I am buzzed into some kind of staging area, still no sign of a front desk or anything like it. There's a window, though, and a woman peers out and through an intercom asks me what I need.

"I'm here to see Kari Francis. I'm her . . . " I haven't thought of lying, but I finish the sentence. "Her husband. I'm her husband."

The woman asks for identification. I pat myself down and struggle to get my wallet free of the jean jacket. I press it up against the glass. She examines the ID coolly. Finally she nods, and buzzes me through another door. I walk around the side of a built-in receiving station.

The woman looks up. Her name tag says her name is Cherry. She notices my face for the first time and scans the rest of my body, down the torso, probably to determine if I'm regular in other ways. Kari always said I had a good body, which embarrassed me. She'd kiss my chest and tell me my pecs were nice, that she envied how lean I was.

"I was hoping to see my wife, Kari Francis. Please."

Cherry is already shaking her head no. "I'm sorry, we can't confirm whether or not a certain person and/or patient is actually in residence. Confidentiality, you know. The new regs are called HIPPA."

"Well, can you at least let me leave her a message? Make sure she gets it?"

"If there's someone here by that name and you're on his or her approved list of contacts I'll see that it's delivered." She hands me a notepad and a pen.

"Why don't you sit down over there to write," she says, the phone ringing. She reaches around to get it. "Center for Healthy Living. How may I help you?"

I go to an area with sofas and a table upon which are pamphlets about organic foods, exercise, and yoga. There's flax gum in a bowl and a Xerox of an article on how mint has been shown to curb appetites. I can see the parking lot through the window, the sun fully up now and glazing the entire area in muted orange. I sit down on one of the sofas and have no idea what to write. I'm defeated and empty. I know Kari's not here. I can sense it. Yet, I want to be certain; I can't take endless hours on the road, searching, if there's a slim chance she's still here.

A few people in lab coats march out office doors and down the hallway. They slide cards through readers at the side of secure entries. I look up and make sure Cherry is still on the phone. I put the pen and paper down quietly as if the movement alone might be evidence against me. For a guard of sorts, she's not that attentive.

The hallway is shiny and smells of Mr. Clean. Much of the staff has not clocked in for the day, their respective offices dark behind a single pane of reinforced glass. I turn the corner and hear voices. There's a copier room and several breakout areas I assume are for group work. I have no idea where to go. I hurry past an open door and take another turn right into a section of the building that seems to be, at least in part, where some of the patients live. It's like a dorm. The hallway is white and untouched, silver handles on the drinking fountains, frosted glass on the many windows. There's a peaceful box garden at the end of the hall where real flowers grow under hazy light. I chance it and peek my head into a room with a door wide open, some light jazz tinkling from a radio. I step inside and spot a man sitting at a writing table. He's heavy, at least 300 pounds, and his white hair is swept back. A gold robe is tightly cinched around his ample midsection. His feet are bare under the table and, strangely, as bony as mine.

There's something in the room that reminds me of childhood. I can't place it; perhaps it's a smell or some small object on a shelf.

The man looks up and smiles, laying his pen on a hefty book with a tassel that marks his place; I can see now that it's a large journal.

"Are you lost?" he asks, motioning for me to sit in the chair next to the desk. He's very relaxed and acting like he's known of me forever—or at least has been expecting me.

"No, I'm here for a reason," I say, sitting. I can't help but stare at him, and there is an awkward silence as he gazes at me, a little smile on his face, his eyes sort of changing as I stare, transfixed. I can't tell what age he is, and just when I think I've settled on a range, his eyes change and he grows older or younger than the number in my head.

I look around the room, the nagging feeling about childhood still there.

"What are you looking for?" the man asks softly. "I don't know," I say, still peering at the shelves hoping to find a scented candle or some toy that is making me feel this way.

"Then are you hiding?" he asks.

"No, not really. Although I'm not supposed to be here."

"Well, you've come for some reason, haven't you?" he asks, his smile still gentle. He doesn't move, not even a twitch or a twiddled thumb, but his eyes still seem to be changing as they take me in, as if what and who I am is affecting him.

"I'm here for Kari Francis," I finally manage. "Do you know her?"

He doesn't answer directly. "Let me see if I can help you."

"Okay," I say, somehow thinking that maybe he can.

"Go ahead," he says, sounding so patient I wonder whether I've stumbled into the room of the center's resident preacher.

"I'm trying to find a woman. Like I said, her name is Kari Francis. She's been here for six months. I need to see her. Her father's sick."

The man nods his head, the movement especially significant since he hasn't used his body at all until just now. "Yes," he says. "She's not here now, though."

"Who are you?" I ask.

"I've been here a long time," he says.

"Did she tell you where she was going?"

"Kari?" he asks. "Not really, but I know where she said she was heading."

"Where, where is she going? Please tell me."

"Virginia. Not far from here really. You can get there if you want."

"You didn't say who you are. What's your name?" I ask. Something moves past outside in the hall, a blurry vision out of the corner of my eye. I'm afraid I'll be caught here, thrown out and away from any chance of finding Kari for not following the rules.

"It really doesn't matter does it?" the man says, nodding.

"No, I guess not. Are you telling me the truth, did Kari really go to Virginia?" It's not much, but finding out even a little bit about where Kari might be is a rush; my heart is pounding.

"Yes, she did. I've got no reason to mislead you. I'm just trying to help." I stand, a little shaky, and offer my hand. The man takes it and pats the top. I ask, "Did she tell everyone this in group therapy or something? Where she was going, I mean?"

He winks. "Just go. If you need anything they know who I am here. Just ask for my room number." He points at the open door. I leave the room and stand outside in the hall, then turn back to look at him. He's again working in his book, writing, head bowed and focused. He peers up from the desk and gives a wave. I wave back and start down the pearly hallway.

Before I know it, I'm on the sidewalk again, the sun warming my head. I want to hurry back to the hotel and wake everyone up and head to Virginia, though I don't know what part. I begin to jog and after a few blocks my lungs are clear and heart thumping. It feels good to run. When I pass a house with children out front, probably waiting for the school bus, they wave. I wave back and jog on. On the outskirts of Durham, I feel changed, or better put, I'm okay with change. I pick up the pace so I can get started toward a new state.

three Roth and Sally are at the breakfast buffet line at the hotel when I come downstairs after showering and feeding Terry a nice bowl of Kibbles and Bits. He ate in my lap from the ice bucket tray, using his darting tongue to work the whole surface over for every morsel. He's asleep on the bed now and we've got two hours before checkout.

Donny is already at a table eating French toast and a stack of bacon, his lips greasy, powdered sugar on his chin. "Why don't they have apple juice? People drink it, you know, for breakfast," he says to me as I step up to the table. It's almost like he's holding me responsible. "All they've got is orange juice and milk. I thought this place was supposed to be fancy. I need apple juice to keep me regular." He shoves a biscuit into his mouth.

"They look happy this morning," I say, nodding toward Sally as she assists Roth with a plate of food at the buffet line, her clothes glittery from some type of silver thread or metal beading in the fabric. Roth is rosycheeked and moving a little better than yesterday with the walker.

"Yep," says Donny. "They should be. You know they did it last night. They told me when I went in to help Roth get ready." I'm stunned.

"It's cool," Donny says, as if to reassure me. "He's all Sally ever talked about anyway, and we were never that serious." The man seems to have grown up some overnight; this other, more mature side of his personality is a refreshing change. "The old guy has actually hired me to be his attendant, you know, his helper. So I guess we'll be seeing a lot more of each other." Donny slurps down the orange juice he said he didn't want. He's a simple man really, I'm starting to see; now that he is needed, he's less needy. "Which is what I was trained in really," he continues. "I was a medic in the army for 10 years. I think I can handle dressing and bathing an old geezer." I frown. "Sorry, I didn't mean it the wrong way. He's probably only 15 years older than me anyway."

Sally waves at me above the crowd of people dining under the high-vaulted ceiling. She nudges Roth and he waves, too.

Donny glugs more orange juice and stops eating, finally, laying his fork down. He seems to be pondering how to ask something. "So, they said your wife or whatever, their daughter," he pauses to take another drink, "she wasn't at the clinic thing?"

"Nope," I say, feeling more optimistic than I should. "She left the center, but still, I've got a lead on where she went. Virginia."

Donny eyes his fork but presses on. "Do you mean that's where her kid is? Although I guess he's probably not a kid now, grown up." He runs his tongue over his teeth and swallows. "That's where he is?" I'm astonished at how Donny is acting, that we are actually able to have a mature conversation. Maybe having Sally attached to Roth has given him a new role to occupy, one that helps him see more clearly how he should behave.

"I guess," I say. "And, yes, her son would be about 20, maybe 21. I don't know where in Virginia, though." I sit down, a chair away from Donny.

"You got a credit card?" he asks, fingering the handle on his fork as he sips coffee. I assume he's watched porn in the hotel room or billed snack bar items to the front desk and is making a preemptive strike.

"Yes, I rented the rooms on it, of course. Why?"

He picks up the fork and begins cutting a sausage link. "Because, if your wife or whatever uses the same account, you could track it to see where she's been. I mean, did she have to rent a car?" Donny chaws on the sausage, peering at me over the cup of coffee he's washing it down with.

"She would've had to rent a car, that's right," I say, pondering his insight. He's not as child-minded as I'd thought.

"I tracked my old lady for about two months that way before I was served a restraining order and she took my name off the card." Donny perks up when he notices Sally beckoning him from across the room. He says, "Shit, I gotta go carry his plate for him. You know, I'm on the clock. I'll be right back." He takes another swig of coffee and hurries to do his new job.

I watch as the three of them walk toward the table, people scattering to make room for Roth's walker. Sally is at his side, carrying her own plate. Roth's mouth is crooked, and it looks like he's telling Sally something about me; he keeps cutting his lulling eyes in my direction. Donny is behind them both, holding Roth's plate, giving me the thumbs up.

When they get to our table, Roth looks to Sally and nods. She opens her big purse and pulls out a folded letter. "Roth wanted you to have this, Hobbie," she says, as Roth pats his heart, trying to show me it's important to him.

four At the top of the letter Sally has written: "It took us about four hours to write this. Roth dictated it to me and I wrote down word for word what he had to say. He loves you very much. He loves Kari very much. So do I. Always remember that. I put a little something from the Catholic Book of Prayers at the bottom. I hope it's okay to say it reminded me of you."

Dear Hobbie:

I wanted to get some things out in the open before we find Kari. I know I've not been a great father to her or you for that matter, but I can say that I love you both more than you can ever know. I have regrets, lots of them. I've already told you how I feel about not protecting you both more, and I truly believe my sin will have to be accounted for, but that's not the point here. All I want to do is give an accurate account of what happened after Kari had the baby in Colorado, what my part in it was and go from there. It's all I know to do to

get things on the right track. I've been a fool for too long now.
Here it goes.

I sent Kari to her grandmother's in Colorado in 1985
where she stayed until the baby came. You were both 16 and
I thought your lives needed protecting, even if I tried too late.
Her grandmother took very good care of her, and while she
never asked me how Kari had gotten pregnant, on her deathbed
I felt she knew. She told me: "Don't blame yourself, sonny. We
just do the best we can."

Anyway, when it was time for the baby to be born, I flew
out to Colorado to be with Kari, but by then she hated me and
didn't want me around. She'd gone through so much I didn't
blame her. I'm sure she's told you some of this, but some of it
only I know and so I'll tell it here. The baby boy was delivered
and Kari held him even though I'd asked that she not. I knew it
was all too much for a 16-year-old. A preacher I used to know
in Colorado Springs had a good adoptive home lined up, and
I took the baby along with a social worker from the state to a
nice young couple there. They'd been part of his congregation
and had prayed obediently for the chance to conceive. To
them, their prayers were answered. Isn't that strange, Hobbie?
That the hell Kari went through was someone else's answered
prayer? Sometimes I think I'll say this to Kari but if I was her
I'd want to slap me for it.

The couple's name was Anderson and they named the
baby boy Stephen. For some years, right up until the time that
you and Kari left Pittsburgh for good, they'd send me pictures
of the little guy. He had those birthmarks on his arms and
face, but he was still handsome and smart, I could tell by his

smile and eyes. I was a coward and never did anything with
the pictures except hide them in the house. Even after you two
were living on your own, living together, and moving around
from place to place like you young people seem to like to do,
I'd still get a photo here and there. And once, I was invited to
meet him when they were laid over in Atlanta coming back
from Florida. But I threw the letter away. I guess I was scared.

Then just before moving from Pittsburgh to Atlanta, I
got a letter in the mail with another picture of the boy. He
was about 13 and gangly looking, a whole mess of metal in
his mouth. He was sick, they said, and needed some family
history, blood type, and that kind of thing. It turned out in
the end that he was fine, had just caught a staph infection that
was treated and he was back to playing baseball by the spring.
Anyway, because I was scared I didn't respond, I didn't know
how to. But being such a coward made me so mad at myself I
couldn't think clearly. Before I knew it I was in the Washburn
Tabernacle parking lot. The church had to pay the victims,
you know that, but I'm not sure if you ever knew they let the
deacon still work there. It made me sick, but he had a huge
number of supporters and they took him back, said it was all
just a bunch of evil teens lying to get attention. Over the years
I'd see him sometimes, way after the scandal had become
ancient history. Once, I was at the Wal-Mart and saw him go in.
I bent the antennae on his car and keyed the paint, but I didn't
feel any better. You kids were living in Minneapolis at the time.
I sat in the parking lot of the tabernacle and waited for hours,
something seething deep inside of me. I knew I was going to
hurt him, and I prayed about it. I asked God to send me a sign

if I wasn't supposed to be there waiting, watching the minutes tick off the clock. Nothing happened. It was beginning to get dark when he finally left the church.

I watched the deacon whistle. He was *whistling*! It'd been 14 years since he raped Kari and I had just as much hate for him then as I did when I first found out. Finally, I got out of my car quietly and crept up behind him. I pretended I had a gun. "Don't move," I said, disguising my voice. "I'll shoot if you move." I told him not to look at me, if he did I'd blow his brains out. "You can have my wallet. Just don't hurt me please. I've got a family." That's what he said. Pleading. And you know, it was that word, "family," that I decided was my sign from God. The sign I should be doing what I was doing.

His hands were sweaty when he handed his wallet over his shoulder to me. I was stuck then, couldn't think of what else to do. Then another sign came: I heard the words "clothes, clothes, clothes" over and over again in my head.

"Take off your damn clothes, asshole," I told him, feeling bad about cussing near a church, even if it was one I hated.

"What?" he asked. "Why?"

"Shut up and do as I say or I'll kill you as God is my witness."

"Come on now, I gave you my wallet, what else do you want?" He started to turn around.

I shoved the corner of his fat wallet in his back. "Don't even think about it or I'll shoot you." He held his hands up higher and said, "Okay, okay." I really think if I'd had a gun I would have murdered him.

He took his shoes off and dropped his pants. "Now the

jacket and shirt," I commanded. He slipped out of the clothes and I kicked them toward my car. He stood there in his white briefs and T-shirt, arms raised and trembling.

"Now the rest of it." He hung his head. "Please, don't make me. I've got more money in the car. Take it." I poked him again. "Lose the rest of it or I'll blow a hole in you."

Slowly, he inched his shorts down and then slipped his T-shirt over his head. He was white as a sheet. I took the underwear and T-shirt and tucked them down my jacket.

"What are you going to do?" he asked, turning his head slightly to look back. The truth was, I didn't know. I stood there silent behind his naked, wretched body, and I wanted more than anything for God to tell me it was okay to beat him to death. But nothing came. I waited. A car drove by and I realized I'd better get on with it.

"Where are the keys?" I asked. He told me they were in his car door, so I reached around him and pulled them out. "When I leave don't even think about turning around or I'll come back and shoot you in the head." He nodded. I walked slowly backwards, picking up his clothes as I went, holding them all in my hand, along with his car keys. I got in my car and pulled a cap down over my head and turned the ignition. For a moment I waited, again hoping God would tell me to run him down and back over him, too. Finally, I did a U-turn and left the parking lot. When I looked back he was still standing naked by his car, arms thrust up to heaven as if he were about to go into a baptism pool.

Out along Madison Avenue, near the city park, I tossed his car keys out the window. There was word of the assault on the local news and the police investigated, but nothing cropped up. They called it a prank.

The deacon died four years ago. He's dead, Hobbie. In hell, too, I'm sure. I know that's no consolation, but he'll never hurt us again, ever. I've made so many mistakes. That's all I know. It's the whole truth. Please forgive me.

Love,
Roth

PS: I've enclosed what pictures I've got of the boy.
PSS (from Sally)

The Stations of the Cross

Veronica Wipes the Face of Jesus: We adore you etc. My most beloved Jesus, Thy face was beautiful before but in this journey it has lost all its beauty; and wounds and blood have disfigured it. Alas, my soul also was once beautiful when it received Thy grace in baptism. But I have disfigured it since by my sins. Thou alone my redeemer can't restore it to its former beauty. Do this by Thy passion, oh, Jesus. I repent with my whole heart for having offended Thee. Never permit me to separate myself from Thee again. Grant that I may love Thee always and then do with me what Thou wilt.

five Terry's acting strange as we pack up our things and double-check the room. He's been walking in semicircles, changing directions, and doing it again. I pick him up and talk into his ear, trying to soothe him. He moves as if he's still performing the turns, his wee head moving in a figure eight.

"What's the deal with him?" Donny asks, zipping up his Mc-Gregor bag, a stick of deodorant peeking from a side pocket.

"I don't know. He's acting weird, that's for sure." I pet Terry's ears and hold him before my face to get a good look at his eyes. Terry does what he always does when I hold him like this; he cuts his peepers to the side as if he's ashamed. Every time I see him do it, my heart aches. I know what it feels like to be inspected.

Donny slings the bag over his shoulder and comes to look at Terry for himself. He sucks on his lip and squints. "He looks a little logy. Has he eaten today?"

"Sure. He ate like he was starving, in fact."

Donny nods and walks to the door. "I'm gonna go check and see if Roth needs anything."

Alone in the room with Terry, I sit down on the bed and cradle him. Roth's letter is heavy in my thoughts, as well as Sally's attempt to illustrate how we're all alike, marred just like Jesus. I appreciate the effort, but I want to get on the road. I pull out the letter and go through the pictures again. The last one must put him around 16, but it's hard to tell. He's got Roth's and Kari's eyes, but other than that, he's a skinny boy with a nice smile and sandy hair. I try and focus, really see if I can find even the faintest trace of the deacon around his mouth or at the tip of his chin, but he's not there. And isn't that an answered prayer? What would have been my reaction toward a blameless boy if he'd looked exactly like his biological father? Hatred? Disgust? I'm not sure, but seeing him as kin to Roth and Kari is what works. In one photo, he's standing with a young girl, the two of them in formal clothes. His skin looks even more perfect in contrast to the brown birthmarks.

I feel something else, too. Am I sad the deacon is dead? It doesn't seem to make sense, but there's something of a homesickness in me.

I suppose all these years I'd hoped to someday run into him; he'd be an old man and I'd still be strong and capable. In my fantasies, I thought about forcing him—still alive—into a coffin and covering him up with dirt, or something crazy like that. But that's never going to happen now, and all I'll have left to dream about is moving on and, while it seems impossible, forgiving him. That's scary, scarier than anything else I can imagine. Roth's retribution doesn't help; his was a father's payback, and I'm glad he had his moment, but it's not the same. Some things have to be completely yours.

Next door, I can hear the three of them laughing, and the door closes with a thud and just like that they're coming through my door. "We heard he wasn't feeling so good," Sally says, stooping to pet Terry's back where a good growth of stubble covers his scar. Her bright fingernails trail over it. Roth makes a moan to show he feels sorry for Terry.

Donny moves forward, carrying Roth's bag on his other shoulder. "We better get down there and see if we can use the computer. They've got a library with an Internet connection."

Downstairs, Sally and Roth are both petting Terry, snuggled up against each other on a sofa, as Donny and I get to work in the business center. Donny plops himself at the computer terminal. "Great!" he says, delighted. "They've got high-speed access." He pops his knuckles and asks me the name of the credit card. In seconds, he's pulled up the credit card company's home page and tells me to give him the billing address, the rented house in the mountains. I think of the bear briefly, and it's like Terry and I are telepathic because he opens his eyes and begins to bark out of nowhere. I try and calm him down as Roth whispers to him through a lopsided mouth. It's as if Roth is becoming his new owner.

"Names on the card?" Donny can type quickly and doesn't seem to make mistakes. He stands up and steps aside like a butler, saying formally, "Enter your account number and it will prompt you to create a password." I sit down but keep one eye on Terry, who is now turning his head from side to side, as if he's watching a ball bounce. I punch in the numbers from the credit card in my hand. Terry's making odd hiccup sounds followed by miniscule wheezes.

"Okay," I tell Donny, my fingers on the keyboard, waiting.

"Now, just click on recent purchases and it should list them. That's the way mine is." The mouse is under my hand, a lump of possibility. I want to click. And I don't.

"Come on," says Donny, nudging me. Terry whines and circles Roth's lap, more like a cat than a dog. I move the cursor and the arrow points right to the "recent purchases" button. My face feels oilier than normal, sort of hot. One click, and a whole new page opens up, springs to life. There it is, a list of purchases. The hotel we've stayed in is already there, but down two lines it reads: Acer Car Rental, Durham, N.C., and above that: Roadside Motel, Lynchburg, VA.

Donny taps the screen hard and hollers, "There you go. She's right there!" He's proud. I try and hold back a self-conscious grin, but he rubs my back in the chair and shakes me, and I'm reminded of a trainer giving his fighter a pep talk. I stand up and Donny says, "You better log out first, unless you want every asshole in this hotel charging shit to your account."

I turn to look at Roth and Sally. "She's in Lynchburg, Roth." I smile and he manages to nod, then gives Sally a look.

Sally clears her throat and speaks. "Hobbie, Roth had forgotten this when he wrote the letter, but Stephen's got a grandfather who's still alive. Other than Roth, that is. His adoptive mom's dad." Sally looks to Roth to make sure she's getting it right. "He lives around Lynchburg."

"Okay," I say, and for some reason I feel more depleted now, like he might be up to his old tricks and keeping secrets. As much as he's made it clear he wants to come clean, it isn't going to be all rosy now. What or who else is going to come out of the woodwork? I think.

I turn back to the computer, where Donny reads an online bass fishing magazine. He says to himself, "Damn, they got lures now that actually take batteries." Suddenly, Terry begins to flail his paws in Roth's lap, turning over and over, eyes rolling white. He groans and lurches, his body seizing up. I'm frozen with fear, and it's Donny who jumps up from the computer terminal and is carefully lifting Terry from Roth's lap. He places the tiny gyrating body on the carpet as if Terry were a bomb about to go off.

"Get back. I'm going to try CPR," says Donny. I kneel down next to where Roth is now, crying and reaching for my arm, grasping at the air. I feel as helpless as I assume he does. Sally prays with her rosary, while Donny pushes two fingers against Terry's narrow chest. He pops open Terry's mouth and blows into it, then goes back to stimulating his heart. Roth is digging his nails into my skin. Donny rubs Terry's body and says, "Come on, little guy. Come on, now." And just like that, Terry kicks his back legs and rolls onto his side. He gets to his wobbly feet and looks right at Donny and begins to lick his hand with a spacey look in his eyes.

Roth manages an "ohhh" and pats my shoulder. Sally holds his limp hand and smiles as if she knew it would all work out. Donny picks up Terry and places him back in Roth's lap. Roth looks tired and smaller than just a couple of hours ago at breakfast. He wipes his mouth to speak, pointing at Terry. "I . . . know," he pauses and sucks in the saliva, "how . . . he . . . feel-suh."

For several long moments we all just stare at Terry resting in Roth's lap. From where he now sits back in front of the computer, Donny says, "Okay. I just did the MapQuest driving directions. They're printing off now. Looks like we're only a couple hours away from Lynchburg." I nod. "Thanks, Donny," I manage. I see Roth is no longer crying. His eyes are serene and he appears to be somewhere else. I want that, too. I need to be out of this hotel and on our way.

six   The others, including Terry, are asleep in the van. For the first time in days, I feel I can think clearly. The radio is on a talk show and two pastors from Virginia are debating the notions of intelligent design and evolution. Neither of them sound all that informed. The one belittling evolution is a professor at Liberty University, founded by Jerry Falwell. I can't take anymore of it, so I hit a preset and find some twangy bluegrass that fits my mood. I've never much liked any kind of country music, but this is playing on a public radio station and it's a recording of a 45. It cracks and pops and the man's voice croons about lost love. I want to remember to tell Kari about it when I see her. In my daydreams, I see us trying new things, taking up jogging and learning to cook gourmet foods; maybe bluegrass will fit into that picture, too.

The van rocks over a bridge as we careen toward the Roadside Motel in Lynchburg. Semis move by, their hefty bodies pushing us over some as they finally make it past and signal to get back over. Outside, green fields dotted with black cattle flip by. White farmhouses with red barns sit back long gravel drives, chickens pecking in the ditches by the road. In the rearview mirror I see Roth sleeping fitfully. Sally is leaning against the opposite window, snoring. I can't help but think about Kari and her son, Stephen. Have they met yet? Had dinner at a nice restaurant at a table with a carnation in a tiny vase? What would they be talking about? I picture the young man in the picture calling the woman who gave birth to him "Kari," or worse, "Ms. Francis." A muscle man in a Jeep honks his horn at my meandering into his lane. He flips me off as he passes, and I think of the weightlifter types in high school who splattered my car window with mashed potatoes and wrote "Pus Face!" in the spuds. But it occurs to me I'm in the wrong, maybe viewing everything as it relates to my past humiliations is something I should give up. I roll down the window and wave to show I'm taking responsibility, but the Jeep is too far ahead now to notice.

When I look back at Roth he's sitting up straight and smiling, that otherworldly expression loose across his face. He sort of scares me looking like that; he reminds me of a ghost I'm pretty sure I once saw at the foot of my bed. I slow down and twist the radio off. "Are you okay?" I ask, trying to watch the road and also look for clues in his face in the mirror. Roth doesn't answer. His eyes open wider and I can see that he's actually not really awake—he's in some kind of a trance. He cups his good hand like he's offering a present to someone, then sort of lovingly fondles the air in front of him.

"Roth," I say, "what are you doing? Can you tell me?" I swerve back in my lane. "Roth," I say again, louder, "Are you okay?" He's looking sort of maniacal now, his hand twisting in front of him like he's touching something, or someone. Both Sally and Donny are snoozing, Terry, too, and I decide to pull over. I slow down and the gravel crunches under the tires as I nose the van next to a railing, a huge billboard above us advertising Angus meat for Hardees.

I shove the van into park and turn around to see Roth. His face is so tranquil now that even his palsied side seems to recess into the soft whiteness of his skin. He's still asleep with his eyes open, his hands slowly making those eerie movements in the air. I take his hand in mine and it's neither warm nor cold.

"Roth, it's me, Hobbie. Lean back and close your eyes. Come on now, go back to sleep." He seems to register this and slowly reclines back into the seat. "Now close your eyes," I say gently. Roth blinks and looks up. He whispers, "You're a fine boy, Stephen. All the people here know that." He spreads his arms, the ruined one barely lifting from his side, and then relaxes back into the seat, finally closing his eyes.

seven I'd envisioned the moment when I would find Kari as being much more sophisticated and charged with emotion, but now, as I leave the van, careful to shut the door quietly because the others are still sleeping, the motel seems as ordinary and stale as a gas station bathroom. Just as I'm about to enter the check-in area, Terry notices me from his vantage point in the van and begins to yap. One by one, the heads begin to wallow around on their necks. I watch as first Donny, then Sally, then Roth are each woken up, dazed. I turn to trot back to the van. Through the window I see Sally already using her compact, eager to see her daughter with fresh lipstick.

I open the van door. "Listen, do you mind if I go in and see if she's here?" They all stare. No one answers. "What I mean is, let me check and see and then we'll figure it out from there."

"Oh, hon, I'd like to be right there to see her, too, even though I'm the last person she'd want to see," says Sally, determined and making moves to get out of the van. "I just want to make it clear how much I want to help her."

"Please," I say, "Let me go in first—alone." Sally gives me a long look and then a half-smile, and reluctantly agrees.

The Roadside Motel is little more than its name, a modest structure probably built in the '50s like a million other motels of its kind. I ring the bell at the front desk, and like a robot working off a faulty circuit, a man appears in a cardigan. He's eating a sandwich, some of it apparently stuck to the roof of his mouth. He mumbles, "Can I help you?"

"I'm looking for Kari Francis. She's my wife and I know she's here because I've already checked our credit card statement online." It comes out too forceful and rushed, arrogant even, but I can't help myself.

The man stops trying to get his mouth unstuck. He looks at me knowingly. "I just rent rooms, pal. What people, married or otherwise, do in them is none of my business." He plops a registry book on the counter. "She's here. Checked in three days ago, but I haven't seen her since."

Sure enough, I see Kari's handwriting looped in blue along a dotted line.

"For what it's worth, she was alone," the clerk says. He places the triangle of white bread on a napkin. "She's in Room 14."

I step quickly to the door outside and he calls after me, "Don't make any trouble or I'll have to call the cops." I nod and look back as he's shoving the last bite into his mouth.

Outside, Sally and Roth and Donny, holding Terry, stand at the hood of the van. Even Donny looks nervous. Sally and Roth are wrapped around one another and whatever strangeness in Roth before—that weird half-awake, half-asleep business—is over. The weather has cleared and a pristine ceiling of blue sky goes on forever.

I walk toward them. "She's in Room 14," I say nervously. Sally fidgets and looks over me toward the row of rooms. I imagine her pushing past me to get to her daughter, but she surprises me. "Let's have Hobbie go in first and see her," she says. "You just take your time, sweetheart. We'll be right out here or in the van waiting." She winks.

I give her a grateful nod and make my way to the rooms. Eleven, 12, 13. I stop before number 14—*her* door—and take a deep breath. My shoes are scuffed, I notice, and I'm a little sweaty. Finally, I knock. No answer, and I peer back at the van. I can make out Roth's hunched back and one side of Sally, but I can't see Donny. The door has a peephole so I think to drop my head out of its view, then change my mind. If Kari's inside, I want her to see all of me—the scar, the whiteheads she's used to anyway, and hopefully, a look of bravery on my face, ready to quit hiding and be a father to her son. Sure, he's an adult, but we've got the rest of our lives to grow old with him, be grandparents, maybe even try again to have a baby of our own, give Stephen a half-brother.

The wind picks up and makes the bright outdoors blustery. I knock again and doublecheck that it says 14 on the door. Somewhere a car starts and a door slams in the interior of the building. A spider's bulbous nest rests in the corner of the doorframe, I notice. My hopes are sinking. I lean back and can see Sally and Donny helping Roth inside the van again. I wait a minute more, then pound on the door and rattle the large pane of glass next to it. Frustration rises in me, and something that feels a little like anger, but at what or whom, I'm not sure.

I can see out the corner of my eye that the clerk from the front desk is making his way toward me. I step closer to the door to act as if everything's normal, but the guy is already saying something intended for me, clearly agitated. He takes long strides and by the time he's to unit 10 I can hear him.

"Stop knocking! The people in 15 are complaining."

I whirl around and face him and he stops short. "Just let me in. Now."

The clerk puffs his chest out and pokes mine with his finger. "No way, crater face. How the hell do I know who you are?" He swishes his tongue around in his mouth, about to spit. "For all I know you could be her pimp. Get the fuck outta here before I call 911."

I say slowly, "Open—the—fuck-ING door, ass—hole." It might just be the first time in my life that I've stood up for myself after being called such a name. Kari's done it before, almost gotten us into several fights over the years, but as for me, I've never found the guts until now. It doesn't work, though. He's whipping out his cell phone, calling my bluff.

"I guess I'm gonna have to call the cops, elephant man."

I can't find any more words, as the singsong tone of three digits being punched into his Nokia sounds like the end to everything. He rests a hand on his hip, a snotty look on his face and the phone pressed against his big ear. "We'll see what the troopers think of your dirty ass." Just then, as if a poltergeist has snuck up behind him, the hand on his hip shoots behind his back. He wrenches forward and grimaces, drops the phone and it explodes into three pieces, battery pack detached.

Donny stands behind him, teeth clenched. I don't know how,

but somehow I didn't see him sneak up on the guy. "Just let this good man into the room, sir," Donny says. "We've got a family emergency here." The clerk squawks and whines as Donny pulls him upright, still holding the arm behind his back.

"It's all right, Donny," I say. "Let him go. Anyway, Kari's not here."

Donny twists harder and says, "Bullshit, he's going to open the door."

I move toward Donny and grab him by the shoulder. "Don—" I start, but he cuts me off.

"Don't touch me," Donny shouts. "I'm trying to help you!"

The clerk pipes up, "If you two assholes will get on the same page I'll open up the fucking shithole so you can see for yourself that your wife's not here. Like I said, I haven't seen her in days."

Donny finally lets go. He looks hurt, probably that I've not recognized his loyalty to me. "I just wanted to fucking help you," he says as the clerk unlocks the door and throws it open.

"There you go, dipshit," says the clerk. "Knock yourself out. But if she files a complaint I'll roll on you two and claim I was threatened." He steps out of my way and toward the inside of the room.

It's dark and the drapes are pulled. I can hear Sally and Roth clambering up the sidewalk. Roth is talking loudly, and although it's garbled, I can make out the words "cross" and if I'm not mistaken, "gun."

The clerk flips on the light switch to reveal a trashed room. There are four empty Domino's boxes, no less than six empty two-liter bottles of Pepsi, a Dunkin' Donuts box with half a chocolate-glazed in it, and a mess of wrappers and fast-food cups. The bed has been stripped, and the blankets and sheets are coiled in a ball on the floor. Something drips from the crappy desk. "Holy shit," says Donny.

The clerk sucks at his teeth. "Told ya. Good thing she paid with a credit card. There's a $50 fee for extra cleaning."

Other than the trash, there's no sign of my Kari. I look at the closet and imagine for a flashed second that a clothes hanger is still rocking back and forth on the dowel, but it's nothing more than a shadow. Kari has always been particular about where we stayed, so it's hard for me to imagine that this was a room rented for the sole purpose of lodging; it reminds me of an addict's den or something. Roth and Sally make a racket coming through the door. They look windblown and out of sorts. Sally's lips are not shiny. Roth's face is absurdly tranquil again, and if I didn't know better I'd think he'd just toked a crisp joint. Donny walks around the room picking things up and stopping just short of sniffing them.

"All right," says the clerk, "I've about had enough of this silly, sad horseshit." He hikes up his pants and jangles some keys hanging off his belt. "Get out so I can have this mess cleaned up."

Donny acts as if the altercation before had never happened and smiles right at him. "We can't argue with that. You've gotta run a business."

I stay planted next to the peeling dresser, water rings over the top. "Are you sure she didn't say where she was going?" I'm beginning to feel a little desperate. "Look," he says, clearly exasperated. "Like I said, I haven't seen her since she checked in."

In the doorway, Roth is trying to speak and Sally is waiting patiently. Everyone turns and looks at Roth, even the clerk. Roth sputters and opens and closes his mouth. Nothing comes out. But Roth is placid, offering up a gentle smile, sort of moving his head around like a blind man at the piano.

I see that Sally looks sad, somehow not her usual positive self.

"He's been behaving strangely today," she says in a low voice. "I know he's tired."

Beside her Roth freezes and bites his lip. Sally sniffs and clutches at her cell phone, which I just now notice in her hand. "I gotta tell you something, Hobbie." Beside her Roth grunts something that might be encouragement.

"We called Stephen's parents in Colorado," Sally starts. "They gave us his grandfather's number here in Virginia." She sucks in some air. "He was going to college in Lynchburg. Religious studies." Sally says. "He was working in a convenience store when it was robbed. He was shot, but he's okay. That was over 10 months ago. Stephen dropped out of school, though. He's been working different jobs ever since. No one can seem to find the boy—apparently he's cut out on his own. They don't know how to reach him." Outside, it's colder and darker, and for the first time in weeks I think to remember what the actual date is. I notice Christmas lights on a live tree near the road. There's a cardboard Santa sleigh next to it but not a Santa or reindeer or anything. It's stupid, but I hear the words to "Away in a Manger" in my head.

Halfway back to the van I stop Sally. "What did he say about Kari? Had she been there?"

Sally nods somberly. "He said she looked bad, Hobbie. Like she hadn't slept for a while. Like she'd been crying for days and days.

I stand dumb in the parking lot. Maybe Stephen had to find a way to hide out, too. After all, in his 20 short years he's had more than his fair share of adults claiming him: adopted parents, Roth, Kari, and a grandfather who loves him but is not blood related. I don't want him spending his life like we have—running away *eight* It's late. Donny and I have our own hotel rooms this time at the Lynchburg Grand Resort. Sally and Roth occupy a nice double with a view over downtown Lynchburg, and Terry's in with them, as Roth had insisted. Smokestacks tower over the James River, left intact to intimate a renovated downtown effect. Percival's Island is not far away; that's what it says in the glossy "Getting Around Lynchburg" magazine in our rooms.

I can't take the tension any longer and throw back the covers. In the bathroom there's a mini sewing kit in the basket of goodies supplied by the big hotel chain. I rip it open with my teeth as I survey my face. The scar from the bear is changing colors. It's gone from purple to red, then pink and now a dead-looking taupe; it's a ridge that tells onlookers to hurry up to the other side, where things get really interesting.

Kari's nowhere to be found. It was stay in Lynchburg or drive more, and no one volunteered to get back on the road. In the morning, we'll check the Roadside Motel again, if the clerk will take my call, and try the credit card tracking system again online, but that's all there is. Stephen's grandfather, who I now know is frail and ill himself, a welder in one of Lynchburg's now-closed factories for more than 50 years, will help if he can, although he's bedridden and cared for by a hospice nurse. He's to call if Kari makes contact or comes back. Kari's on a binge so I might as well take a step toward sweet release, too, dig in, and find the problem.

I twist the hot water handle and steam rises up toward my head, fogging a small section of the wall mirror. There are four or five spots that are ripe and I squeeze fast and hard. I run the tip of the sewing needle under the water. It looks as if I might really be sewing as I skip from bump to bump, probing and ducking the needle into the skin. I step back and view my face, red and raised, glistening in the mirror. The ice machine in the hall moans as I begin the ritual of washing up.

The truth is, this process no longer holds any sort of salvation. We're in trouble, I think, when even our unhealthy responses to disappointment don't work. When that happens, you've either got to pretend they still work and fake relief or find another way. I dab up pinkish droplets of blood and wipe the counter and try to remember when just two days ago I felt so good, so ready to change. Now, thinking of my life ahead without Kari, I toss the towel under the sink and click off the light, walk to the bed. I'd been silly anyway, thinking I could be the father to a man whose real father hurt his real mother and made both Kari and me scared of the world. I don't know what I was thinking I could've offered him.

I unzip my suitcase and find the pictures of Stephen. In all of them, his birthmarks are visible from different angles. In an eighth-grade school photo, a dark oval peeks out from an open collar.

I zip up the pictures in the suitcase and take three Tylenol PMs from my shaving kit. I go to the window. We're on the 11th floor. Christmas lights blink in various patterns over the city, some blues and reds and greens in the shape of pines, reindeer, and the occasional snowman against the dark sky. A lone car sits at a traffic light. It seems so absurd for a person to be sitting there in isolation, waiting for an electronic cue to move on. Finally the car sputters through the light. I press my face on the window and feel the cold glass. It's soothing. I decide to crawl in bed, wishing I had some wine to speed up the pills. There's a slight rapping on my door. I can hear Sally whispering, "Hobbie, Hobbie."

I fumble around trying to find my jeans and pull them on in a rush as Sally continues at the door. "Hobbie!" she says louder. I paw at the light switch and find my shirt. I open the door, hoping my face isn't too hideous from the picking. Sally's wearing a long black piece of lingerie I hope wasn't lost on Roth.

"What is it, Sally? What's wrong?"

"I don't know, hon. Roth and Terry are gone. I can't find them. I thought maybe Roth got up and the dog followed him to the bathroom or down the hall." Sally wrings her hands. She's not wearing any makeup, of course, but she's just as attractive. I notice some age lines that are normally concealed, but they only create a prettier, more vulnerable look to her dark eyes.

"Don't worry," I say, "I'm sure they're around here some place." Although I can't imagine where. Or how they've managed to go unnoticed. "Where's Donny? I could use him to help look."

Sally rolls her eyes. "He's either dead to the world in there or out at a bar. I knocked and knocked and even called his room."

"Try again. I'll put on some shoes and grab my cell phone. Call me if they come back or Donny shows up." Sally nods and proceeds to pound on Donny's door.

I check with the front desk. "I haven't seen them," says the desk attendant, a slender, pale kid not much older than Stephen, I would say. "I would've seen them on one of the cameras if they left out the front entrance." He points to the row of flickering gray-blue TV sets under the counter. He uses his radio to call security.

"I'm going to keep looking," I tell the kid. "By the way, he's kinda senile." Inside the glass elevator in the lobby, I can see all the potted plants and white lights and two majestic fake Christmas trees the hotel has on display as I ride up to the 11th floor. I'll start with the stairwells and check out each floor. The elevator doors part, and there stands Sally.

"They're on the roof," she says, seeming relieved, which I can't understand. "Donny's up there with him."

"How do you know?" I ask, my brow tight.

Sally holds up her phone and says breathlessly, "I called Donny." She pats her forehead with a balled-up tissue. "We should go up there, hon. Donny said Roth's acting strange again." Her eyes shimmer wet and a crinkle appears above her nose. "Last night he was talking in tongues." She leaves it there, perhaps needing help with the idea.

"Really? Are you sure he wasn't just mumbling? I mean, I don't know much about speaking in tongues, but doesn't it sound a lot like gibberish?"

"It was tongues all right. Once, back when we were early in love, Roth said I made him speak it. We'd be kissing and tearing at each other's clothes and he'd start in." She touches her hair. "I'm sorry, hon. Too much info, probably. Anyway, yes, he's doing it. I hadn't heard it in years." She's got a daydreamy look in her eyes.

"I'll go get them down," I say.

"I'll go with you," says Sally.

"No way. You'll freeze out there in that."

"I'll change, won't take long," she says turning toward the elevator.

"I'm going up there now, Sally. Just stay here," I say, leaving her standing there as I rush back to the elevators. "By the way, how'd they get on the roof? Isn't the roof door locked?" I ask, calling over my shoulder.

"Donny," she says. "He can jimmy anything."

I take the stairs quickly. At the top, the door reads: Authorized Personnel Only. I twist the handle but it's locked. I pound on it. No one comes. I put my lips up close to the door jamb and shout, "Donny, it's me, Hobbie, open up." I step back from the door. The stairwell is quiet and cold, metal everywhere, dangerous. I peer down the center and it makes my head woozy. I knock again. What could take so long? "Donny? Roth? Are you guys out there?" A ping and a swoosh of air echoes in the stairwell, some type of machine turning on.

Finally the door handle moves and Donny's eye is visible. "Are the security guards with you?"

"No," I say, irritated. "Now let me out there so we can get him down."

"That's not going to be so easy," says Donny, opening the door wider, still acting as though they've hidden out up here after a bank heist.

I step onto the roof. I'd imagined a drop-off with no edge to keep Roth from falling to his death, but there's a wall that goes up almost past my head and tables and chairs for lounging when it's warm. There isn't a pool, but clearly this is an area for recreation. In the cold month of December the roof looks depressing and useless.

"Where is he?" I ask, as Donny pulls his collar up against the wind.

"Right over here," he says, pointing to a trellised area that has empty plant containers lined around the base, floodlights shining on the dirt. Terry yaps from somewhere, and as we walk toward the fenced-in area I can hear Roth and his blessed tongues. Roth's outline comes into view, and Terry is sitting on the chair opposite him. There's a tenderness to Roth's babble, a kind of cadenced prayer. There were men at the Washburn Tabernacle who spoke in tongues. It was all pretentious and put on, a ploy to seduce newly divorced women from a church group at the tabernacle called Ladies of His Grace. But now I can't help but find the babble soothing.

Roth doesn't seem to notice us. "Roth," I say, "come on down with us now, it's cold up here." No response—it's as if I'm not there. "Let's get you back in the room with Sally. She's worried, Roth."

Donny rubs his hands together and blows into them. "I told you. He's not going anywhere. I've been trying to get him to leave for 40 minutes."

"Why'd you bring him up here in the first place?" I ask, knowing as I speak that my tone is too accusing.

"Hey, it wasn't me, man. He came and knocked on my door and said he wanted to go for a walk. He's my boss now, you know. It took us 20 minutes to climb two flights of stairs."

"What about the door, I suppose Roth picked the lock?"

"Screw you, man," says Donny, tensing, moving away. "He wanted to come out here and kept pointing and looking at me and then he started doing that shit he's doing now and what was I supposed to do?" He shrugs. "Besides, I'm not about to piss off a preacher who pays me."

"Roth isn't a preacher," I say, but it doesn't matter to Donny, who has now walked to Roth and is rubbing his back in small circles with the palm of his hand. "Come on, Roth. He's all better now, you've healed him. Let's go get some sleep in the fancy hotel."

Terry is eye-locked with Roth and seems to be enjoying the attention. I step closer, right up next to Donny, and notice that around Roth's neck is Sally's rosary, and in his lap is a Bible, probably from the hotel room. "Terry," I call. "Here, boy. Come!" I'm hoping if he moves, Roth will come out of whatever trance he's in, too, but it doesn't work.

I walk to the other side of Roth and squat down next to him. I can see he's got that same contented expression on his face, meek and hopeful, as he did in the van yesterday. He's still chanting, his drooping lips forcing out the nonsense words. "Roth," I whisper, the wind now howling around us. "You've helped Terry. He's well now. Sally needs you downstairs."

I take off my jacket and droop it over his shoulders; Donny tucks his around Roth's midsection. Terry begins to yelp, sort of in response to Roth's chanting, and the two of them sound so comical that I can't help but grin to myself. Terry picks up the pitch, his tiny muzzle pointed into the air as he tries to hit a note, and for a moment it's as if they're howling in synch.

I can't hold it in any longer and let out a giant guffaw. I can't stop laughing. And just like that, the chanting stops, the barking, too, and Roth turns his head slowly toward me, a sly smile creasing his face. Then Donny busts out laughing, too, and the three of us laugh and laugh.

I wipe my eyes and notice that Terry has begun to whine and shiver. I tuck him inside my shirt; he feels cold and bristly against my skin. Donny helps Roth up. The moon is full above us, or close to it, and there's a buttery aura around the edges. Roth points to the sky and grunts. I'm close to him, close enough to smell his soap and a douse of liniment. We all stare at the sky. Roth reaches over and takes my hand. In the clearest voice, as if the stroke had never gotten him, he says, "My God, I love you." I look at him and he's still got that dreamy look on his face. I'm not sure it was meant for me.

nine After getting Roth back to his room, Sally kissing him all over as if he were a newborn, the Tylenol PM finally kicked in and I fell into a weird slumber. I didn't dream of the bear, but a version of it. The deacon was on all fours, growling, his furry feet with dangerous claws sticking out. I wake up when he leers at me.

My head is woozy and I'm still sleepy, but can't sleep. I can see the gray light of morning ebbing from around the drawn curtains. I roll over and see the clock reads a little after six. I've slept in my clothes, and a damp sweat covers my chest and mats the hair at the base of my neck. I turn on the television. Two anchors, a man and a woman, jibe each other about what they've gotten their Secret Santas. It's a local affiliate morning show and it's annoying, yet I can't turn it off. The inane sound of their supposed unscripted banter is somehow comforting, just like the Christmas tree on the set behind them.

I leave the TV on and hop in the shower. The steam swirling around in the bathroom makes me think of Roth the morning of his stroke. I can see his body laid out on the floor, ochre-colored, and I feel a bawl catch in my chest. I try and hold it back, keep it at bay, by scrubbing harder with the soap, but it's no use. Clearly, the lack of sleep is catching up with me, and I miss Kari so much I punch the wall, feeling stupid as I do it. I can hear myself crying, completely exhausted and discouraged. I stay in the shower until there's nothing left to let out.

Later, I've dressed and pulled myself together and sit at the computer station in the hotel's business center. I begin a search for my credit card's Web site. Once I find the page, I type in the account number and password. The computer screen goes blank for a second and blips back with our spending history. Just as the man had said at the Roadside Motel, there's a $50 cleaning charge tacked on.

I scroll up, then down some and find a new charge. Under this hotel is another. I can't believe what I'm seeing. The word "Lynchburg" is printed next to the hotel name. I log out and turn off the computer and rush through the lobby and approach the desk. The kid from last night is still on duty. He's swiping a batch of card keys through a magnetic device. He looks up and says primly, "I saw you guys up there." He points to his monitors. "I'm glad you found your friend, but please stay off the roof. I was about to send a guard up."

"Sorry. Sure," I say, distracted. "Where's the Ridgebaker Hotel and Suites?"

"The Ridgebaker? It's just down two blocks and over one, near the courthouse. It's nice, but not as nice as this one. Here we have continental breakfast until 11, and there they stop serv—"

I can hear his voice trail off as I shoot out the revolving door, getting trapped briefly by an elderly man and his luggage. Out on the street the air smells clean and cold, windswept and scoured by falling temps. This isn't like Durham, when I sensed we'd already missed Kari. She's got to be at the Ridgebaker. I start out jogging, but shift into high gear and run down the sidewalks like a man on fire, soles slipping so much I have to sort of skate to take the corners. Cold air lifts my bangs as I take a turn. I run past a bagel shop and then a Dunkin' Donuts, where a line of people snakes out the door. A delivery van is backing up to a loading dock as I check both ways and cross the street. The Ridgebaker is in view and I turn it all on, sprint down the decline and reach a set of revolving doors that lead into a hotel that looks very much like the one I just left.

I pause and try to catch my breath. My lungs burn. We could move to Lynchburg and get jobs, I think, and I could take up running again, make the last few blocks part of my daily run, a tribute to how we found each other again.

I suck in four quick gulps of air and can feel my vitals slowing down. I walk to the front desk. "Could I have Kari Francis' room number please?"

The young woman on duty is chipper but firm. "Oh, no, we don't give out room numbers. But you're more than welcome to call her." She swings her hair back and hands me the hotel phone. "Just punch in the first three letters of her last name." I pause to think things through. I can't take another near-brush with Kari; if I call and get her, she'll be on to me and that will be that. In the state of mind she's likely in, she'll just keep running away from me.

"Excuse me," I say to the woman, giving her my best doting husband look. "It's our anniversary and I want to surprise her. She's here on business and doesn't know I'm in town. Couldn't you make an exception just this once?" She gives me a long look, up and down, but she's not looking at me like I'd expected, that kind of pitiful once-over that says: Awww, look, isn't that cute. See, everybody can find love if they just keep trying.

"Well, all right," she says, looking around. "But don't tell anyone." She slides toward her computer and hits the space bar hard several times, scratches down something and folds it up.

"Here," she says in a hush, handing me the square of paper. She actually whispers, "But if I were you I wouldn't go up there empty-handed. Our gift shop opens in 15 minutes. They've got a few long-stemmed roses." She winks and nods her head toward the shop window where a plastic Rudolph is blinking his schnozz and a tribe of tiny teddy bears is clad in elf hats.

I offer a curled smile and turn to leave quickly before she gets it in her head to personally walk me to the gift shop herself. The orange numbers above the onyx elevator doors slowly count down, skipping some floors altogether, stopping on others and making my wait unbearable. My mind is racing, thinking of Kari, of what it will be like to hold her again, and for some reason, I also think of Roth. I can't get the image of him up on that roof, Terry in his lap, out of my head. Finally, the elevator doors open. I've forgotten to check the room number and quickly open the folded paper in my sweaty hand. In blue ink it reads *Room 507*.

The elevator dings and I step off onto the fifth floor. I take a left and before I know it I'm standing right in front of 507. A "Do Not Disturb" sign dangles from the door handle. I pause to think what I'm doing. I could knock and tell her it's me, or I could just sit out in the hallway and wait until she leaves the room or comes back; the sign on the door is no guarantee she's in there, I know. Over the years, on special occasions or just for a change of pace and scenery, we'd check into a hotel in the same suburb we lived in and just watch cable and order room service. And in all those times, Kari never once changed her habit of immediately putting the "Do Not Disturb" sign on the door as soon as we checked in. "I don't want anyone bothering us," she'd say. "Besides, we're only here for one night—how many towels can we possibly need?"

I listen for any movement inside, a toilet flushing or the TV blaring, but it's quiet. I realize I've been sleeping in so many hotel rooms lately that I'm getting used to stained carpet and corny equine prints hanging on the walls. The image of Roth up on the roof and Terry howling along with the tongues flashes in my head. It makes me smile. I rock back on my heels and decide to walk down the hall and think. I go past the other rooms, trying to appear nonchalant so I can think without someone getting suspicious and maybe assuming I'm stalking the occupant of 507. Static clicks under my feet as I walk slowly to the end of the hall and turn around.

It's come down to this. I really *am* stalking my common-law wife in Lynchburg, Virginia, loitering outside her door, trying to figure out an approach that will work. I shake my head as if to clear it. I can't let myself think of seeing Kari in person after so long or I'll bust down the door and take whatever is left of her in my arms and beg her to marry me in the lobby while a bellman officiates.

An idea occurs to me. I hurry back to the elevator area and spot a hotel phone. The placard reads: 6+room number. I hit the digits and listen. It rings and rings and I'm close enough to Kari's room to hear the phone ringing in there, too, after a millisecond of delay. I let it ring five more times, then tell myself I'll hang up after 10, then 15. I place the receiver down and stand before the elevators, at a total loss. The doors begin to shudder as the elevator prepares to stop on this floor. The back of my neck tingles. It could be Kari, I think. Quickly, I check my face in the oval gold-framed mirror on the wall, pat down my hair. She's about to step off the elevator and into my arms, I think. A rubber seal on the doors wiggles and the seam begins to part, slowly.

It's empty, not a soul inside. The mirrored interior only offers up different angles of me as I step inside.

Downstairs in the lobby I'm feeling a little dizzy as I approach the front desk. The woman from before acts as if she's been waiting for me to return. "I didn't notice this when I got the room number for you, but your wife's actually not checked in. She was supposed to be here last night, but like I said she didn't check in." The sleep medicine is still trying to do its job and my face feels clammy. She looks at me with a wary frown. "Are you okay, sir? Maybe you should get some air."

I lean against the wall and feel my legs buckle a little. "No," I say, waving her off. "I'm okay, just a little headache. I'll be fine."

"Are you sure, because I could call someone for you," she says.

"No!" I almost yell, acting like a jerk. I tone it down, seeing her frown. "I'll be fine."

The walk back to the Lynchburg Grand Resort is dreary and too short. Shops have started to open up and holiday music clashes with other holiday music. A Santa Claus is setting up in a department store window along with a real-life little person as his elf. Both of them have yet to put on hats and their hair is nearly the same color—mousy, and sticking up—so close in color they could even be related, I think.

In just a few minutes I'm back inside my own hotel and exhausted. I sit down on one of the fancy couches in the lobby and bow my head. The carpet is a twilled Berber and I start rubbing the soles of my shoes over it, digging into it so hard I believe I can tear right through and hit concrete. I've got no choice now. It's time to go home, I think, wherever that is. I'd thought Kari was waiting to see how I would love her in this new world we inhabit, where she's a mother and a whole lot thinner, and where I could be counted on to change, too, walk out of the shadows and take a place beside her.

My feet are gouging the carpet even harder. The noise of people milling about seems amplified. I look up. In the middle of the lobby is a faux waterfall trickling into a lighted pool, and it makes me think of the time Kari and I went on a picnic. It had been overcast with brief pockets of sunshine, and once I'd set up the blanket and opened the basket, put all the food out and popped the wine, lit a candle even though it was daytime, it had started to sprinkle. Kari was happy, though, and even as it started to thunder and lightning and pour down rain, we stayed right there where we were. In the storm we ate our picnic and made love, not considering the risks. It was, I think, the only time in our lives together that we were ever brave, when we didn't get up and run to another place. Now, I sit and listen to the water in the fake wishing pond and it sounds like nails on a chalkboard.

Finally, I stand up and someone is instantly next to me. "Shit," says Donny, breathing hard. "There you are." He looks panicked and pale. He grabs me by the arm. "Come on, we've got to get back up there to Roth. We think he's having another stroke." I'm yanked toward the elevators as paramedics come running into the lobby. The sirens are loud and piercing, right outside the hotel doors. They had to have been there for some time, I realize, but the truth is, I hadn't even known they were there until just now.

ten The rooftop looks entirely different now in the morning sky, gray and severe over Lynchburg. Roth is lying on a stretcher, an oxygen mask over his face, and an itchy looking wool blanket covering his body. I stare at it and can't find a focus. Why do they always use those awful, coarse blankets? Don't dying people deserve more comfort?

Donny holds Sally, but she's taller than he is so his head rests under hers, making it look as though he's the one being consoled. The paramedics busy themselves with taking Roth's vitals and applying another one of those damn blankets. Off in the distance, just above the spire of the bank building, a dot of a helicopter grows larger as it whacks its way toward us.

"Remember," the paramedic says as I go down on one knee next to Roth, "don't touch him." The straps on the oxygen mask dig into

Roth's soft skin, and I can see silvery beard stubble and a rosy glow on his apple cheeks. He looks healthier than ever, but according to one of the paramedics, he's in grave danger. "His system is shutting down," he yells. "We'll have to medevac him to a hospital that has a specialist."

The helicopter circles over the hotel and swings back around, tree leaves and wrappers swirling in a conical whorl as one paramedic clutches his badge to keep it from flying up into his face. Donny grabs a hold of his cap. Sally seems like she couldn't care less that her long nightgown is flapping in the strong wind, exposing her underwear, and Donny tries to hold it down. I watch as the helicopter pilot talks into his mouthpiece and lowers the helicopter perfectly onto the center of a bull's eye. Before I can even stand up, the paramedics are rushing toward the whapping blades, ducked down and expert in their moves to get Roth onboard in seconds. The noise is so loud I can't hear myself crying. Donny hobbles toward me still clutching Sally.

"Here," he yells over the blustery airstream, and hands off Sally to me; she falls against my chest and stays huddled there. "I should be the one to fly with him," Donny yells. "You get her fixed up and get to the hospital pronto!" With that, he sprints toward the helicopter like a pro. One paramedic stays behind as the helicopter lifts off the rooftop and flies off with the grace and speed of a dragonfly. In an instant the area is as cold and silent as a walk-in freezer.

In the stillness the tall paramedic booms, "Come on. It's too damn cold up here." He takes Sally from me and helps her through the rooftop doorway.

My face burns a little, probably from the wind and the cold, and I put my fingertips to my skin as I walk behind them through the door and down one flight of stairs to the elevator. Skin has been an obsession for me so long, I'm only half aware that I'm playing my cheek like a piano.

My back hurts from too much time leaning over Roth's hospital bed. I'm in the parking garage of Lynchburg General, sitting with the minivan door open and smelling gasoline fumes, a triad of oil spots gleaming ominously on the concrete at my feet. It's 10 p.m. I hadn't wanted to leave Terry in the car by himself when I was inside with Roth, but there was no other choice. He's starving now as I feed him turkey loaf from the cafeteria. He licks the Styrofoam container, his pink tongue darting into each of the different compartments. Roth's stroke was "substantial." That's what the specialist had said nearly 12 hours ago. It's nighttime now and the garage is barren and lonely, only a few vehicles left near the stairwells. Every 15 minutes or so a man in a patrol car with a flashing yellow light cruises by and waves. He's about to turn down our aisle again so I quickly close the door and shut Terry and me into the van. He snuggles into my lap as I lay back on the middle seat. The harsh security lighting overhead slashes in through the windows and keeps me from dozing, but Terry is out like a light, ripping off little snorts just like always. Maybe he's dreaming of Roth's chanting in tongues last night or the bear attack or maybe even all the commercial Christmas junk that he's seen in the past couple of days. Terry has always loved Christmas, when he gets to perform his one and only trick: ripping open presents with his sharp, little teeth. He starts at one corner of the package—tearing even strips, then another and another, until the whole present is unwrapped. It can take him 20 minutes to open a shoebox with a chew bone inside, but what he lacks in speed he makes up for in meticulousness.

I wish I had some sleeping pills. Terry's chest rises and falls as he dreams in my lap. I dial Kari's number at the Center for Healthy Living—which I've memorized—out of desperation; I know it will go unanswered. My head won't lie flat in the seat while I listen to a recorded message tell me that the number is not active. Wherever Kari is, she's trying hard to avoid us, and it makes my head ache.

I toss the phone onto the floorboard and try and sleep. It's difficult to get comfortable, and I don't want to disturb Terry by turning over on my stomach and putting him on another seat. In the end, I just lie awake, eyes open, and experience the familiar feeling of being stuck. I could do so many things: get up and go back to Roth's room and tell Donny and Sally I'm driving to Durham to see if Kari's gone back; take a flight to Colorado to meet Stephen's adoptive parents and explain to them who I am, who Kari is, maybe even tell them about the deacon and between us we can find forgiveness of a sort; or make myself get some real rest so I can think better about the whole mess in the morning. But none of these trigger my will to take action. After all, it hasn't worked so far. I've forced myself to take steps in reclaiming Kari, but all I've managed to do is pull off a botched road trip, replete with another Roth stroke. I remain in the minivan and opt for a compromise. I'll doze and wake in the morning, get up early, and relieve Donny and Sally so they can eat breakfast in the hospital cafeteria.

The flashing light from the security car approaches the minivan, strobing into the windows and making me feel guarded rather than protected. I can hear the specialist who saw Roth in my head: *What language he did have will be even further reduced. His day-to-day care will require a great deal of intervention and support. Don't be alarmed if he's confined to a wheelchair. Your loved one may be unlike him/herself from now on. Remember, a stroke of any magnitude is serious.*

The security guard finally passes by at a speed that can be no greater than 3 to 4 mph. I sit up, Terry still in my lap. I place him on the floorboard and cover him with a sweater. He doesn't even flinch, belly full and soft palate vibrating like a reed. I lie back down and fold my arms over my chest. It's cold in the van but not unbearable. With a few adjustments, I'm comfortable and can imagine sleep.

People do change. It either comes in one big blast like with Roth, or glacially, as is the case with Kari and me. It could be the added weight around your waist or a new pock at the corner of your cheek, either way the end result is the same; at some point it's complete and you wake up different, and those around you have to learn to love a whole new person. It's that solid idea that finally puts me to sleep.

eleven It's starting to get warmer. Sunlight beams strong on the front lawn, toasting the bushes and coaxing maroon buds from their tight bullets. Atlanta's spring comes early. Mid-February is the starting point, and from this moment up until the second week of June, the subdivisions will be aflame with baby pinks and stark whites, dusky reds and bright cherries, azaleas in the fulcrum of extended color. Today is supposed to be near 70 degrees and I want to get Roth outside, let him take in the splendor of his own yard—after all, he's the groom.

The ramp Donny built from the back of the house trails gradually down to an area near the deck, a spot that is now lit with full sunshine. Before Donny and Sally left for the grocery store, they worked in tandem to bathe Roth in his new roll-in shower. They are now experts in dressing him and getting his deodorant and cologne on in equal measures. He smells nice as I push the wheelchair down the ramp, the cool breeze making the sunlight feel even warmer in comparison. They've put him in an Izod zip-up jacket and given him the option of wearing gloves, which now lie in his lap next to Terry. Terry loves to be on Roth's thighs as the wheelchair is pushed; he lifts his head and enjoys the air as it passes over his droopy ears.

Parked in the sun, Roth grunts and points with his chin toward the sunglasses hanging on a cord around his neck. His verbal communication is rudimentary, less than before, for sure, but he uses sounds like a form of pidgin to get his point across, and his eyes are as clever as they were before.

"Want your shades on, huh?" I ask. He nods, and I fumble as I put them on him, accidentally sticking one of the arms in his ear. He chuckles, helping to keep me from impaling his earlobe by turning his head slightly. "Sorry about that," I tell him. Once he's got the sunglasses on, I position his chair to catch a full dose of the warm rays. Terry is sitting up now, and it occurs to me that Roth looks like an actor posing for a glamour headshot, shades on, his white hair combed back and his best pal on his lap. It could be the caption of some tabloid photo: "The elderly but wise silver screen star at home, talking candidly about his life and loves."

I leave Roth with Terry and roam around the backyard, bending to pick up sticks that have fallen after a strong storm yesterday. The lawn needs mowing, something Donny said he'd gladly do at dinner last night. It was my turn to cook. We had a pasta dish one of the women in the office told me about. For more than a month now I've been working at Simon's vet clinic, saving money to get an apartment not far from Roth's house, where I've been living since he got out of the hospital. Every day, Terry can come with me to work, where he usually sleeps under my desk. I'm using my tellering skills to do the billing and answer phones. Tomorrow, I've agreed to go with Simon to see his dermatologist in downtown Atlanta; the first procedure will take almost three hours. I'm actually excited about the prospect of healing my face. It's a new treatment, one I've never tried, and according to Simon's face and the "before" pictures he's shown me, I may be in luck.

Next to the fence a clump of purplish, tiny flowers is blooming. I don't know what they are, but decide to wheel Roth over for a look. Halfway across the yard, with Roth's head jostling back and forth over the ruts, I think I should've just picked one and brought it over for him. Most of the time I'm afraid I'll hurt him and send him into another stroke, one he won't be able to endure. Terry is alert as we take our little ride, his eyes wide and serious, almost scared. I sometimes wonder whether he still holds the memory of the bear attack all those months ago. I know I do. The dreams still come, but farther apart, and while I abused the sleeping pills for a while, I read now until I'm exhausted. The job helps, too, wears me out in a good way, keeps my mind off of things.

It's cooler by the fence and sparrows flitter in a birdbath. I point to the flowers. "See, aren't those nice, Roth?"

Roth puts his hand to his face so slowly it seems his arm is controlled by hydraulics. He sputters, "Air—eeeeee." I recognize the sound as the one he makes to say "Kari." "Did she plant those for you?"

Roth nods, and tries to pat my hand.

"That doesn't surprise me. She always has good taste." His eyes tear up.

"Would you like me to pick one for you?"

Roth taps his knee once. He and Donny came up with the system: one means yes, two means no, because Donny felt Roth got tired of shaking his head. I squat down and pick two of the flowers, my new running shoes sparkling in the sun, the night-glo strips like iridescent snake skin. I've taken to running a three-mile course daily in Roth's subdivision, stopping every other day to pick up Simon and his wife to join me, both excellent runners.

I hand the flowers to Roth. He puts them to his mouth where a permanent wetness always gleams. Roth sometimes gets his senses mixed up. When he wants to smell something it goes directly to his mouth; if a news program is on and he can't hear it, he'll occasionally sniff the air. He is slow to recognize the mistake, but when he does, he proceeds to diligently correct it. Now, he gradually moves the now-soggy flowers to his nose, inhales.

It's Sunday and we're due at church in an hour, but we don't have far to go. Today, we'll have our regular service and Roth and Sally's wedding ceremony, too. After Roth came home and he'd completed his intensive OT and speech therapy, all of us attended service at his church with the electronic Bibles. Sally and Donny fiddled with the touch screens and were intrigued. Sally wore her rosary around her neck and even genuflected, which was met with awe and confusion by the rows of evangelicals close enough to see her.

Since we'd been gone and on the road trying to find Kari and Stephen, the church had installed a newer, grander stage. The pulpit was now as big as most worship halls and it rose up, replete with built-in spotlights and wireless microphone. The pastor gave a sermon on how God wanted us to roll in his riches, and not just the spirit, but the earthly gold, too. "Did God ever write a commandment that said Thou Shall Not Live in Luxury?" he hollered.

Later, after the service there, on the drive back to his house, Roth struggled to speak. We were sitting in traffic. "N-n-n-no!" he sputtered. It was clear that we would not be going back to that church.

With Sally's help, we organized a different way to attend church, one that would please Roth and accommodate his needs. Donny was the one to ask, "Why don't we just have a service here, in his house? Roth could even lead it." In the end though, the house was too small, so we looked for something close by. Sally was thrilled to get to drive the hour to a monastery in Georgia to purchase a whole worship kit: rosaries for us all, heavy metal crosses for the walls, prayer cards, and even a Bible so large it has its own stand. Simon and his wife come to our services, and some neighbors from the subdivision.

We meet in an empty storefront next to Simon's vet clinic. He's rented it for a grooming salon that I will eventually operate, but we're waiting until the interior is completely finished. For now, it's the perfect home for a temporary suburban church, even if it's more quirky than suburban. People bring their pets, and the dress code is very informal. Every Sunday there's a new development in the place as it moves closer to becoming a pet salon—the bare walls are painted; the mural of a kitty and puppy are colored in more; a set of tanks used to shampoo pets is installed—but Sally's Catholic artifacts remain in place. The cover of the gigantic Bible has some specks of white paint on it, and the stand is frosted with drywall dust, but other than that, the workers are careful not to break the candles or move the heavy cross that hangs by the mural. It looks like the cartoon kitten and dog are about to pounce on it during their rambunctious play.

Roth does in fact lead the service, but it's not your typical sermon. He opens up each service sometimes speaking in tongues, and at others in just his regular garbled speech, which to some sounds the same as the tongues. But for those of us who know him well—as does most of the congregation—it's more than clear that he's making a point about redemption and forgiveness or, say, the genuine nature of God.

Roth taps his wrist to indicate we should get going. Terry yawns, then whines some. The flowers Kari planted for Roth are wilted in his hand. It's grown even warmer out, a perfect day for a man to marry his one true love all over again.

twelve Donny and Sally are unloading the grocery store items out of the minivan in front of the church, hauling things through the front door, which is propped open by a concrete block. They've bought trays of cheese and fruit, and platters of rolled luncheon meats with dipping sauces in the center, all tightly wrapped with cellophane, which catches the sun.

"Sally, let me do that," I say, watching her pay close attention to her dress, making certain it doesn't get soiled. She's wearing a long red dress for the occasion, her hair up in a bun, little ringlets dangling around her neck. She smiles and switches places with me behind Roth's chair.

Donny quips, "Hey, isn't it bad luck for the groom to see the bride before the wedding?" He's donned a black suit with a tie that has pictures of a goofy looking Tasmanian devil on it. Donny will be an usher, along with Simon.

Sally stops before rolling Roth inside. "Hon," she says, "That's only if you don't believe in destiny." She winks and bends to Roth's puckered kiss, his hand trying to pat her cheek.

"Tomorrow's the big day, huh?" Donny says, turning to me. "You go get a face treatment, right?" He's holding stacks of paper cups and boxes of clear plastic tableware.

"No. Today's the big day, Don." I grab the last grocery bag full of two-liter sodas and the brown bag with a bottle of champagne out of the van.

"Well, there can be two big days, can't there?" Donny smirks. He has a cigarette dangling from his lips, and I reach over with a free hand and yank it out, toe the thing into the pavement. I sweep out here on weekdays when the vet office is slow, so I'm certain I'll get to clean it up.

"Well," Donny says. "What your docs have done so far has really helped. You look good."

Cars are pulling into the parking lot, some of them tooting their horns when they see us. Inside, an old woman named Mrs. Duskas is playing the rented keyboard. "Come on, this shit is getting heavy," says Donny. He pauses, "How do I look?"

"You look great, and I like the devils." I point to his tie.

The RSVPs came in at just over 30 people, friends from way back, even a couple Sally and Roth knew in their days in Indy when Roth was contemplating Bible school and Kari wasn't even born.

As we enter the church, it bustles with hushed activity. The women from the vet's office have done a superb job decorating the place. Gold and silver balloons hang in clusters like enormous grapes from the tiled ceiling. Streamers of the same color flutter in the air coming through the door from outside. Three large folding tables hold homemade food and a punchbowl filled to the rim with a pink drink. No fewer than 10 dogs are in attendance. Terry lies on a mat with a new friend of his: a poodle mix with a furry blond mane. The dog's name is Pinty and he's got permanent brown tears under his eyes that make him look like a sick pirate. Pinty and Terry are a good match; they doze and wake to watch the other dogs in the room before slipping back into slumber, Pinty resting his head on Terry's shoulder. He hasn't had a seizure in months, and Simon's prediction is that Terry will live the last part of his life in comfort.

After people have signed the registry and taken their seats, Mrs. Duskas, perched on the keyboard seat like a hen, hits the notes hard and commences the ceremony with a momentarily off-key version of "All I Have to Do Is Dream." Sally and Roth are holding hands, facing the small crowd. I'm at Roth's side, hand on his shoulder, and Sally's asked Simon's wife to stand next to her. People begin to notice that the music is trailing off and the chatter dies down.

Sally touches her rosary as she speaks. "Roth and I would like to thank you all for coming. This is an informal ceremony, so please make yourselves comfortable." She smiles at the crowd and pats the top of Roth's hand. He stands and says with some effort: "Thank you . . . for sharing this . . . day . . . with us." He smiles and hands Sally a note. He kisses her and says, "Go a . . . head," motioning toward the crowd with his heavy arm.

"As some of you know, Roth has had a change in the way he communicates, but he wanted me to read a message from him today, too." She opens the folded square of paper and clears her throat. Roth looks up at her. "It's a wonderful blessing to have you all here for this special day. Almost 50 years ago I met this fine woman and we were married. Back then we made lots of mistakes, but that's behind us. Today I ask that you join us in the spirit of God and share our love for one another, our families and each of you. Amen." Sally folds the paper back up, teary-eyed, and bends to kiss Roth on the forehead, her rosary touching his stomach. "And please, if each of you could include our beautiful daughter Kari in your prayers, we sure would appreciate it."

For 10 minutes a pastor Roth knows from his short-lived days at the Bible college reads from Psalms and talks about love. The traditional vows are taken, Roth's "I Do" sounding like: "I Duh." We all clap and pull ourselves up to give Sally and Roth a standing ovation. Donny steps forward and speaks, ducking his head and acting shy in a way I've never seen before. "This is a buffet-style reception. Please help yourselves to whatever you like. We've got plenty of food. Beer and wine, too, if you partake." He motions with a grand arm movement toward the folding tables.

I slip away and go outside through a back door that opens onto the alley. It's even warmer out now. I take off my jacket and roll up my shirtsleeves. Some early bees buzz around a plant that's not yet flowered. I try and remember if I've ever noticed spring this much in my entire life. I'd always thought of the seasons changing as something that happened on a farm or out in the frontier—not in strip malls, not in suburbia. Kari and I would know that the seasons were changing by the holiday junk that showed up in the CVS or by the way chain restaurants put new specials on their menus: "Shrimp Fest on the Fourth," "Ribeye Wednesdays Are Autumn-some!"

Kari. It's hard not to wish she were here. I picture her invitation to the wedding today sitting in some plastic tub in the Durham post office marked undeliverable, unopened, and lost.

Behind me the cheery chitchat of Roth and Sally's guests mingles with the sound of laughter. I find a cinder block in the alley and sit down, tilting my face fully into the sun. I'm reminded of the poem that Rocky wrote in the movie "Mask." It made Kari and me cry when we heard his voice recite it at the end of the movie, after he was laid to rest in the cemetery. The poem listed the things he liked, like the sun on his face. Then his voice listed the things he hated, and the sun on his face was included there, too. I miss Kari terribly, but it's different than before. Now, I realize chasing her would never bring her home, even if we'd been successful and brought her back. If we'd done that, she might've been present, but not here, not really.

I lean back against the alley wall and can't help but think of the procedure on my face tomorrow. Simon's doctor had started with the bear scar. He lasered it and buffed it and reduced the contrast of the skin on each side. I was reluctant at first, afraid of the cost and the procedure, and of taking someone's help, but in the end Simon insisted. "I take care of this doctor's four champion Irish setters. He wants to help you free of charge." Simon smiled. "Besides, he sees us as his true calling. He gets tired of operating on wealthy Atlanta housewives with a single blemish on their facelifts."

The sun glares bright in the superbly blue sky. I'm about to stand up and go back inside when a shadow to my left emerges from the door. I look up but can't see very well from the sun. "So this is where you're hiding." It's Simon. He walks in front of me and sits on his haunches, then leans back on the wall like me.

"Wow, it's gorgeous out here, huh." For several minutes we sit basking in the sun in silence. Then he says, "This is going to be a nice place for the grooming business." We've talked about this over and over during breaks and lunchtime. I agree. To have real hope about something is a foreign emotion for me. Off in the distance, crows call, then flash black over our heads just seconds later.

"You scared about tomorrow?" asks Simon, his voice even.

"I think so," I say. We both know it's a long haul, that while the procedures are painful, it's more scary to take the risk, to sit in a chair under bright light and expose your face to a technician and then the doctor. After many sessions of this first part, I'll get to undergo something called Levulan Photodynamic Therapy, a new treatment, which they say does well on severe cystic acne. I like the name. Something about it seems futuristic.

Simon gets up and stretches; he's a tower of a shadow. I stand, too. "I wouldn't worry too much if I were you," he says. "They knock out your face with local anesthesia. The first and second procedures are tougher than the other ones, but you'll be glad you did it, trust me."

Inside the music is turned up and Donny is speaking over a microphone that really isn't needed. As the feedback whines and pops, I can hear him say, "Is this thing on?"

Simon and I stand in the sun and listen, amused, waiting for Donny to announce what we know is next. "If you'd all take your seats, Roth would like to lead us in prayer." We can hear the mike bumping into objects, crackling with feedback and an intelligible whisper as Donny passes it to Roth. Finally, there's breathing. Roth begins his sermon by weeping, apparently with joy. Out in the alley, Simon says, "She sure makes him happy."

thirteen I'm alone in the house. It's midmorning and just as nice as yesterday. In a few days it will be April. I'm due at the clinic in downtown Atlanta at 1 p.m., so I've got time to dawdle. I read the newspaper and have a light breakfast. The before-care instructions tell me to avoid a large meal because some people can get sick from the anesthesia. There will be 12 sessions in all. They also warn not to get overly optimistic about the results from the first several procedures. "Take care to realize that your facial appearance will look somewhat worse at first. You should be prepared to take a few days off during the first three sessions. Symptoms will include: skin bubbling, extreme redness, swelling, clear discharge, and pain."

The house is quiet. I slip into the study and get Kari's burlap-covered photo album and the new one of Stephen that Sally put together over a rainy weekend just a couple weeks after we got back from our fruitless road trip. She'd sat at the kitchen table and on each sticky, cardboard page applied a prayer card and a photo of Stephen that she'd gotten from his grandfather. The cards are laminated and have a tiny piece of cloth pasted on them next to a picture of a saint. The dot of cloth has these words printed around it in a circle: "This piece of cloth has been touched to His relic."

By nightfall on Sunday, Sally was showing her creation to Roth, describing the saints, why she'd chosen him or her, and how the prayers on the backs of the cards were carefully chosen to protect Stephen in different ways. "This one is Saint Francis. See, it starts out like this: 'Lord, make me an instrument of your peace.' It'll keep Stephen from harm, I know it." Roth had smiled and asked her to go over each one again.

Now, as I step outside and approach Kari's patch of purple flowers, I sit down in the grass and open up her album. Right away I notice that Sally has also stuck prayer cards next to pictures of Kari, too, covering all her bases. The scent from a mimosa tree drifts over the fence into the yard. The spring sunshine seems to clean me without water, and I can feel my hair warm against my scalp. When I turn the pages of the album, sunlight dances over the plastic.

I stand and pick a bundle of the little violet flowers, then sit back down and start in. Next to each photo of Stephen, and right next to the prayer card, I put a flower and smooth the plastic sheath back down over it to make certain it's secure. I want to meet him, tell Stephen that the real silver bullet is family, a lesson that's taken me too long to learn.

I start on Kari's photos and do the same with the flowers. There are pictures of us, as well as the all-too familiar baby picture of Stephen when he was still her "cousin's poor deceased infant." The flowers look preserved under the plastic, still purple, their green stems like neon-green hooks; each one takes a different form, bent slightly one way, the petals splayed. When I'm done, it still feels like something is missing. I glance at my watch and see I've got to leave soon or risk getting caught in lunchtime madness on the connector downtown.

I put Stephen's album back in the study but keep Kari's with me. The nervousness I feel in the pit of my stomach belongs to the skin doctor, and I want to pick. I take the album in the bathroom with me where Sally has redecorated, using Greek-style prints, applying plastic ivy above the towel racks. Donny is supposed to paint the walls soon in a forest green.

I put Kari's album on the sink and open it to a page that holds her yearbook picture and two snapshots of Roth and me watching television, eating off of trays. We're having spaghetti that I remember Kari made, and if I squint, I can make out that we are watching "Trapper John, M.D.," Roth's favorite TV show in 1985. Near the bottom of the page is my newly applied violet. I take the needle from my shaving kit, the one I've always used to abuse my face before, and peel back the plastic. I place it on the sticky cardboard, right next to the flower. I use the palm of my hand to smooth the whole page back down, then stand and look at it there. If I don't leave now, I'll miss what I've got to do.

The waiting room at the doctor's is too warm. I've been handed a portfolio with pictures and information explaining the procedure. Inside there's a quote. " 'There is no single disease which causes more psychic trauma, more maladjustment between parents and children, more general insecurity and feelings of inferiority and greater sums of psychic suffering than does acne vulgaris.' Sulzberger & Zaldems, 1948."

Then there are pictures of patients. The first is a man with a black bar over his eyes, I guess to protect his identity. His skin is about as bad as mine in the first photo, cratered and maroon, the skin on his brow like a textured ceiling. In the middle picture he looks monsterish; his face is so bubbly and red that I'm reminded of a gelatinous underwater sea creature. Tiny grape-like structures cling to his nose and cover the slim brow. I feel a little sick. Turning to the "after" picture, I read: "6 months later, 13 procedures." First there's dermabrasion, then chemical peels, and finally, after 18 months of monthly treatment, the Levulan Photodynamic Therapy. In this shot, the black bar over his eyes is gone and he is smiling, sitting up straight. His face is slightly pink, but nearly perfect. The surface is smooth and clear, and it's even more impressive when I realize the photo next to it is a blown-up version focusing just on his face. Even this close, it's like he's removed a mask, with not a trace whatsoever of his former mugshot. There's a disclaimer that tells me that not all patients experience such dramatic changes, and it reads like a sweepstakes' fine print. I've never won anything in my life, not even a scratch-off or a free two-liter under a cap.

On the backside of the photo page is his testimonial: "I used to feel like one of those ugly ghouls in that Michael Jackson video. I was scared to show my face anywhere. I've lived most of my life avoiding mirrors and ducking my head. I've hidden myself from most everything and everyone. If you can be reborn, this is it."

I close the book and feel a little breathless.

"Mr. Hobbie, they're almost ready for you," says the nurse at the front desk. "Can I get you a drink of water while you wait?"

"No, thank you."

She grins knowingly and uses her intercom to call back to wherever I'll be heading shortly. She says into the intercom, "That's what I think, yes." Then she turns to me. "Mr. Hobbie, I've been given instructions to offer you a sedative. Would you like something to put you at ease?" She's already up and unlocking a cabinet. I wonder whether she sneaks in there sometimes for herself. After all, watching person after person walking through these doors with such botched, desperate faces and witnessing their gradual transformation has to be taxing, even if the rewards must be great as well.

"Okay," I say, and she's there by my side, holding a little paper cup of water and an opened pill bottle. "Hold out your hand," she says. When the pink pill falls into my palm and she hands me the water, all I can hear is Sally reciting words for communion at our strip mall church. "Do this to remember me. The blood of Christ. Bread up in heaven, the cup of life shed for you." As I swallow, I remember Sally placing a bit of saltine on Roth's tongue, crumbs falling onto his dark shirt.

fourteen Donny is now pulling double duty. He knocks on my bedroom door and turns the handle. "You need anything, Hobbie?" A tray of warm water sits next to my thigh, two neatly folded white hand towels draped over the edge, and a handheld mirror tilted against the container of salve I'm supposed to apply liberally. Donny brought the tray in earlier and didn't look me in the eye. He set the stuff down and slipped back out. I wonder whether his not looking at me is a suggestion from Sally, who has most definitely seen me up close. Last night, after the painkillers wore off and I managed to get to my feet, she came into the room as if she'd been waiting outside the door the whole time. "Oh, hon," she'd said, "let me get whatever it is you need."

"I've got to pee."

"Well, sugar, you better take care of that yourself." I assume it was this interaction that made her convince Donny he'd need to care for me as well as helping Roth.

My head hurts as I tell him, "No, I'm okay, Donny. Thanks." I watch the door handle ease upward and I can hear his feet brush the carpet as he makes the trek down the hall, probably to Roth's room. I push myself upright and arrange the pillows behind my back; for some reason, this position reminds me of riding a roller coaster with Kari at King's Island, the rush of wind through our hair, and her hand tight around mine.

I dip one of the towels into the water and wring it. Leaning back some, I place the towel over my face and immediately it feels as though the water is bleach; the spots on my face burn and the pain burrows into my cheeks. Thankfully, the pain lessens and I think of the new terms I've got for my face. It's true I've got *acne vulgaris*, but Simon's doctor was more precise. "Actually, your condition would best be described as *acne conglobata*, a form of *acne vulgaris*." His terminology sounded ridiculous to me; here, all along I thought of myself as a *vulgaris* when I was really a *conglobata*. I miss Kari and the fact that this silliness would not be wasted on her drives me to remove the towel and apply the antibiotic ointment. I want to be a healthier man for her, and the truth is, I want to look better for her, too.

I also learned that my zits are called comedones. The bundle of literature I was given sits on the nightstand. I lean over and take a sip of Sprite from a bottle with a straw, which Sally left for me. Taking more painkillers would be the way to go here, but something in me says not to, that I need a clear head. I switch on the television and flip through a triad of shopping channels, a black-and-white movie, and more inane reality shows than I can stomach. I decide it won't be long until there's one about guys with *acne conglobata*. With the room quiet and my head aching, I feel my eyelids grow heavy.

Two days later, I'm up and about. Terry is in my lap at the dinner table and we've got a window open. Atlanta is starting its full bloom and the air is heavy with the scent of hyacinth. My head feels heavier, a condition the pamphlet says is due to the excess drainage. I'm self-conscious at the table, but Sally pipes up as she pulls a shred of lettuce from a fork tine with her perfect teeth. "Hon, you look rugged." She turns to Roth. "Shoog, you remember when we saw that boxing match at the state fair? Doesn't Hobbie look like that big handsome fighter who won?"

Roth nods, appearing sleepy but generous, his busted smile peaceful. Donny eats a wad of garlic bread and adds his two cents. "Yep, he's gonna heal up good and be back in the ring in no time." All of this is supposed to make me feel better and it does, not because I believe it, but because they are making the effort, trying to help.

"I hope it doesn't bother any of you," I say, the bubbles on my face heavy. "I could eat in the other room if you want."

Roth frowns and tries to speak.

"Nonsense," says Sally, scowling.

Through the open window I can hear a car door shut. Donny cranes to see. "We've got visitors," he says, narrowing his eyes. "A young couple with a baby and a woman." Roth begins to rock a little, a calm look on his face.

"I think I better go to my room," I say, and start to stand.

Donny looks hard at Sally, then me. "I don't think you should. I think that's Kari." His voice is firm.

I turn to look out the window. Her hair is the first thing I see, longer, dark, and beautiful, and then I see that she's as slim as she was in 10th grade. With her are a young woman holding a baby and a man, as Donny had said. Stephen, I think. I can make out a birthmark on his neck, another on his forehead. That's Stephen, I think again, a little dizzy. With Kari. *With his mother.* I take a deep breath, let it out.

They pause on the front walk and the young woman hands the baby to Kari. I see that Stephen's right arm is stiff, I assume from the shooting, even after all these months. They make their way up the walk, nervous chitchat coming to us through the window. I look at Roth and see that his eyes are filled with tears. Beside him, now standing, Sally is wringing her hands and grinning. "She's here, Roth," she says, voice wavering. "She's finally here."

Kari's voice is clear through the window, cooing at the baby, "It's okay, sweetie, don't cry." It hits me: Kari has become a grandmother at 38. I can feel my face sting a little from a big dumb grin I can't seem to contain. This is the start of moving from anonymous jokes to beloved freaks, I think. I hope Kari sees it that way. I hope, I hope.

There's the knock at the door and I can hear the baby squeal with delight. I listen as they all laugh, now just outside the door, literally steps away from me.

"Aren't you gonna get that, hon?" Sally asks, looking at me and biting her lower lip. Beside her, Roth's face is tipped up and he's gazing at me with that peaceful look of his, and Donny stands just behind them both, a shy smile on his face.

"Yes, of course," I say, looking to Roth. I can move any time, I think, just open the door and take them all into my arms, this family of strangers. And when I do it, I'll look awful, even though underneath, it's all getting better and better.

Book Club Discussion Questions

1. Early on in *The Flawless Skin of Ugly People* we learn that Hobbie and Kari are in a relationship that started when they were just teenagers and rocking out to the heavy-metal band Quiet Riot. Now they're older and perhaps wiser, and trying to live differently. Do you think their relationship will survive these changes? Are healthier people "better" people? Were Hobbie and Kari in love because they were mutually in pain?

2. Hobbie tells us from his perspective the role that Kari and her father have played in his life. Is Hobbie a likeable narrator? Is he a reliable narrator? Do Kari's letters make for more questions or give the reader clues to her biggest secret as the story unfolds?

3. Did the deacon cause Hobbie's face to break out and Kari to gain weight? Why or how?

4. Hobbie and his father-in-law of sorts share a past filled with secrets. What does this tell you about Roth? Can carrying secrets around change a person? Is Roth different at the end of the novel? If so, what part of his change can be attributed to his finally releasing/telling these secrets?

5. One of the themes of the novel is a desire to know the meaning of beauty. Hobbie and Kari see themselves as akin to a freak show, hiding out from the world in the anonymity provided by malls and soulless apartment complexes. Do beautiful people have it easier in this world? Who defines beauty for us?

6. Think about the role of religion in *The Flawless Skin of Ugly People*. Is Hobbie spiritual? Who is the most spiritual person in the novel? Is spirituality the same as religion? The deacon has shattered Hobbie and Kari. Do you think they can ever trust religion or religious people again?

7. In Part III, Hobbie describes how a hotel clerk looks at him: "She gives me a long look, up and down, but she's not looking at me like I'd expected, that kind of pitiful once-over that says: Awww, look, isn't that cute. See, everybody can find love if they just keep trying." What has it meant for the characters in the book to live their lives with a "mark"—something that makes them "different"? If Hobbie's mark is his face, and Kari's her weight, what is Roth's? Sally's? Stephen's?

8. Throughout the book, the characters must deal with failing, imperfect bodies. They change, though, both on the inside and the out. What is your view regarding the ability of a person to change his or her essential personality? Is it okay to spend lots of time trying to look better on the outside, whether it's with Botox, a pair of Manolo Blahniks, or as with Kari, by checking into a diet clinic? Which should come first, a focus on how a person looks on the outside or how he/she is on the inside—the heart and soul?

9. Are there differences between how generations in your own family view love, beauty, and faith? In the end, the story leaves us with an essential choice: live life under a veil of sorts, or embrace it as you are. Are there any other options beyond these two? Which view do you believe in?

10. Finally, what does the novel tell us about ugliness?

© Nancy Brooks-Lane

The Flawless Skin of Ugly People, a finalist for the William Faulkner Prize, is Doug Crandell's first novel. He is the author of two memoirs, *Pig Boy's Wicked Bird* and *The All-American Industrial Motel,* and lives in Douglasville, Georgia. Visit www.dougcrandell.com.